Jackson studied Bentley's profile.

The perfection of form and feature, the flawlessness of color and texture. It was a look, a perfection, that had to be coaxed and cultivated. Like a hothouse flower.

How could one not be sucked in by something that looked so soft and fragile, so beautiful?

He knew better than to be fooled by appearances. And yet with Bentley...

Jackson stiffened, realizing the danger of his thoughts. No. All he had to do was remember the lesson of the rose. The beauty invited you in for a closer look, a caress....

There, the thorn waited.

Dear Reader,

Welcome to Silhouette **Special Edition**, where each month, we publish six novels with *you* in mind—stories of love and life, tales that you can identify with.

Last year, I requested your opinions on our books. Thank you for the many thoughtful comments. I'd like to share with you quotes from those letters. This seems very appropriate now, while we are in the midst of the THAT SPECIAL WOMAN! promotion. Each one of our readers is a *special* woman, as heroic as the heroines in our books.

We have some wonderful books in store for you this June. *A Winter's Rose* by Erica Spindler is our THAT SPECIAL WOMAN! title and it introduces Erica's wonderful new series, BLOSSOMS OF THE SOUTH. Not to be missed this month is *Heart of the Wolf,* by Lindsay McKenna. This exciting tale begins MORGAN'S MERCENARIES.

Wrapping up this month are books from other favorite authors: Gina Ferris (*Fair and Wise* is the third tale in FAMILY FOUND!), Tracy Sinclair, Laurey Bright and Trisha Alexander.

I hope you enjoy this book, and all of the stories to come!

Sincerely,

Tara Gavin
Senior Editor
Silhouette Books

Quote of the Month: "Why do I read romances? I maintain a positive outlook to life—do not allow negative thoughts to enter my life—but when my willpower wears, a good romance novel gets me back on track fast! The romance novel is adding much to the New Age mentality— keep a positive mind, create a positive world!"

—E.J.W. Fahner
Michigan

ERICA
SPINDLER

A WINTER'S ROSE

Silhouette®

SPECIAL ▼ EDITION®

Published by Silhouette Books New York

America's Publisher of Contemporary Romance

For Metsy Hingle,
a genuine "Flower of the South"
and
a true friend

Love ya, Mets!

SILHOUETTE BOOKS
300 East 42nd St., New York, N.Y. 10017

A WINTER'S ROSE

Copyright © 1993 by Erica Spindler

All rights reserved. Except for use in any review, the reproduction or utilization of this work in whole or in part in any form by any electronic, mechanical or other means, now known or hereafter invented, including xerography, photocopying and recording, or in any information storage or retrieval system, is forbidden without the permission of the publisher, Silhouette Books, 300 E. 42nd St., New York, N.Y. 10017

ISBN: 0-373-09817-0

First Silhouette Books printing June 1993

All the characters in this book have no existence outside the imagination of the author and have no relation whatsoever to anyone bearing the same name or names. They are not even distantly inspired by any individual known or unknown to the author, and all incidents are pure invention.

®: Trademark used under license and registered in the United States Patent and Trademark Office and in other countries.

Printed in the U.S.A.

ERICA SPINDLER

believes in love at first date. Because that's all the time it took for her and her husband, Nathan, to fall in love. "We were too young. We both had to finish college. Our parents thought we should see other people, but we knew we were meant for each other," Erica says. Thirteen years later, they still know it.

Erica chose her home—New Orleans—the same way. She went "way down yonder" for a visit, fell in love with the city and decided to stay. "I may have been born in the Midwest," she says, "but I'm a true Southerner at heart." It is that continuing love affair with the people and customs of the South that inspired Erica to write the Blossoms of the South trilogy.

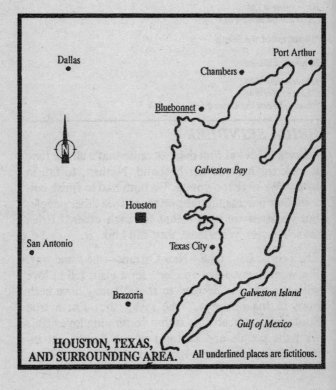

Dallas

Port Arthur

Chambers

Bluebonnet

Galveston Bay

N

Houston

San Antonio

Texas City

Galveston Island

Brazoria

Gulf of Mexico

**HOUSTON, TEXAS,
AND SURROUNDING AREA.** All underlined places are fictitious.

Prologue

The shop, Small Miracles, was nestled into a corner of the Houston Galleria's second level. Although not usually interested in antiques, Bentley Barton Cunningham stood outside the shop's front window, transfixed by a domed box displayed there.

The piece measured about eight inches in height and four inches across. Its glass dome rested on a luminous wood base decorated with gold filigree; inside the dome stood the figure of a southern belle, her hands filled with bunches of tiny, star-shaped flowers.

Although exquisite, it wasn't the beauty of the piece that had beckoned Bentley back to this window again and again. Bentley moved closer to the glass, her heart beginning to race. No, what had drawn her was the uncanny resemblance between herself and the figure inside the dome.

I could have posed for it, Bentley thought, studying the belle's face. Delicate, chiseled features; full, almost pouty mouth; almond-shaped eyes that slanted exotically up. Even the smile—the slight lifting of the lips that she'd been accused of fabricating but which had been hers almost from birth—was the same.

She wanted to buy the box; so much so, the want gnawed at her.

She hadn't even allowed herself inside the store for a closer look.

After tomorrow she wouldn't be able to afford it, Bentley acknowledged. The box or anything else. A sliver of fear speared through her, and she called herself a coward. She was a grown woman with both a college degree and a divorce under her belt. She should be able to support herself. She should be able to *do* something.

But what?

An ache, now familiar but no less disturbing for being so, settled in her chest. Bentley drew in a ragged breath. She was a twenty-six-year-old woman who had never done anything but look good.

Tears sprang to her eyes. She fought against them and the feelings of failure and frustration that had been with her for as long as she could remember. The feelings that had intensified with her marriage. And divorce.

Bentley lifted her chin a notch. Sink or swim. She had to find out if she could do it, find out what she was made of. And if she discovered she was made of nothing tougher than wrapping paper, then at least she would know.

"Well, sugar," a woman drawled from the doorway of the shop, "why don't you just come on in and take a look."

Bentley dragged her gaze from the domed box to the woman, surprised to see the husky, southern drawl attached to a woman who looked amazingly like a pixie. Bentley smiled hesitantly. "This is your shop?"

"Sure is." The tiny woman held the door a bit wider. "Welcome to Marla's Small Miracles. I'm Marla. Come on in."

Mouth dry, Bentley followed her inside, feeling like a giant alongside the other woman. "I was noticing the—"

"Music box," Marla supplied, plucking it from the window. "For about a week now."

Bentley laughed. "It *is* lovely."

"Turn of the century," the pixie woman said, placing it in Bentley's hands. "The base is pecan wood, the filigree twenty-four-karat gold. The figure inside is hand-fashioned porcelain."

As the shopkeeper talked, Bentley ran her fingers over the smooth, polished wood, over the filigree. "May I wind it?" Marla nodded, and Bentley turned its small gold key. As the lilting tune played, the figure inside the dome circled the base.

"It's as if she's offering her flowers," Bentley murmured, charmed. She met the other woman's eyes. "How much is it?"

"Fifteen hundred."

"Oh." Bentley's heart sank a bit. Last week she wouldn't have thought twice about spending that on something she wanted a lot less. But last week she hadn't realized just how much money that was.

"Now, sugar," Marla coaxed, "I bet you spend that on a dress. This is, after all, a piece of history."

Bentley looked from the piece to Marla, the blood beginning to thrum in her head. "Do you know where it's from? Who owned it?"

The little woman nodded. "Another tragic southern story, I'm afraid. It's from a Mississippi plantation. The family has fallen on hard times and has been forced to sell their heirlooms. I understand that one of the last surviving fam-

ily members is trying valiantly to hold on to the property.
I've gotten some other lovely things from that plantation.
Ashland, it's called.''

"Ashland," Bentley repeated softly, a fluttering sensation in the pit of her stomach. Panic, she acknowledged. If
she didn't buy the box today, she couldn't tomorrow. This
was her last chance.

She had to have it.

Bentley lifted her gaze to the shopkeeper's. "Is she anyone?" Bentley asked, referring to the figure. "Do you
know?"

"Sorry, hon, I don't." The woman smiled, the curving of
her mouth slow and satisfied. "The resemblance *is* amazing. Saw it right off."

She knows I'm going to buy it, Bentley thought, lightly
touching the glass. *She knows I can't resist.*

And she couldn't. With a feeling of inevitability, Bentley
handed the woman her gold card.

Chapter One

Her mother had already arrived.

Bentley smoothed a hand over the hip of her raw silk skirt, wishing she could soothe her nerves so easily. Sink or swim, she told herself for about the billionth time. She would never know until she tried. Telling her parents what she planned to do was her first step into the water; she'd already prepared herself for their response.

Prepared or not, it would be difficult. She hated disappointing them, but she couldn't go on the way she had been.

Smiling with a confidence she far from felt, Bentley crossed the sunny, plant-filled café to where her mother waited. The older woman looked up as she approached. As always, Bentley experienced a moment of stunned admiration at her mother's beauty. Tiny, curvaceous and totally pampered, her mother was as much art object as flesh and blood woman.

"Bentley, darling, you look wonderful." Her mother smiled and stretched out her hands.

Bentley clasped them, bent and brushed her lips against her mother's unlined cheek. "Thanks, Mom. Where's Daddy?"

"He had to cancel." The older woman pulled out her compact and inspected her face, making sure Bentley's kiss hadn't marred her makeup. Satisfied, she snapped it shut. "You know how his schedule is."

Bentley did know. Only too well. She slipped into the chair opposite her mother's, acknowledging hurt and disappointment. She'd told her father that she had an announcement, that it was important to her that he be here. Business had still come first. But then, Nick "The Slick" Cunningham hadn't built an oil empire by kowtowing to the demands of his wife or children. Or anyone else.

"You've changed your hair-style," her mother murmured, studying Bentley.

"Mmm." Bentley laid her napkin in her lap. "Suzanne altered the angle of the cut so it would fall away from my face."

Her mother smiled. "I approve. It's very flattering." Reaching across the table, she brushed an errant wave from her daughter's cheek. "There. Now it's perfect."

Bentley automatically lifted a hand to her hair to assure herself it was, indeed, perfect, then dropped it again, annoyed with herself and the self-conscious gesture. What was it about her mother that made her feel thirteen and lacking?

As she gazed at her mother, Bentley remembered being ten and overhearing one of her father's business associates say that one look at Trixy Cunningham confirmed his faith in both God and His gender. She hadn't realized, until this moment, how much that comment had affected her.

The waiter arrived with the menus and took their drink order. "Were you waiting long?" Bentley asked after he'd walked away.

"Not long." Trixy scanned the menu, then set it aside. She met her daughter's eyes, her own serious. "Bentley... honey, we have to talk."

Bentley frowned and set her menu aside. "Is something wrong?"

"Yes." Her mother leaned forward slightly, lowering her voice. "Honey, in Texas, you are only as good as your family name."

Bentley knew exactly what her mother referred to, and the heat of anger—and shame—stung her cheeks. "We've been through this before, Mother. I didn't take David's name with me after the divorce. I didn't want it or anything else of his."

Trixy Cunningham lowered her voice even more, her drawl becoming as sweet and thick as molasses. "Weaver is a fine old name. Almost as distinguished as Barton. Besides, David will take his daddy's seat in Austin one day. The connection wouldn't hurt."

"Well, I guess I'll just have to try to stumble my way through without it," Bentley said stiffly as the waiter approached with their mineral waters.

After he'd taken their lunch order, Bentley turned to her mother. She didn't want to argue, nor did she want to talk about her ex-husband, her marriage or her divorce—all favorite topics of her mother's. No, today she wanted to talk about her own life. Her own dreams and ambitions.

Taking a deep breath, Bentley leaned toward her mother. "I asked you and Daddy to lunch because I have something I want to tell you. Something I think is wonderful, and I hope you will, too."

Her mother's eyes lit up. "You've met someone."

"No, Mother. I—"

"You and David are getting back together?"

"No," Bentley said, tensing.

Trixy Cunningham raised her eyebrows. "Then, I can't imagine."

Of course she couldn't. Bentley laced her fingers together in her lap, fighting feelings of helplessness and failure. She drew in a deep breath. She *could* do this. "The wonderful thing is, I've made a decision about my life. I'm going to work."

"To work," her mother repeated as if she'd heard incorrectly. "What do you mean, 'work'?"

"I'm getting a job."

For several moments her mother sat in stunned silence. Then she shook her head. "But why, Bentley? You have everything. We've given you...everything."

And that was the problem. They'd given her everything. She'd never had to work for anything. She'd never had to struggle, never had to stretch. Her beauty had been an effortless accomplishment; her social position, the gift of her birth.

She'd always yearned to be more. To achieve something on her own and for herself. But she'd never had the courage. Until the last of David's humiliations had pushed her to the edge.

But she hadn't gone over, she reminded herself. And she wouldn't. Not without a fight.

Bentley caught her mother's hands. "For a long time I've felt like I was...drifting. Like there was nothing to connect me to the real world, nothing that was mine—that I'd created or worked for." Tears clogged Bentley's throat, and she fought to clear it. But still, when she spoke her voice was husky. "I've felt useless. And I think if I had a job, I would feel—"

"You're just rebounding from your divorce," her mother interrupted, squeezing her daughter's fingers, then releasing them. "If you and David had tried harder, or if you'd been able to get pregnant..."

Bentley dropped her hands to her lap. Her inability to conceive had been a great source of pain during her marriage; she still ached every time she allowed herself to dwell on the fact that in all probability, she would never be a mother. But an even greater source of pain was her own self-doubt and cowardice. Would she ever have the guts to tell her mother the truth? About her nightmare of a marriage? About David?

"Don't you understand, Mother? This has nothing to do with marriage or pregnancy. This has to do with how I feel." Bentley pressed a hand to her chest. "With the kind of person I think I am."

Trixy made a small, breathy sound of exasperation. "You're a beautiful woman, darling. You come from a good family. You don't *have* to do anything."

Bentley looked at her mother. Trixy Cunningham had devoted her life to maintaining her physical beauty and her place in Texas society, and to enjoying the life-style she had been taught to expect as her due.

Her mother would never understand, Bentley realized, tears stinging the backs of her eyes. Her mother would never give her the approval she so desperately wanted. Bentley blinked against the tears. She had to move on without it.

Bentley reached into her pocketbook for her credit card case. Knowing that the act would change the course of her life, she handed it to her mother. "Give these to Daddy for me."

Her mother looked blankly at the case, then at her daughter. "I don't understand, Bentley. What is this?"

"My credit cards. I won't be using them any more."

"You can't be serious."

"I've never been more serious about anything." Bentley drew in a deep breath. "I'll be out of the town house by the end of the month."

"But where will you live?"

"As soon as I get a job I'll find something else, something I can afford on my salary."

"Oh . . . my." The older woman sank back against her chair, looking totally befuddled. "And the BMW?"

Bentley thought of her beautiful little car, knowing that in all probability she would have to sell it. "That was a birthday gift. I'm going to keep it. But from now on, I'm paying for the insurance and upkeep. I'll have the policy changed over immediately."

"But what are you going to . . . do?"

Bentley paused, some of the wind going out of her sails. "I don't know," she said softly. Thinking, oddly, of the music box and of the beautiful doll inside, she stiffened her spine. "I'll find something. I have a college degree."

Trixy gazed at her eight-karat diamond solitaire as if it were a crystal ball. After a moment, she looked at her daughter. "Are you sure you've thought this through, darling? Why don't you take a vacation. The islands are wonderful this time of year, and I'm sure if you—"

"A vacation from what, Mother? From shopping? From manicures and lunch with my friends?" Bentley caught her mother's hands once more, hoping to lessen the sting of her tone. "I *have* thought this through. In fact, I've thought of nothing but this for weeks now. My mind is made up."

Their food arrived then, and they picked at the seafood salads, exchanging an occasional bit of gossip, neither of them addressing the subject foremost on their minds.

And as the minutes passed, Bentley's mood fluctuated between exhilaration and terror, confidence and doubt.

A week later her mood swings had become less dramatic—and less positive. Curled up on her white leather couch, the music box on the end table beside her and the *Houston Chronicle*'s want ads spread out before her, Bentley wondered if she'd been crazy to think she could do this.

Her liberal arts degree qualified her for nothing. Every job seemed to require specific or technical degrees. And experience. Even the lowest-paying and least prestigious of jobs preferred experience.

She'd never even baby-sat.

Bentley picked up the music box and gazed at her look-alike trapped inside the dome. "What am I going to do?" she wondered aloud. A dozen employers over the past week had taken one look at her and ever-so-politely told her no, thank you. Another dozen had refused to even see her.

Frowning, Bentley wound the music box and watched the figure slowly circle its base. How naive she'd been. She had imagined some entry-level position, a nice office complete with a helpful co-worker willing to train her. Embarrassment stung her cheeks. In a week, she hadn't even been able to get an interview for such a position.

Maybe she *had* been too hasty. . . maybe her mother was right and she hadn't thought this through. Bentley sighed and touched the dome's cool glass. When she'd made her decision, all she'd known was that she had to make a change, that she had to try to make her way on her own.

The phone rang; Bentley jumped for it. It was her mother.

"Darling, I didn't wake you, did I?"

"No." Bentley shifted her gaze to the newspaper, determined not to let her distress or doubts show. "I was going through the want ads."

"Any luck?"

"Some possibilities. Nothing definite yet."

"Then I'm in time." Her mother paused dramatically. "I've found you a job."

"A job?" Bentley repeated, not sure she'd heard correctly.

"That's right. And not," the older woman hurried to add, "with Cunningham Oil." She paused again. "The position is with an environmental group over in Galveston. Baysafe, it's called. They're in desperate need of help, and, well . . . nonprofit is a good career for a lady."

Bentley wrapped her finger around the phone cord. "We talked about this, Mother. If I'm going to make it on my own, I need a salary."

"It's a paid position," Trixy responded stiffly. "I do listen when you talk."

"I'm sorry," Bentley said automatically. "I know you do."

"So? What do you think?"

Bentley drew in a cautious breath. "I appreciate your help, Mother, really I do. But please try to understand, I prefer to find something on my own."

The silence on the other end of the line was deafening. After a moment, Trixy murmured, "Forgive me. I was only trying to help."

At the hurt in her mother's voice, Bentley sighed. "I know, Mom. It's late and I'm tired. Tell me about the job."

"Very well." The older woman cleared her throat. "Baysafe is a very well-respected group, and you would be working directly under Jackson Reese, Baysafe's originator. They're in need, and the position comes without the annoyance of having to apply . . . or the humiliation of being turned down."

Bentley shifted her gaze to the *Chronicle*'s classified ads, the humiliation of the past week—and with it all her self-doubts and insecurities—barreling into her.

In the past seven days she'd been turned down for everything from receptionist to waitress. What if no one would hire her? Bentley imagined having to tell her parents she had failed, imagined asking for an extension on the town house or worse, to borrow back one of her credit cards.

She caught her bottom lip between her teeth. Wasn't the point not about how she got a job, but about doing it and supporting herself?

"They really want me?" Bentley asked, hating the tiny tremor in her voice.

"They're ready and waiting."

Bentley drew a deep breath. "All right," she said. "I'll take it."

"You did what?" Furious, Jackson Reese faced his thirteen year-old daughter, Chloe.

She inched her chin up defiantly. "I called Mom. I told her how horrible you are."

"You called your mother," Jackson repeated slowly, carefully. "The one who is vacationing on the French Riviera, to tell her what a terrible parent I am."

Chloe glared at him. "That's right."

Jackson worked to hold on to his temper. "And what did she say?"

"She agreed with me." Chloe tossed her head back. "She thinks you're mean, too."

Jackson counted to ten. Once, then again. He wouldn't say the words that begged to jump off his tongue, words like, "But I'm good enough to raise you." And others like, "If I'm so awful, then why did she dump you with me?"

But he didn't—and couldn't—say them because they would hurt Chloe too much. It wasn't her fault her mother was selfish and irresponsible. Nor was it her fault that his and Victoria's marriage had ended almost before it had started.

Besides, in her heart of hearts, Chloe already knew the truth. And knowing that hurt him more than any of the things his daughter could say to him.

"Mom said," his daughter continued, "that you were being silly, and that as far as she was concerned, I'm entirely too old for a baby-sitter."

"Did she?" He lifted his eyebrows. "And who did she say should watch you while I'm working?"

Chloe's chin tipped up another notch. "I can take care of myself."

Her tone was as haughty as a princess's. She'd inherited that from her mother. Along with her exotic looks—the waterfall of thick, blond hair, the full, pouty mouth and large, almond-shaped blue eyes.

That she was so beautiful and poised, so mature looking at thirteen, scared him silly.

That her behavior so closely resembled that of her mother frightened him more.

"Chloe," he said wearily, "you get kicked out of boarding school for the third time and yet you expect me to believe you're mature enough to take care of yourself while I'm at work? And what about when I'm out of town? Did your mother think of that?" Jackson shook his head. "No way, kiddo."

Chloe stomped her foot. "You're so unfair! I hated that place. They made me—"

"What?" Jackson interrupted. "Eat your vegetables? Study? Follow rules designed to protect you?"

"But, Daddy," she wheedled. "If you'd just give me a chance..."

In the background Jackson heard the phone ringing, heard Jill Peters, his office manager, greet someone. "I don't have time for this, Chloe. The subject is closed. Until you go back to school, you will have a baby-sitter.''

"I hate you!'' she shot back, tears flooding her eyes. ''I wish I never came here. I'd even rather be at that dumb boarding school than here with you!''

Her words tore at him. It wasn't the first time she'd said them, yet they hurt no less than the first. He'd never imagined that his child would say that to him. But then there were so many things about being a parent he'd never imagined.

''Well,'' he said stiffly, ''maybe you should think of that the next time you feel the urge to call your headmistress a—''

''Jackson—'' Jill opened the door and poked her head inside. ''Bentley Cunningham is here.''

Jackson met his office manager's gaze, and she rolled her eyes. Great, he thought. Just what he needed. Another spoiled princess on his hands.

Realizing his own thoughts, guilt plucked at him. If Chloe was a spoiled princess, it was as much his fault as Victoria's. He'd been a lousy father, and the hell of it was, he didn't know how to become a better one.

Jackson flexed his fingers, torn between his desire to make it right between him and Chloe, and the urgency of Baysafe's situation. Damn it. He didn't have time for this. Every moment had to be spent scrambling to come up with donations to replace the ones that had been pulled.

Donations. Bentley Cunningham. If he hadn't needed Cunningham Oil's yearly contribution so badly he would have turned Beatrice Cunningham down flat.

But he *had* needed it. Badly. Lobbying in Washington to change environmental legislation took money. Saving the precious coast and her wildlife took money. Lots of it.

Money Baysafe didn't have. Time was running out for the bay and her wetlands. He would do whatever he had to to save them, even swallow his pride and take on a spoiled debutante who wanted to dabble at a job.

Jackson looked at his daughter only to find her staring at him, an expression in her eyes he hadn't seen in a long time. Part vulnerability, part yearning, part hero worship. His heart lurched. He hadn't realized just how much he'd missed that expression.

He reached out to her. "Chloe, I—"

"Jackson, line one. It's Washington."

Making a sound of frustration, Jackson dropped his hand and turned away from his daughter. He kept the conversation brief, but when he turned back to Chloe, gone was the soft expression of moments before, in its place was the petulance he saw so often these days.

A feeling of futility washed over him, and he fought it back. Putting his arm around Chloe's shoulders, he steered her out of his office, ignoring when she popped her gum. "We'll get this worked out, sweetie. We're still adjusting to living together. I have some things to do, but when I'm done, we'll get an ice cream. Okay?"

Chloe rolled her eyes. "Ice cream? Get real, Daddy." She ducked out from under his arm, crossed the room and plopped noisily down onto the waiting room sofa.

At the commotion, Bentley turned from the series of photographs she'd been studying to face Jackson Reese. Her first glance at him took her breath. He was tall, at least six-three, with broad shoulders and a big outdoorsy build. He filled the small reception area, towering over his secretary and a young girl she assumed was his daughter. Even at five foot ten, Bentley felt dwarfed by him.

But it was more than his physical size that filled the room; it was his physicality, his very presence. Jackson Reese was all man, all Texan. Judging by the lines radiating from his sky-blue eyes and the healthy wind-burned look of his chiseled face, Jackson Reese had spent a lifetime enduring the fickle Texas elements, be it the unrelenting sun or the cold, wet wind. His sandy-colored hair and bushy eyebrows were streaked from the sun and with hints of premature gray.

Bentley moved her gaze over him, taking in the faded jeans and cowboy boots, the flannel shirt and sheepskin-lined denim vest. Jackson Reese was the antithesis of David and her father, corporate sharks who wore Brooks Brothers suits and deceptively civilized smiles. Yet something in his expression suggested a man capable of the same ruthless cunning, of a determination to win that precluded everything—especially tenderness.

Even though her insides fluttered like a field of butterflies, Bentley stepped forward and held out her hand. "Mr. Reese."

He took her hand and smiled. The curving of his lips was broad and handsome, the kind of smile that won votes and stole hearts. It didn't reach his eyes. "Ms. Cunningham."

"Please, call me Bentley."

He nodded curtly and dropped her hand. She couldn't help but notice he didn't offer her the same courtesy, and a ripple of irritation moved over her. She was unaccustomed to such brusque treatment, especially from men.

"You've met Jill, my office manager?" He motioned to the woman who had first greeted her. "Yes." Bentley looked at Jill; the woman nodded briefly, then returned to her paperwork.

"My daughter, Chloe."

Bentley turned to find the youngster's too-adult gaze assessingly upon her. Bentley had the feeling that if asked, Chloe could quote how much her suit cost, identify her watch as Piaget gold and diamond, her shoes as Gucci.

Even though she would have been able to do likewise at the same age, Bentley was unnerved. She shook off the feeling and smiled at the exotic-looking girl.

In response, Chloe snapped her gum. "I was kicked out of boarding school. He's stuck with me until after Christmas."

Bentley stared at the beautiful child in shock, then shifted her gaze to Jackson, even more shocked when he did no more than send his daughter a narrow-eyed glance.

Then he turned to Bentley. "We need to talk," he said, motioning to the office he had just emerged from. "Have a seat, I'll be right in."

Resisting the urge to wring her hands, Bentley moved around him and into the office. The room was sparsely and crudely furnished, a far cry from Cunningham Oil's executive offices. Here, as in the reception area, photographs of the wild and varied Texas coast lined the walls.

Caught by a photo of a whooping crane bursting into flight, Bentley moved closer to examine it. Ethereally white, the bird glowed against the background of lush green as it cut with seeming effortlessness through the air.

How wonderful to be able to soar, Bentley thought, tipping her head, still studying the photo. How wonderful to be able to—

"Beautiful, isn't it?"

Bentley whirled around, startled. Jackson Reese stood not three feet behind her, his eyes also on the photo. "Yes," she managed, turning back to the photograph. "I was thinking it almost magical."

"Magical," he repeated, moving closer until he stood directly behind her. "That's a pretty good description. But like any sleight of hand trick, now you see it, now you don't."

He smelled of the outdoors, of the Gulf and the sun. The scent, natural and somehow wild, was foreign to her. The men she knew smelled of colognes and after-shaves and fancy soaps. Not of wind and water and hard work.

Unnerved at the way her blood stirred, Bentley turned and tipped her face up to his, meeting his eyes. "Sleight of hand? I'm not sure what you mean."

He looked at the photo of the whooping crane. "That picture was taken not ten years ago. But that place is gone, replaced by a pricey waterfront housing development." He met her eyes once more, the expression in his hot and hard. "Where do you think that whooping crane nests now?"

Bentley swallowed, a funny ache in her chest. "I don't know."

"Exactly. Sleight of hand, Ms. Cunningham." He motioned to the chair across from his big, battered desk. "Have a seat."

She sank into the chair and crossed her legs, willing their trembling to stop. "I'd like to thank you for this opportunity, Mr. Reese. I'm excited about the chance to work with—"

He cut her off with a wave of his hand. "Let's dispense with the niceties, shall we? All this gratitude and appreciation isn't necessary. In fact, it's not even necessary that you show up."

Shocked, Bentley straightened her already ramrod spine. "Pardon me?"

He made a sound of annoyance. "I don't have time for games right now, Ms. Cunningham."

She resisted the urge to look away and met his eyes boldly. "I understood I was to check in as soon as I arrived. If now is an inconvenient time to acquaint me with my responsibilities, just name another."

Jackson stared at her. Bentley stared back. Slowly, he moved his gaze, raking it over her, taking in her dress-for-success suit, her obviously new briefcase, her unmarred suede pumps.

Bentley knew exactly what he saw; she had taken great pains to achieve a professional, confident look for their first meeting. Yet, as Jackson Reese assessed her, she had the feeling that what he saw lacked. That when he looked at her, he saw the same emptiness she did.

A place in her chest, dangerously near her heart, tightened, and Bentley sucked in a quick, silent breath. She wouldn't let this man intimidate her. "Is something wrong?" she asked, her cool, modulated tone one lie she promised herself Jackson Reese would not see through.

"I expected someone younger."

She lifted one perfectly arched eyebrow. "Did you?"

"Yes."

"May I ask why?" He raked that assessing gaze over her again, and Bentley decided she didn't like him. Not one bit.

"I should think that's obvious." When she didn't reply, he cleared his throat. "May I be blunt, Ms. Cunningham?"

Bentley arched her eyebrows a fraction, sending him a look that suggested he already had been, and that he was no gentleman. "Please do."

"There is no job here."

Nonplussed, Bentley stared at him. "I'm sorry. I must have misheard—"

"You didn't." He picked up a pen and rolled it between his fingers. Bentley couldn't help noticing how large and rough his hands seemed compared to the sleek, silver pen. "Your mother is one of Baysafe's contributors. She called. She said you needed a job..." Shrugging, he let his words trail off.

Bentley filled in the blanks, and embarrassment hit her in a debilitating wave of heat. Insecurity and self-recrimination followed. Her mother had not only found this job, Bentley realized, she had bought it for her.

Just as she had bought her everything else in her life. Including her ex-husband.

She should have known, or at least suspected. She should have checked this job out herself. She should have questioned her mother more thoroughly, should have—

Bentley curled her fingers into fists. The humiliation of being turned down for the jobs she'd applied for was nothing compared to the humiliation she felt now, sitting across from this arrogant man and knowing what he thought of her.

What was worse? she wondered dizzily. Having this man think she couldn't find a job for herself, or that her mother was so sure she couldn't?

Her own breath threatened to choke her, and at that moment Bentley thanked God for her years of etiquette classes, for the hundreds of excruciating teas and nerve-racking beauty pageants, for the countless times she had hidden her feelings behind a brilliant smile and perfectly modulated conversation.

Now she drew her training around her like a suit of armor. "Apparently, there's been some miscommunication here. I very much want to work with an environmental group. Mother had heard of you, she said you had a position for me."

Bentley sent him her most winning smile; to her chagrin he seemed totally unaffected by it. "Although I had several other offers, I wanted to work with the best. I understand that's you?"

"We like to think so."

Bentley laughed lightly and shook her head. "Mother's precious, really, but sometimes she gets...carried away. I've learned to live with it, she does mean well." And when she saw her next, Bentley silently added, she would wring her beautiful neck.

"Many groups need volunteers, Ms. Cunningham. But Baysafe is—"

"I'm not volunteering," she corrected quickly. "I need to earn a living. I intend to."

"I'm sure you do."

At the disbelief, condescension even, in his tone, heat flew to her cheeks. Arrogant, she silently fumed. He was an arrogant, self-important jerk. "Exactly how did my mother pay for this job?"

Jackson paused. "She makes a yearly contribution. This year's was unusually sizable."

"I see." Bentley could just imagine what *sizable* meant. Humiliation warred with fury—having a worthless daughter could get expensive. No wonder Jackson Reese looked at her with such contempt. Bentley worked to keep her thoughts—and feelings—to herself. "I'm sure that was quite a grand sum of money."

"It was."

"And I'm sure you really needed it."

He frowned and tossed down the pen. "We did."

She collected her things and stood. "When would you like me to start?"

Jackson followed her to her feet. "Ms. Cunningham... Bentley, there is no job."

"I'm afraid you're mistaken." She faced him regally. "Carried away or not, my mother bought and paid for this job and, as I see it, a deal's a deal."

Jackson slid his gaze slowly up to hers, a muscle jumping in his jaw. "Tell me, Ms. Cunningham, what do you think of Texas?"

"I beg your pardon?"

"I bet you think of Texas in terms of bright, shiny cities and the thick, black liquid that gushes up out of her to out-fit you in designer clothes and fancy cars. I bet you think of the coast only in terms of fresh seafood and of browning in the sun while sipping some exotic drink. Not in terms of cranes and egrets and herons, certainly not in terms of live oaks and marsh grasses and algae. I bet you don't know the first thing about what we do or what we're up against. So, why don't you go back to Mama and Daddy and let us do what we need to."

He was right. She did think of Texas in those terms. She had no idea what Baysafe did. But that didn't change the fact that she was not going to run home, that she was not going to let him scare her off.

Fuming, Bentley met his gaze. "If I go, Mama's dona-tion goes with me. I don't think that would be too good for your cause. Do you?" At the anger that flared in his eyes, she smiled. "I'm afraid you're stuck with me, Jackson." She moved to the door, turning to him when she reached it. "I'll see you tomorrow morning."

Chapter Two

Hours later Jackson stood in front of the Victoria House Hotel, gazing at its elaborate nineteenth-century facade. In the gathering darkness the curling ironwork cast ornate shadows against the masonry. He shook his head, a smile pulling at his mouth. He should have known Bentley Cunningham would take up residence at the most expensive and elegant hotel in Galveston.

And on The Strand, no less. His smiled deepened. That suited her, too. Once called the Wall Street of the Southwest, the recently restored historical district was about as classy as Galveston got.

Jackson hiked his collar up against the bite of the damp night air. Not much else about this quiet little island would suit her, of that he was certain. Galveston, a barrier island bounded on one side by the Gulf of Mexico and on the other by Galveston Bay, promised plenty for a family to do and see on a three-day vacation, but compared to Houston the shopping was abysmal, the restaurant choices few and the nightlife nonexistent. A jet-setter like Bentley Cunningham would consider Galveston a cultural wasteland. She would be bored silly. Experience had taught him well.

So why had she come?

Jackson drew his eyebrows together. Not for one moment did he buy her song and dance about wanting to work with an environmental group. It didn't fit. Nor did he buy her needing to earn a living. Women like Bentley, from families like hers, didn't earn livings. They lunched and shopped, they married, they volunteered. Again, experience had taught him well.

Crossing to the hotel, Jackson nodded to the doorman as he sprang forward to open the door for him. Inside, Jackson took the marble entry steps two at a time, then headed for the elevators.

He should despise her. He wanted to. She stood for the power of money and all it could buy and bulldoze. He resented being pushed into something he didn't want to do, resented like hell having to kowtow to Cunningham Oil's money.

But he couldn't deny a reluctant appreciation. Not for her looks, although he wouldn't be a man if he hadn't noticed them. Jackson punched the number for her floor. No, it was the way she had stood up to him and all he'd dished out that had earned his grudging admiration.

He'd dished out plenty—contempt, barely veiled criticism for her and her type. He'd hoped to embarrass—even bully—her into running back to Houston. And out of his hair.

But she hadn't run. She'd stiffened her spine and dug her heels in.

But so had he. This wasn't over yet.

Jackson paused a moment outside the third floor's prestigious corner suite, then knocked on the door. She swung it open almost immediately, and his gut tightened at the sight of her. Even without one speck of makeup, she was a sensational beauty. Her face had no doubt inspired men to wild fantasies, flowery poetry and ruinous acts.

Jackson trailed his gaze slowly over her. She wore an emerald-colored robe, cinched at her waist and made of some slippery, silky fabric that had his fingers itching to touch and stroke. The robe concealed more than it revealed, but what he could see of her skin looked smooth, petal soft. Perfumed and pampered, Jackson thought, acknowledging his own cynicism. He'd known her kind of woman before. Hell, he'd made the mistake of marrying one.

He brought his eyes to her face. Her hair was a deep rich brown with just enough red to make it unusual—even exotic. Knowing in his gut that it wasn't bottle-enhanced, he lowered his eyes yet again, taking his time even though she was annoyed, even though he could feel the irritation ripple off her in almost palpable waves.

Jackson smiled. There was nothing he liked more than stirring up an opponent before the big battle.

Except making love.

He dropped his gaze to her bare feet. Her coral-tipped toes peeked out from beneath the hem of her robe, and he lingered a moment, his blood stirring.

When he finally brought his eyes to hers, she arched an eyebrow, all cool, unflappable arrogance. "Inspection over?"

Jackson smiled slowly with appreciation. No doubt she'd leveled many an impertinent servant with that particular tone and look. "Yes, ma'am," he drawled. "There's nothing quite like a long, leisurely gawk at a pretty woman."

The eyebrow arched a bit more, and she folded her arms across her chest. "Now that you've had your gawk, is there something I can do for you?"

He slipped his hands into the front pockets of his denims and cocked his head. "Pretty fancy digs for a working girl."

The ice in her eyes became fire. "I don't see where it's any business of yours, and I certainly don't remember issuing an invitation to call."

"Well, that's good," he drawled, "because I didn't receive one. The mind, they say, is the first thing to go."

She expelled her breath in the tiniest huff. The sound had him grinning. He leaned against the doorjamb, studying her once more. He'd made her angry. It was there in the flashing eyes, the stain of heat on her cheeks, the way her chest rose and fell with her quickened breathing.

At that moment, he found Ms. Bentley Cunningham appealing. Dangerously so. He'd thought Victoria had forever cured him of his taste for pampered princesses.

Apparently not.

He called himself a fool, a glutton for punishment, but still he leaned teasingly toward her. "Are you going to ask me in, Bentley Cunningham?"

She bristled. "I don't believe so."

"A drink, then? A cup of coffee? We could go out."

Bentley gritted her teeth. The man was impossible. Smug. Arrogant and condescending. Ridiculously good-looking. "As you can see, I'm not dressed."

"Too bad."

"For you, yes." She pushed impatiently at the curls that tumbled across her forehead. "What *can* I do for you, Mr. Reese?"

"Jackson," he corrected. "And I'm here to talk business."

He flashed her a bone-melting smile. She swore silently when it did just that. "You disappoint me. I thought, perhaps, you'd come to apologize."

"For my boorish behavior?" Jackson tipped his head back and gave a hoot of laughter. "I'm sure that's the type of treatment you're accustomed to. Sorry, m'lady, but I never apologize. I came to talk about your job."

Her job? The blood rushed to her head, but she lifted her eyebrows haughtily. "Does this means you're acknowledging I have one?"

His smile didn't falter, but it seemed to tighten around the edges. "You gave me no choice. Remember? I'm stuck with you."

"So?"

"So... let's talk business. What can you do, Bentley Barton Cunningham?"

Bentley inched her chin up even as panic curled through her. *Nothing.* "Name it," she said instead. "Anything."

"Anything," he drawled, amusement—and challenge— twitching at the corners of his mouth. "I doubt that."

Bentley narrowed her eyes, panic forgotten at his affront, anger replacing it. "Name it," she said again.

"Ever baby-sat?"

As she met his eyes, he lifted his eyebrows rakishly. She shook her head as realization dawned. His wayward, kicked-out-of-school-again daughter. "That's not what I came to Galveston for."

"It's a job. Of course—" he lifted his shoulders "—if it's not a good enough one, not important enough for someone like yourself, you could run back to Mama and Daddy."

That was exactly what he wanted. It was what her mother wanted, also. Bentley gritted her teeth, furious. "You are a pig, Mr. Reese."

Jackson laughed, the sound rich with amusement. "And you are a princess."

Now she understood the origin of the expression spit bullets, Bentley thought. Because at that moment she felt like she could, indeed, spit them.

She jerked her chin up. This man would not daunt her, could not intimidate her into giving up. She would be the best damn baby-sitter ever. She would tame his unruly, ill-mannered daughter—or die trying.

"How long?" she asked.

A frown tugged at his mouth. "Chloe's been suspended until after the Christmas holidays. But I doubt you'll last a day, let alone six weeks. Last week Chloe went through three sitters in four and a half days. She can be...difficult."

An aching sadness slipped into his expression, and Bentley lifted her hand to comfort him. Realizing what she was doing, she dropped it. "And if I do last?"

He met her eyes, and she suspected by the softness in his that he had been, for that moment, far away. "Pardon?"

"If I go the distance with Chloe, will you give me a shot, a real shot at working at Baysafe?"

Jackson drew his eyebrows together, and considered her through narrowed eyes. "Why Galveston? Why Baysafe?"

"I already told you, I want to work with an environmental group. I heard you're the best."

"Yeah, you told me. I didn't buy it then, I still don't."

"What?" She tilted her head back and met his eyes. "That you're the best?"

"That you give a flip about the environment."

Bentley's cheeks heated, and she cursed their color. "That's your problem, isn't it? Do we have a deal?"

Several seconds ticked past, then Jackson nodded and handed her one of his cards. "Here's my address. Be there by eight and I'll fill you in."

As he started down the hall, she called, "Why me? What makes you think I can handle your daughter, even if only for a day?"

Jackson stopped and turned to face her. He met her eyes and smiled. "You handled me, didn't you? Besides, I'm desperate. See you in the morning, Princess."

Desperate, Bentley thought, watching as he stepped into the elevator and the doors swished shut. Now, there was a commendation. For long moments she stood in the doorway staring at the empty hall, his business card clutched in her hand.

She shook her head and stepped into her suite, closing the door behind her. He'd said she'd handled him. Had she? She felt like a punch-drunk boxer, too tired to go another round, but too dazed to understand the time had come to call it quits.

But, in a way, she had won. If she could go the distance with Chloe, Jackson would give her a real job at Baysafe. She would have *earned* that job. And that felt good. Really good. She smiled.

All she had to do was figure out how to cope with Chloe. How hard could it be? She had been Chloe's age once. And a baby-sitter couldn't be that different from a nanny, and she'd certainly had enough of those growing up.

But that didn't make her an expert, just as having once been a child didn't make every adult a good parent, she reminded herself.

A thread of self-doubt worming through her, Bentley crossed to her music box look-alike. Picking up the box, she wound it and watched the figure circle the base. David had told her that it was for the best she hadn't been able to conceive, because she would have been a terrible mother. She didn't know why he'd said that, didn't know what he'd based his opinion on. The comment had been just another of his cruelties, another of his calculated blows to her self-esteem. Bentley tightened her fingers on the music box's base. In truth, she'd been too devastated to even ask.

She still was.

She shook her head and fought back tears, focusing again on her look-alike belle. Bentley smiled, somehow comforted by the figure. David was wrong. She would prove it—to herself, to the world. Tomorrow she would win Chloe's trust and affection, and earn Jackson's respect.

Tomorrow came fast, and by seven forty-five the next morning, Bentley was scared witless—over baby-sitting a thirteen-year-old. She shook her head, feeling more than a bit ridiculous at admitting it, even if only to herself.

Shaking her head again, Bentley turned onto a lovely street lined with oleander bushes and restored Victorian cottages. The concierge had called this the Silk Stocking district. A smile pulled at her mouth. Jackson Reese lived in the Silk Stocking district? It just didn't fit.

But the house did. Bentley pulled to a stop in front of his home, a raised Victorian cottage with a minimum of gingerbread and a wide, shaded front gallery. She turned off her car and took a moment to study it. He'd left the yard to nature, in a sort of contained wildness. Two large live oaks dominated his property, and oleander bushes, climbing vines and winter blossoms abounded in disordered profusion. Although far from the pristine, manicured lawns and landscaping of the surrounding homes, his garden was beautiful. It reminded her of him.

Disconcerted by the thought, Bentley checked her appearance in the mirror, then took a deep breath. This was it. Stepping out of the car, she headed up the walk. Inset into his front door were two leaded glass panels, and the diamonds of glass caught and splintered the light. She pressed the buzzer.

Moments later Chloe answered the bell, her expression defiant. When Bentley smiled Chloe glared at her, then without speaking turned and stalked into the house. So much for fantasies about winning trust and friendship, Bentley thought, waiting at the open door a moment before following the youngster inside.

The house was charming, with high ceilings and lovingly restored woodwork and floors. Sun spilled through the abundance of windows, dappling the interior in warmth and light. Bentley stopped in the middle of the front parlor, hesitant to venture farther without an invitation.

Just as she started to call out, Jackson came around the corner, his expression thunderous. "Sorry about Chloe's rudeness," he said, yanking on his tie, tightening it.

Bentley worked to appear confident and in control. "It's not your fault."

"Isn't it? I'm not so sure." The tie ended up short; he swore and started over. "Come on in."

Bentley followed him into the large, light kitchen. Here, as elsewhere in the house, instead of renovating and updating, the interior had been meticulously restored. Chloe sat at the table, her expression sulky.

Bentley turned to Jackson. "Your home is lovely."

"Thanks." He poured himself a cup of coffee and held the pot out to her. She shook her head, and he set the coffee on the warming plate just as smoke began to billow from the toaster. Jackson swore again, popping up the now-blackened bread. He looked at it for a moment, as if deciding whether to eat it anyway, then tossed it into the trash.

Bentley clasped her hands in front of her and told herself she was not charmed by his domestic ineptitude. "Did you do the restoration yourself?" she asked.

"Mmm." He dropped another slice of bread into the toaster. "Bit by bit. I bought it before the area was considered anything more than an eyesore. Now, it's—"

"Mother hated it," Chloe interrupted. "She said it was old and ugly and should have been demolished."

"Chloe..." Jackson said, a warning in his tone.

The girl's chin inched up. "She says Daddy could have been somebody, but that he preferred to throw his life away on lost causes. She says—"

Jackson wheeled around to face his daughter. "That's enough, young lady! Up to your room. Now!"

Chloe jumped to her feet, her eyes filling with angry tears. "Fine, I won't talk. I'll be a good little girl and keep my mouth shut, just like you want me to." Turning, Chloe fled the kitchen.

For long moments, Jackson stood and stared after his daughter, a vein throbbing in his neck. Bentley checked the ridiculous urge to put a hand on his arm; instead she clasped both of them in front of her. Jackson Reese, she suspected, would not appreciate the show of sympathy.

Silence stretched between them until, finally, he turned to her. The expression in his eyes—made up of frustration, anger and despair—tore at her and she tightened her fingers. It would not be smart to soften toward this man; he would use it against her. But still, seeing this big, strong man made weak from fear and love for his child made her soften. She couldn't help herself.

"Chloe wasn't always this way," he murmured, a catch in his voice. "She used to be so bright, so eager to please, so happy. There was always something...hopeful about her." He shook his head and met Bentley's eyes. "Or maybe it was that looking at her made me feel hopeful."

Jackson popped his toast up. "It's only been in the last year and a half that she's changed. She was living with her mother. It wasn't working. They fought. Her grades slipped until she was flunking out of school." Jackson rubbed his eyes wearily. "Then, eight months ago, Victoria just up and sent her here. No warning for either of us."

"I'm ..." Bentley let the words trail off. After all, what could she say? She was sorry? That she understood? Those platitudes would mean nothing to him. She said instead, "That would be hard to adjust to."

"We haven't, yet." He laughed, the sound raw and without humor. "Maybe we never will. I don't know."

Bentley bit her lip. The situation with her own parents couldn't be more different, and yet something plucked at her, something begging to be noticed and commented on. But whatever it was, it remained just beyond her reach.

"After Christmas she goes back to boarding school," he continued. "They're giving her one more chance." Jackson checked his watch and made a sound of frustration. "I've got to go. I'm already late."

Bentley's stomach sank at the thought of being left alone with Chloe. She worked to keep her distress from showing. "Wait..." She sucked in a quick breath. "What do you want me to do with her today? What do you expect?"

Jackson met her eyes. "Just keep an eye on her. Keep her out of trouble. Keep her ... safe. Last week she ditched one of her sitters by climbing out her bedroom window. Scared me to death. She was gone all day."

"Oh." Bentley's stomach plunged a bit more. "Is the mall okay? Or a movie?"

"Sure, whatever." He breathed a sigh of frustration. "If this doesn't work, I don't know what I'll do. I have a trip to Washington scheduled ... never mind." Jackson pulled out his wallet and dropped a couple of twenties on the counter. "See that she gets what she wants."

Jackson looked at his watch again and started for the front door. He stopped at the bottom of the stairs and looked up, his expression hesitant. Bentley found herself hoping he would take a moment and go up to talk with his daughter. He didn't.

"I'm late," he said. "I've got to go."

And then he left. Without talking to Chloe, without even calling out a goodbye. Bentley didn't know why that made her so sad, but it did. Jackson wanted it to be right with his daughter; she felt his frustration, his pain. Bentley shook her head. It made her—

"I bet you want to get into my dad's pants."

Shocked, Bentley swung around to face Chloe. The girl stood at the top of the stairs, chin tight, eyes narrowed in challenge.

And now, Bentley thought, the fun began.

Bentley narrowed her own eyes. "I don't believe I'm going to dignify that with an answer."

"That means you do." Chloe laughed. "Mama says women always fall for his big, macho type. And then they want to get into his pants."

"Well," Bentley said breezily, not wanting the child to know just how disconcerted she was, "your mama's wrong. Because I have no desire to, as you so delicately put it, get into your father's pants."

Chloe sniffed and sauntered down the stairs. "Mama says women lie."

Bentley drew in a deep breath. She didn't know Victoria Reese, but she knew she didn't like her. "Then perhaps she's the one who's lying here."

Color flooded Chloe's cheeks. "Don't call my mother a liar!"

"Then don't call me one."

Without waiting for a reply, Bentley turned and stalked to the kitchen. There, needing something to occupy her hands, she poured herself a cup of coffee although she detested the stuff. She counted to ten. Then twenty. Finally, when she heard Chloe crossing the parlor, she pretended great interest in the coffee and the scene from the kitchen window.

A moment later, Chloe stomped into the kitchen. When Bentley didn't look at her, the child huffed and sighed and muttered to herself. Finally, she plopped noisily onto one of the kitchen chairs. "What are we going to do today?"

Bentley took a sip of the coffee and angled the girl a glance. "I'm open to ideas."

"There's an R-rated flick playing over at the mall. Take me."

"Sure."

Chloe's eyes widened. "Really?"

"Certainly. We'll just call your dad to make sure it's okay with him."

"You're old enough to get me in."

"True." Bentley took another sip of the bitter-tasting brew. "But an R rating calls for parental guidance. I'm not your parent."

Chloe scowled, obviously annoyed that Bentley wasn't responding as she wanted—or expected—her to. "Do you smoke grass?"

Bentley's heart stopped, and she counted to ten again. Chloe was trying to shock her, and doing a good job of it. But she wasn't about to let the youngster know she had the upper hand. She leveled the child with a cool stare. "No. Do you?"

"No." Chloe inched her chin up. "But I know some kids who have."

"Well, I suppose that makes you, and them, all grown up."

"You're a drag, just like the others."

Bentley dumped her coffee. "And I happen to think that people who take drugs are ignorant."

Chloe stomped her foot. "Do you know who my mother is?"

A few choice guesses, ones like Wicked Witch of the West, jumped to her tongue, but Bentley swallowed them all and turned regally toward the child. She arched an eyebrow. "I'm quite sure I don't."

"Victoria Ellerbee, that's who. My granddaddy founded Ellerbee Oil." The girl fixed Bentley with a triumphant stare. "We all but own Dallas."

"All but own Dallas? Is that so?" Bentley narrowed her eyes and faced the child, her fists on her hips. "Well, do you know who *I* am? Bentley Barton Cunningham. Cunningham as in oil, Barton as in one of the first families of Texas, as in the Daughters of the Texas Revolution Bartons, as in governors and Senator Barton. My mama took tea with Rosalind Carter, and my grandmama took tea with Mamie Eisenhower. So don't you try to pull family connections with me, young lady, because family connections are something I have plenty of. Do you understand me?"

Chloe nodded, her eyes wide with surprise. "Yes, ma'am."

"Now then, let's get something straight, shall we? You treat me with respect, and I'll treat you the same way. If you act like a spoiled brat, I'll treat you like one." Bentley folded her arms across her chest. "Do we have a deal?"

Chloe pouted and stubbed her toe against one of the chair legs. "I guess so."

"Good." Bentley smiled. "Then, how about some shopping? I'm in the mood."

"In this hick town? Give me a break."

"Houston's only an hour away. We could go to the Galleria. And out to lunch."

Chloe's head snapped up. Excitement, pure little-girl delight, lit Chloe's eyes. A second later it was gone, replaced once again by bored cynicism, but in that moment, when she caught sight of the child beneath the veneer, Bentley could understand some of what Jackson was going through.

"So, what do you think?" Bentley asked. "Houston, shopping and lunch? Or TV game shows here?"

"Shopping." The girl shrugged. "If you want."

Bentley could see Chloe struggle for indifference, and she fought back a grin. She'd won the first battle, no doubt about it. And if she had any say in it, she would win the war, as well.

Smiling, she picked up her handbag and slipped it over her shoulder. "Let's go."

Chapter Three

Bentley and Chloe spent the next several days as they spent the first, at the Houston Galleria, going from one shop to another, with Chloe trying on and buying outfit after outfit. As each day passed Chloe's bored facade slipped a little more, giving Bentley glimpses of a thirteen-year-old who was vulnerable, eager to please and in great need of attention. That child reminded Bentley of herself at the same age. And tugged at her heartstrings.

Bentley shook her head at the thought, watching as Chloe, juggling their soft drinks, made her way across the busy food court. Outwardly she and Chloe were nothing alike. Chloe was fair, she was dark. Chloe's behavior was...well, less than ideal. Growing up, Bentley had been the model of southern grace and manners; she'd striven to be the perfect daughter, had gone on to be the perfect debutante and sorority sister and, later, the perfect wife with the ideal marriage.

Perfect wife, perfect life. How often had David said those words to her? How many times had they replayed obscenely in her head while he belittled and ridiculed her? Bentley shuddered and dragged her thoughts away from herself and her nightmare of a marriage and turned them back to Chloe.

She and Chloe were nothing alike, and yet they were. In the past three days Chloe had charged a small fortune without thinking about it once. With each purchase she had brightened, as if buying things made her feel more whole. And as if looking good somehow validated her existence.

Suddenly melancholy, Bentley trailed her fingers over the scarred edge of the tabletop. She could be reading herself in Chloe without justification. She could be simply transferring her own faults onto Chloe because they had been so much on her mind of late. But she didn't think so.

She let out her breath in an exasperated huff. All this brooding was nonsense. She should be happy that her time baby-sitting Chloe was passing without incident, and that Jackson seemed pleased. She should be elated. She was proving herself and earning the position at Baysafe that Jackson had promised her.

Bentley frowned. But she didn't feel like she'd earned anything. In her heart of hearts, she didn't feel like she'd done Chloe—or Jackson—any favors.

Bentley shook her head again and focused on Chloe. She'd stopped to talk to a boy she seemed to know. Bentley drew her eyebrows together, watching as Chloe blushed and giggled, as the boy leaned close and whispered something in her ear.

The boy looked too old for Chloe and too...experienced. A ripple of apprehension moved over Bentley, and just as she wondered if she should intervene, Chloe motioned at her, said goodbye to her friend and started to the table.

A moment later Chloe set the drinks in front of Bentley. "Sorry," she said a bit breathlessly, sliding into a chair. "He's an old friend."

Old being the key word, Bentley thought, studying the youngster's flushed features. She felt it her duty to question Chloe about the boy, but she didn't want to raise the young girl's ire. If Chloe became angry and defensive, she wouldn't get a thing out of her.

"He's cute," Bentley murmured, taking a sip of her soda. "Do you know him from school?"

Chloe looked at her, then away. "I go to an all-girls school. Rick's an old family friend." She fidgeted with her straw. "Daddy knows him."

"You mean, his parents are family friends?"

"Yeah, that's what I mean. The Ables and the Ellerbees have been friends forever."

Able. The name belonged to one of Texas's most prominent families, a family the Ellerbees would socialize with. Reassured, Bentley smiled. "He certainly is a looker."

Chloe blushed and lowered her eyes. "He'd never be interested in me."

"Are you kidding?" Bentley leaned toward her. "Not only are you gorgeous, but you're rich, too. In Texas, that means you can write your own..." Bentley let the thought trail off as she realized she was reassuring Chloe with the same words her mother had said to her at the same age. The realization left her feeling discomfited.

"Write my own what?" Chloe asked.

Bentley looked at the girl and forced a smile. "What I'm trying to say is, you're a really great girl, Chloe. You're smart, you're beautiful, you can be whatever you want to be. Never sell yourself short." Bentley laughed. "In other words, you're going to have more boyfriends than you'll know what to do with."

Chloe colored with pleasure. "You really think so?"

"I do. Trust me on this." Bentley patted her hand. "I had a good time today. How about you?"

"Yeah. I had a lot of fun." Chloe traced her finger through the beads of moisture on the side of her glass, her smile fading. "The last couple of days reminded me of—" She bit back the words and shook her head. "Never mind."

"What?" Bentley prodded. "You can tell me."

Chloe was quiet for a moment, then she shrugged. "Mom and I used to do this all the time. Before—" Chloe shrugged again, this time with such adult nonchalance that Bentley ached "—before she met *Jacques*. Then she didn't have time for me any more."

"Oh, Chloe..." Bentley let her words trail off, unsure what to say and wishing she had something better, something more profound, to give Chloe than "I'm sorry."

"He's a real slimeball, too. But it didn't matter what *I* thought, she married him anyway." Chloe met Bentley's gaze, hers filled with defiance. "That's why I'm here, you know. I got in the way. That's why she shipped me off to that...prison." She jutted her chin out. "Now I'm in Daddy's way."

"That's not true!" Bentley said quickly, hurting for the child and wanting to reassure her. "I can't speak for your mother, but your father—"

"What?" she interrupted sarcastically. "My father *loves me very much?* Get a life." Chloe jumped to her feet and began to gather up her purchases. "You know, I thought you were different, I thought you were pretty cool. But you're just like the rest. Grown-ups always stick together."

"Chloe, wait." Bentley grabbed her hand. "I didn't mean to upset you, or to imply that your feelings weren't valid. It's just that, yes, I can tell your father loves you...very much. Maybe he just doesn't know how to show it. Maybe he—"

"Save it." Chloe snatched her hand away, her eyes filling with tears. "You don't know anything about me. Neither of them wanted me. They still don't."

Bentley swore silently and stood. "You're right, I don't know much about you. But I know what I see. I know what I feel." When Chloe wouldn't look at her, Bentley touched her arm. "I am trying to be honest with you."

Fighting tears, Chloe shrugged. "This whole thing is totally lame. I'm ready to go."

"Fine," Bentley said, wishing she could solve Chloe's problems, ease her pain, with just a smile or a word. But she couldn't, she didn't have that kind of magic. So instead, she linked her arm with Chloe's and said, "Let's go home."

Several hours later Bentley waited for Jackson. Upon returning, Chloe had retreated to her room, giving Bentley a lot of time to think about what the child had told her. And the more she thought, the more concerned she became. She needed to talk to Jackson about his daughter, to bring up some of the things that were bothering her.

And talking to Jackson, she suspected, would not be easy to do.

Tossing aside the fashion magazine she'd hardly glanced at, Bentley jumped to her feet and crossed to one of the windows that faced the road. She wasn't a teacher, she reminded herself. She wasn't Chloe's parent or guardian. She was a sitter, a paid playmate. Just as Jackson had asked, she had kept Chloe safe and happy. She had done her job.

So what if Chloe had her own American Express gold card? So what if Bentley had seen a crumpled pack of cigarettes in Chloe's purse? So what if Chloe thought her father considered her nothing more than an annoyance? Bentley's heart wrenched even as she sternly told herself that it was none of her business.

She caught her bottom lip between her teeth and pushed aside one the lace sheers. Moments later Jackson pulled into the drive, and as she watched he climbed out of the car and started toward the house. He looked tense, tired and irritable. This was probably not a good time to broach the subject of Chloe with him, Bentley realized.

She would anyway.

The light that spilled from the windows into the darkness bathed him in half shadows; the backdrop of light and dark transformed Jackson's silhouette from that of civilized man to warrior. He looked up and met her gaze, his expression fierce. Bentley shuddered and told herself to either move away from the window or acknowledge his glance, but instead she stood still, immobilized and light-headed, her eyes locked with his.

Something hot and heavy moved over her, something sweetly pungent, like a profusion of blossoms in a still, dark room, like forbidden desire. Shaken, breathless, Bentley dropped the lace curtain and stepped away from the window, her heart a freight train in her chest.

She sucked in a deep, steadying breath and pressed a trembling hand to her mouth. Dear Lord, what had happened to her? For a moment, she had felt ... everything a woman could feel when she looked at a man—desire and regret, power and powerlessness. The need for connection, the fear of it.

She didn't turn as Jackson opened the door and stepped inside. He shut it behind him with a soft click. The sound seemed to resound in the quiet room, and Bentley pulled in another calming breath. Nothing had happened, she told herself. Nothing.

She faced him then, and called herself a liar.

"Bentley?"

She heard the concern in his voice and realized that he would be worried about Chloe. She attempted to smile and found she could not.

"Is something wrong?"

"No. Everything's fine." She cursed the tremor in her voice and clasped her hands together. "Chloe's upstairs. I think she's trying on some of her new things."

He drew his eyebrows together and lifted his gaze to the stairway. For long moments he stood that way, then he turned to her. "Great. Thanks, Bentley. You can go now."

She told herself to do just that. She reminded herself that Chloe and Jackson's problems were none of her concern. She forced a smile. "Good. I'll see you tomorrow."

After collecting her purse and coat, she started for the door. There, she stopped and looked at Jackson, her heart lurching as she saw that he once again gazed toward the stairs and Chloe's closed bedroom door. In his expression she saw frustration and fear, she saw a father who yearned for his daughter. And one who had no idea how to reach that daughter.

Calling herself a dozen kinds of fool, Bentley swung toward him. "Jackson?"

He dragged his attention from the stairs. "Yes?"

"I...wanted to talk to you about Chloe. Something's bothering me, and—" She paused, searching for the right words. When they wouldn't come she settled for the ones that jumped to her tongue. "Don't you think it's a little permissive to allow Chloe her own gold card?"

"What?" he asked, narrowing his eyes almost imperceptibly.

"A gold card. It just seems—"

"Permissive by whose standards?" he interrupted tightly. "Yours? That's rich."

Bentley stiffened at the sarcasm in his tone. "It just seems to me that by allowing her to shop like that, you're only reinforcing—"

"I find this odd criticism coming from the queen of the shop-till-you-drop set." He leveled her a deadly cold stare. "Good night, Bentley."

Angry heat flooded her cheeks, and she tipped her chin up. "It wasn't criticism, it was concern."

"I see. Well, thank you for your *concern*. I'll take it under advisement." Without another word, he turned and crossed to where the day's mail had been stacked and began thumbing through it.

The heat in her cheeks became fire. He was dismissing her! As if she were no more than an annoying fly buzzing around his head. Bentley narrowed her eyes. The arrogant, self-important Neanderthal! She would make him listen whether he wanted to or not.

Stalking across the entryway, she grabbed his arm, forcing him to face her. "What is Chloe's punishment for getting kicked out of school?"

He lowered his eyes to her hand, then lifted them to hers. "Excuse me?"

"Her punishment," Bentley repeated. "What is it? Being allowed to shop every day, spending however much she wants? Being allowed to go to movies and out to lunch?"

A muscle twitched in his jaw. "Amazing. A couple of shopping trips with my daughter and you're an expert on parenting. My, my...you must be some sort of prodigy."

She flung her head back, so angry she shook with it. "You know what I think? That you're punishing yourself."

Jackson leaned toward her, the expression in his eyes dangerous. "What exactly were you the queen of? All belles worth their salt reign as some sort of royalty, and you're just reeking of it. What was it, Princess? The Azalea Ball? Cotton Carnival? Or maybe even the Rose Festival?''

Bentley sucked in a sharp breath. "You are a complete bastard."

"Really," he murmured, arching his eyebrows, mocking her. "I thought I was a pig."

She wanted to shout, she wanted to slug him. She lifted her chin regally instead. "There aren't enough expletives to describe you, Mr. Reese. Good night."

Turning, she crossed to the door. Again, she stopped and looked at him. "You've given up on your daughter, haven't you? Why, Jackson? Your own guilt? Exactly what sin are you paying for?''

Without waiting for an answer, she let herself out. Struggling for control, she forced herself not to slam the door behind her, not to hurry. Even as she prayed he wouldn't follow her, she knew he would.

And he did. Showing none of her control, he slammed out of the house seconds behind her, his fury almost palpable in the darkness. Shivering, she stopped and turned slowly to face him.

He halted inches from her, his breath making frosty clouds in the cold air, fury flashing in his eyes. "You don't know anything," he said, flexing his fingers. "Not about me. Not about Chloe."

"No?" Bentley flung back. "Then why are you so angry?''

"Damn you." He caught her arms and dragged her against his chest. "Damn you to hell."

Bentley tipped her head back and met his eyes, hers filled with challenge. A muscle jumped in his jaw, betraying the depth of his fury. He tightened his hands at her back. She didn't flinch. She didn't beg him to forgive her hasty words, her unladylike emotions. She'd never been so bold, but then

she'd never been so angry, never allowed herself to be. Now
the adrenaline of fury, a lifetime's worth, pumped through
her, and with it a freedom that was both terrifying and ex-
hilarating.

"Damn me to any place you want," she said softly, her
voice as even and sharp as the edge of a razor blade. "It
won't change a thing I said. It won't change the truth."

In that moment, as the words slipped from her lips,
something passed between them. Something hot and pri-
mal and teetering on the edge of control. Bentley sucked in
a deep breath, wanting to deny the heat spiraling through
her, but finding she could not. Sensations, like the perfume
of winter roses, spilled over her, intoxicating her with their
powerful sweetness.

He felt it, too. She saw it in the subtle darkening of his
eyes, felt it in the way his fingers convulsed at her back,
heard it in his quickly indrawn breath.

That Jackson felt the same as she only made the moment
that much more dangerous. She told herself to move away
from him before control topped that edge. Instead, she
brought her hands to his chest, to his thundering heart, and
curled her fingers into the fleece of his jacket.

"Damn you," he said again, lowering his gaze to her
mouth.

She swayed toward him, the blood thrumming in her head
until she was dizzy with it. One moment became two, became a dozen. The night, with its subtle, sultry sounds,
surrounded and enfolded them—the sigh of the wind, the
murmur of distant traffic, the whisper of the small night
creatures.

The sound of Chloe calling her father.

It jarred them apart. Bentley fought back a sound of disappointment even as relief barreled over her. The last minutes had been a mistake, they had been madness. If so, then

why did sanity seem so empty? And why did she wish so desperately that Jackson had kissed her?

The front door opened, light spilled through the rectangle and over them. Jackson made a move to leave, and for the second time that night, Bentley caught his arm. He met her eyes, his own glittering in the moonlight. "You have such contempt for me," she said softly, battling for both breath and control, "yet you're encouraging Chloe to become me. Think about it."

Jackson searched her expression for a moment, his own shuttered. Then, without a sound, he turned and walked away.

Hours later Jackson prowled the quiet house, his mood as dark as the midnight sky. What the hell had happened between him and Bentley?

He shook his head, scowling. She'd been right, he did have little but contempt for her. He knew her type, he knew how she'd been raised, what she stood for. He'd promised himself he would never again make a mistake like the one he'd made with Victoria.

Bentley Cunningham was so much like his ex-wife they could be sisters. And his marriage to Victoria Ellerbee had been a match made in hell. He shook his head. A shrimper's son and an oil baron's daughter. If he hadn't been so besotted he would have seen it from a mile away—trouble with a capitol *T,* a lifetime of paying for one monumental mistake.

Now he saw it coming with Bentley so clearly it chilled him. Even so, electricity crackled between them, and his blood stirred every time he looked at her. And the arousal he'd felt only hours before had been undeniable. Jackson made a sound of disbelief. Undeniable? Earth-shattering had been more like it. Its intensity had stunned him. He'd felt that way only once before, and then he'd been a randy youth, ruled by hormones and an unquenchable sex drive.

Jackson swung toward the picture window that faced the garden where he and Bentley had angrily confronted each other only hours before. Good God, he was nearly forty years old. Too old for the lure of illicit sex in a moonlit garden. Too old to have considered throwing caution to the winds, even if only for a few, brief, shattering minutes.

Crossing to the window, he pushed aside the curtain. Moonlight soaked his wild garden in pale gold, and he imagined it falling over Bentley's smooth, white skin. Warming her. Softening her.

She hadn't needed warming or softening tonight. The picture-perfect beauty had been transformed into a real woman, one alive with anger and indignation. And heat.

His gut tightened. That woman had been unbelievably, dangerously alluring.

Jackson fisted the material in his fingers, pushing away those disturbing thoughts to focus on even more disturbing ones. What was he going to do about Chloe? As much as they had infuriated him, Bentley's words made sense. In the last hours he'd replayed those words in his head, and each time they had sliced deeper, closer, carving out tiny pieces of his heart.

Bentley was right. He hadn't been paying attention to what his daughter was doing. He'd been so relieved that she wasn't climbing out of windows and disappearing, so relieved that he hadn't had to deal with a new sitter and new crisis every day, that he let her do whatever she wished. He hadn't wanted to rock the boat.

Jackson swore. When it came to Chloe, he'd done everything wrong. She had owned his heart from the first moment he saw her, red-faced, wrinkled and howling with indignation. He'd never felt that way before. He remembered smiling stupidly at her through the nursery window, his heart near bursting with pride and love, the thought that he was a father playing over and over in his mind.

Had the guilt started then? Jackson pressed the heels of his hands against his eyes. Or had it started when he'd allowed Victoria to take his daughter without a fight? Or when that first sweet wave of relief had hit him at Victoria's leaving?

Even now, twelve years after the fact, guilt twisted in his gut. He'd let her go. He'd felt relief. What kind of father was he?

And what would he do if he lost her?

Needing air, Jackson wheeled away from the window, crossed to the front door and yanked it open. He stepped outside, the punch of the December air stunning him. He breathed deeply, welcoming its shock, letting it steady him.

When Chloe had been small, he'd been able to cuddle her, buy her an ice cream or a doll, and she'd loved him for it. He'd been able to fascinate her with stories about growing up in a fishing village, been able to hold her rapt with nothing more than a card trick. Being a parent had been easy.

It wasn't anymore.

He had to do something.

Jackson shoved his hands into the front pockets of his denims and looked at the moon. A cloud moved across it, momentarily obliterating its light. This time, he vowed, he wouldn't make any mistakes.

Fingers of sunlight inched across her bed. Bentley gazed at them, thinking of Jackson and wondering what madness had occurred between them the night before. Reaching out, she touched one of the warm rectangles. She hadn't slept. She'd tossed and turned and relived every one of those heady minutes in Jackson's garden.

Bentley frowned. She hadn't found the answers she longed for. Reassuring ones. Ones that made sense. That calmed.

Instead, she'd had to face the truth. And the truth was far from logical or calming. A sexual pull existed between her and Jackson, one so strong that it had left her weak and wanting. She'd never felt that way before. Never.

Dismayed, she sat up. She didn't want the pull; she didn't like it. She would deny it. Bentley inched her chin up. She wouldn't allow herself to be caught up in a destructive relationship with an egomaniac. Once in a lifetime had almost destroyed her.

Throwing aside the covers, she climbed out of bed and crossed to the floor-to-ceiling windows that overlooked Ship's Mechanic Row and its restored nineteenth-century buildings. Cracking the blinds, she gazed down at the still-deserted street.

Bentley smiled, remembering the way she had faced Jackson. She'd told him exactly what she thought, without worrying about how her anger made her look, without worrying that the world would think less of her for having expressed her true feelings. Without doubting herself.

And she'd stood up for Chloe. Even though she'd known Jackson would not be receptive, even though she'd known that, put on the defensive, he would attack.

Every other time in her life she'd backed down. She'd never told David what she'd thought of him. Oh, she'd divorced him, but quietly. She'd let other people—even her own mother—whisper and cluck about *her*, had let them believe that the reason the marriage had ended was that she was selfish and spoiled. She'd allowed David to get away with trying to break her—then with telling the world that it was *she* who was the loser.

She'd let him. She'd given him all the power.

Bentley spun away from the window, her breath about to choke her. Squeezing her eyes shut, she fought the wave of helplessness and self-criticism that flooded her, threatening to drown her.

No. David had been wrong. He was a cruel, sick man. From now on she didn't second-guess herself, she didn't whip herself for decisions and choices she couldn't change. Bentley took a deep, healing breath, then another. Never again would she punish herself for other people's sins.

With that thought, she started to dress.

Within an hour she was not only dressed, but stepping through Jackson's front door. As she did, Chloe raced down the stairs, eager to start for Houston. She had obviously forgiven Bentley their exchange of words the day before.

Bentley angled Jackson a questioning glance from the corner of her eye. He hadn't acknowledged her other than with a generic good morning. He hadn't acknowledged their confrontation of the night before.

A thread of irritation wound through her. She had expected something to have changed. She had expected some sort of reaction to the worries she had expressed about Chloe. She'd been sure he would leave orders that Chloe do something today. Or even that they go nowhere.

Instead, he wished his daughter a good day, gave her an absent smile and headed out the door. So she and Chloe shopped, and again the youngster did as she wished and used her charge card with abandon. And as the hours ticked past, Bentley's irritation turned to anger.

By the end of the day, she was furious. Jackson Reese was a stubborn and arrogant man, she fumed as she waited for him to return from work. He hadn't even thought about what she'd said! Instead, he had thumbed his nose at her and her opinion. Well, she wasn't going to stand for it. If all he wanted was a brainless playmate for his daughter, he could hire a chimpanzee.

When Jackson finally stepped through the front door, Bentley glared at him, ready for a fight.

He lifted his eyebrows. "Something wrong?"

"Daddy!" Chloe came barreling down the stairs. "Can we go out to eat tonight?"

Jackson smiled at his daughter. "Sure, honey."

The youngster beamed at him, and Bentley rolled her eyes. Jackson had no idea he was being manipulated. And even if he did, she thought sarcastically, he probably wouldn't care.

"Can we go to Tony's?"

"Sounds good. Anytime you're ready."

"Great! I'm going to wear one of my new outfits." She started up the stairs, then stopped and turned to him. "Can Bentley come, too?"

"Sure." He shrugged out of his jacket and tossed it on the chair. "Anything you want."

Bentley muttered several unladylike expletives and grabbed her coat.

"You say something?" He angled her an amused glance.

She tipped up her chin. "Not anything I'd care to repeat. Good night." She marched to the door and yanked it open.

"Not coming to dinner?"

Bentley arched her eyebrows in disbelief. "I don't believe so."

"Party pooper." He grinned.

She felt the curving of his lips to the tips of her toes, and swore. "I'm not a party pooper," she said haughtily, "I'm just choosy about who I break bread with."

She started through the door. He laughed, caught her hand and pulled her back. She glared at him.

"Are we upset about something?"

"We?" Bentley flexed her fingers. *"You* don't seem upset about anything."

"Should I be?"

She sucked in a quick, angry breath. "You didn't even think about what I said last night, did you? What you did tonight is a perfect example of what I—" She bit the words off. "Never mind."

She tugged at her hand; he laughed again and tightened his fingers. "Come to dinner. It'll make Chloe's night."

Bentley narrowed her eyes. "She'll survive."

"Come on." He tugged her hand once more, inching her farther inside. He deepened his voice and met her eyes teasingly. "It'll make mine, too."

Her blood pressure skyrocketed, her knees turned to Jell-O. She fought the sensations off. *"Did* you think about what I said?" she asked, the huskiness of her voice shocking her.

He paused, his smile slipping, the teasing light fading from his eyes. "Yes," he murmured. "I've thought of almost nothing else."

"And?"

He paused again, searching her expression. "And I don't know." He laced their fingers and tugged her the rest of the way inside. "Come to dinner. As a thank-you for your concern. As an apology for reacting like a horse's behind."

Bentley hesitated. This time not because she didn't want to go, but because she now wanted so desperately to go. Because now her pulse hammered and her senses were swamped with him. Damn it. If only he wasn't being so sincere.

She let out a long breath. "Jackson, I just don't think—"

"Ta da!"

Bentley and Jackson swiveled toward Chloe. She stood at the top of the stairs, wearing pink denim straight legs with a matching rhinestone-studded jacket.

"What do you think?" she asked, posing. Jackson whistled. "Pretty swell duds for dinner with your old man."

"Well . . ." She started down the stairs. "I wanted to talk to you about that. You know the radio station that plays all the hits all the time?" Jackson lifted his eyebrows, and she rushed on. "Well, they're hosting a beach party, right there at Tony's. Isn't that great? They're going to have a band and drawings for free records and—"

"No."

"But, Daddy, we're going to be right there!" She batted her eyelashes. "I'll be perfectly safe, and Randa and Billie are going to be there, too. Please?"

Jackson hesitated, and Chloe looked imploringly at Bentley. "You'll help him watch me, won't you, Bentley? You'll be able to see me from the restaurant, and I promise I won't leave your sight or talk to any weirdos or anything." She looked at Jackson. "Can I go, Daddy?"

"Bentley hasn't said whether she's coming yet." Jackson looked from his daughter to Bentley. "Are you?"

"Please, Bentley!"

He'd cornered her, the rat. She sent him a withering look, then turned to Chloe. "All right, I'll come."

With a squeal, Chloe raced for the front door.

Chapter Four

Tony's restaurant was located along the ten-mile seawall that protected Galveston Island from the Gulf of Mexico. Built on a pier that jutted out over the beach and into the Gulf, Tony's wasn't much more than a burger joint with a great view.

After her first look at the place, Bentley had considered not eating. But now, after consuming half of the biggest, best-tasting hamburger she'd ever had, she understood why Jackson and Chloe had chuckled at her apprehension.

Bentley didn't know whether it had been the incredible food or the laid-back atmosphere that had affected her nervous system, but at that moment she was dangerously relaxed. Pushing her plate away, she made a sound that was part pleasure, part pain. "Delicious."

Jackson dragged his gaze away from the window and the beach party in progress below. "Told you so." He eyed her plate, amused. "You did a pretty good job on that sandwich, Princess."

She arched her eyebrows. "A gentleman never comments on what a lady eats. It's unseemly." She moved her gaze lazily over him. "But then you, sir, are no gentleman."

Jackson laughed again and held up his hands. "Guilty as charged. Although my mother did her best to instill in us some of the southern code, she was, I'm afraid, outnumbered. Five sons and a husband who had about as much need for cloth napkins and finger bowls as he did for suits and ties."

"Four brothers?" Bentley repeated, incredulous. "Are they as big and mulish as you are?"

He grinned. "Bigger and more mulish."

Bentley fanned herself as if overcome by the vapors. "The poor woman."

Jackson eased back in his chair, a smile pulling at his mouth. "That poor woman kept all five of us in line." He shook his head. "She's not much better than five feet tall and speaks with the softest little drawl. The softer that drawl got, the bigger the trouble we were in."

His eyes alight with amusement, Jackson leaned toward Bentley. "Mama would say, 'Jackson, darlin', you were brought up better than that, now weren't you?' Of course, by then I always knew I was in big trouble, partly because of the drawl and partly because of the way she was slapping her wooden spoon against her palm. So I would just nod and say, 'Yes, ma'am,' as pretty as I could. Of course, manners that late in the game never did any good, but I always hoped."

Bentley laughed. "You're teasing me."

He held up his right hand. "This is the God's truth. Anyway, then she would say to me, sweet as molasses,

'Now, honey, you go apologize to Miss Leigh-Anne and her mama, then you come on back here for your punishment.'" He laughed. "She broke that spoon over my backside more than once."

"I don't doubt you deserved it."

"Oh, I did. I was bad." He cocked his head. "Although my brothers were worse."

"Worse?" Bentley smiled, charmed by the picture he'd painted of his family. And envious. Her childhood had been so regimented and elegant, so…lonely. She took a sip of her tea, swallowing past the lump in her throat. "Are these bad brothers of yours all grown?"

"With kids of their own. Two are shrimpers like Daddy. Bobby's a lawyer and Lee's career Navy." He glanced out the window, spotted Chloe, then turned to Bentley. "What about your family? Any brothers? Sisters?"

Bentley tightened her fingers on her glass, thinking of the ever-present comparisons between her and her siblings. "Two brothers. They're just like Daddy. Wildly successful. Busy." She carefully set aside her drink, then dropped her hands to her lap. "Both are considerably older than I am, and by the time I was in grammar school, they were away at academy."

For long moments, Jackson studied her. His eyes were the light, clear blue of an early morning sky, his gaze uncomfortably direct. She had the feeling he saw things about her she preferred to keep secret.

Unnerved, she looked away. "It was the next best thing to being an only child."

Jackson opened his mouth to comment, then shook his head as if deciding otherwise. Frowning, he looked toward the beach again. "I can't imagine having grown up without my brothers. Without any siblings. It certainly isn't what I wanted for Chloe."

Bentley followed his glance. Chloe was on the beach, laughing with her girlfriends. As if sensing their scrutiny, she looked up and waved.

"She'll be fine," Bentley murmured.

"Will she? I'm not so sure."

He spoke from the heart, and Bentley felt a tug of sympathy. "I know."

"She's a lot like her mother." He drew his eyebrows together. "In every way."

"Is that all bad?"

He turned to Bentley. "I think so."

Bentley lowered her eyes. She didn't know the other woman, but from what she'd heard about her from Chloe, she had to agree. And from what she knew of Jackson, Victoria Ellerbee seemed like the last person he would fall for, let alone marry.

Bentley trailed her fingers over the battered vinyl tablecloth, stopping on a particularly deep scar. She ran a finger gently over it. "How did you meet Victoria Ellerbee? You couldn't have traveled in the same circles. And it doesn't sound as if Galveston was her idea of heaven on earth."

"Through Baysafe." Jackson laughed without humor and curled his hands around his coffee mug. "It's ironic, because she hated it so much."

Remembering, Jackson looked down at the beach, making sure Chloe was still there, then met Bentley's eyes once more. "Ellerbee Oil was my first sponsor. There'd just been a major spill in the Bay, the damage was sickening. At the time of the spill, I was working with the Gulf Coast Marine Research Institute. We all pitched in to help with the cleanup operation. I was astounded to learn there wasn't an organization set up specifically to protect the Bay."

"So, you started one."

"Yeah." Jackson lowered his gaze to his coffee and frowned. He shouldn't be sitting here talking with her like this, shouldn't be feeling so comfortable. He tightened his fingers around the mug. And he sure as hell shouldn't be thinking the thoughts about her that he was. Thoughts of him and her, of a cool, dark room and a big, soft bed.

Those kinds of thoughts had gotten him in trouble before. The kind of trouble a man couldn't turn his back on. The kind of trouble that followed him forever.

Annoyed with himself and his fertile imagination, Jackson continued. "I grew up here, on the Texas coast. My daddy instilled in me a reverence for the land and water, for her bounty, her magic. He always called it the work of the Lord, not man."

Jackson made a sound of disgust. "He talked plenty about the work of man, too. When the shrimp weren't running, Daddy worked on the rigs. The violations he saw were a sin. The land and water were changing, man was changing them, right before our eyes."

"I'm sorry," Bentley murmured.

And she was. The truth of that kicked him squarely in the gut. Even though she wasn't responsible, even though she could give a thousand reasons why it wasn't her responsibility, she was taking blame anyway. Bentley Cunningham wasn't what he'd first thought her, not completely anyway.

Jackson swore silently. Of course she was. This was some sort of game, just like her wanting to work was a game. Right now she wanted something from him. He'd best remember that.

"Back then," he continued, "oil was booming. We had an energy crisis, they said. Nobody thought much about what kind of damage the search for oil was doing. Big Oil could afford to throw some money my way. It made them look good. It paid my rent. It was an impossible situation, a double-edged sword, but back then it worked."

"And now?"

"Now it's not working so well. Now people are aware of what's going on, and of how very fragile the earth is. Now we're making a difference, putting some heavy pressure on Oil and other industries that have always had free rein to do what they liked no matter the consequences."

"And they don't like it," she murmured. "They're pulling their donations."

"Exactly." He picked his coffee up, then set it down, memories tugging at him. "Anyway, I was Lee Ellerbee's pet of the moment. He liked to hold me up to the social set as a shining example of what he was doing for the great state of Texas. I met his daughter at a party."

"You fell in love."

Jackson laughed, the sound cynical. "Not exactly. Although I think at the time I considered myself in love." He angled a glance at Bentley. "We fell in lust. She was the most beautiful, most exotic woman I had ever known. Pampered. Elegant. There wasn't one place on her that wasn't smooth and soft and perfumed. Like she'd never even gotten her hands dirty."

Jackson shifted his gaze to the beach. "Chloe looks like her." Although the size of the crowd had increased, he found Chloe immediately. Her golden hair stood out like a beacon. His heart wrenched with a peculiar combination of love and regret.

"We married six months after we met," he murmured, still gazing at his daughter. "I had no idea she expected me to give up Baysafe and work for her father. That all along she'd assumed I would." He shook his head. "I was so stupid, I thought she understood and was proud of what I did. I had no idea she'd never even considered living on my salary. She laughed when I told her she should. She thought what I did, how much I made, a joke. Anyway, she left and took Chloe with her. Chloe wasn't quite two.''

"I'm sorry."

He brought his gaze to Bentley and shrugged. "It's in the past."

"Is it?"

An ache in his gut, he looked down to where Chloe danced with her friends. For long moments he stared at her, then he shook his head. ''No, I guess it's not. And it won't ever be. Some mistakes are irreversible.''

Bentley opened her mouth to speak; he stopped her. ''I don't want to talk any more.'' He caught her hand across the table. ''Go to a party with me?''

"But—"

"Shh . . ." Even as he told himself it was madness, he curled his fingers around hers, stood and tugged gently on her hand. ''Come on, Princess. No more talking. Let's go listen to the music and pretend we're fifteen again.''

He smiled, and Bentley's stomach crashed to her toes. The man did have a way with a smile. How could the simple curving of his lips make her pulse flutter and her knees weak? It ought to be impossible, illegal.

Even as she told herself to run as far and fast as she could, she got to her feet. ''Fifteen's no good. I had to wear a retainer.''

He laughed. "Sixteen, then."

"We'll cramp Chloe's style."

"That's not a negative."

Laughing, Bentley capitulated, and after paying the bill and collecting their coats, they walked down to the beach.

Instead of releasing her hand, Jackson laced his fingers with hers and as they walked, their joined hands swung between them. Bentley's pulse stirred, and she scolded herself for being an idiot. She wasn't sixteen and she couldn't allow herself to believe that this man was anything other than what she'd first thought. And she definitely couldn't allow herself to be drawn into his life or his problems.

Bentley caught her bottom lip between her teeth, acknowledging that she was too late for her own warnings and that she had a problem. A big one.

The music hit them in a throbbing wave; the energy from the teenagers hit them harder. In the midst of the party, it proved more difficult to find Chloe than from above, and when they finally did, she wasn't pleased.

"Daddy!" she exclaimed, shooting a mortified glance at her girlfriends. "What are you doing here?"

"Bentley and I decided to crash your party." He grinned at her friends. "We're going to pretend we're sixteen."

"Dad!"

Bentley noticed as a handful of boys standing nearby scattered. One seemed familiar, but when Bentley went to take a second look, he'd disappeared into the crowd.

"It was all his idea, Chloe." Bentley laughed and held up her hands. "Really. I tried to talk him out of it."

"Any of you girls want to dance with me? Ever heard of the twist?"

Chloe's cheeks flamed; her eyes filled. She looked like she wanted to die. Remembering the tenderness of that age, Bentley took pity on the girl and grabbed Jackson's arm. "Come on, Jackson," she said, pulling him away. "You're embarrassing her silly."

"Yeah, but did you see those guys take off?" He sent Bentley an amused glance. "They'll think twice before giving her the eye again."

"You'll be lucky if she ever forgives you."

Jackson's smile faded. *That was exactly what he was afraid of. What if she never forgave him for being such a lousy father?*

He stuffed his hands into his pockets. "Would you rather walk or sit?"

"Whichever you prefer."

"Let's sit, then. I don't want to stray too far from the party."

They chose a place far enough from the party not to be deafened by the music, but close enough to keep an eye on Chloe. Bundled in their coats they sat on the sand, and by unspoken mutual agreement, stared out at the dark water.

After a time Jackson cocked his head and studied Bentley's profile. Her beauty reminded him so much of Victoria's, even though they didn't resemble each other at all. The perfection of form and feature, the flawlessness of color and texture, were the same. It was a look, a perfection, that had to be coaxed and cultivated. Like a hothouse flower.

How could one not be sucked in by something that looked so soft and fragile, so beautiful? He knew better than to be fooled by appearances. And yet with Bentley...

Jackson stiffened, realizing where his thoughts were going. No. All he had to do was remember the lesson of the rose. Its beauty invited you in for a closer look, a caress. There, the thorn waited.

"Did you know," Jackson asked suddenly, "that at one time Galveston was the capital of Texas?"

Bentley met his eyes, a question in hers. "No."

"In fact, after the Civil War Galveston was the state's largest and wealthiest city and its principle seaport." He looked out at the Gulf. "Then along came the hurricane of 1900. Except for patches of homes and commercial buildings, the city was completely destroyed. Winds reached one hundred miles an hour, tides in the city reached twenty feet. Six thousand people died."

Jackson plucked a stone from the sand and hurled it out at the quiet water. "They built the seawall, raising the city seventeen feet behind it. But despite the monumental achievement, it was too late. Houston had surpassed Galveston in both size and importance."

Bentley dug her fingers into the sand. "You have a point here?"

Jackson turned and met her gaze. "Chloe sure has taken to you."

"I've taken to her, too."

"Six sitters before you, she despised them all." Jackson found another stone and curled his fingers around it. "But then, they didn't have the right credentials."

Bentley cocked her head toward him and let the sand slip through her fingers. She drew her eyebrows together at the tightness of his expression, at the change in his mood she felt as much as saw. "Credentials?"

"Mmm." He looked at her. "Your club membership, Princess."

Bentley stiffened. He couldn't give her credit for having done something well. Instead, he wanted to turn her success with Chloe into a negative.

"What exactly are you saying?" she asked, her hands trembling so badly she clasped them in front of her.

"Chloe and her mother spent a lot of years the same way you and Chloe have spent the last few days."

The truth hit her then, and Bentley caught her breath. It was so obvious, she couldn't believe she hadn't seen it before. "Victoria is why you have such contempt for me, isn't she?" She caught her breath. "You think I'm like her."

"Yes."

Fury blindsided her. She didn't know why his opinion should make a difference—all her life she'd been judged by other people's rules and notions, by things that had nothing to do with her. It shouldn't matter.

But it did make a difference. It did matter.

She wanted to slap him, she wanted to shout. Instead, she straightened her spine and met his eyes evenly. "You want to believe that. You want to believe the only reason Chloe likes me is that I'm like her mother. That way you can discount my criticisms of how you're raising her. And you can discount me that way, too." She balled her hands into fists. "Well, I'm not like her. You don't know anything about who I am or what I feel."

Her words hit their mark, and Jackson sucked in a sharp breath. Reaching out, he cupped her cheek in his hard palm. "You move like Victoria, you carry yourself the same way. You even sound like her. And it all reeks of money, of a kind of power that doesn't have to be earned but is given at birth. Admit it, Princess, you're a card-carrying member of the Lucky Sperm Club."

Bentley jerked her head away from his touch. "If that's true, then why are you here with me? If I'm so despicable, why are you looking at me like you're aching to kiss me?"

Jackson stared at her, shock warring with fury inside him. She was right. Even knowing all he did about the type of person she was, he wanted to kiss her. Worse, he had allowed himself to forget the lessons of his past—even if only for a couple of hours.

She started to scramble to her feet; he caught her hand and pulled her down beside him. She landed on her knees in front of him, and he caught her other hand. "What is your story?" he asked, his tone scathing. "Why are you here? Daddy take the credit cards away? Or maybe you're searching for the real you." He tightened his hands around hers. "Or is this some sort of rebound trip?"

"Bastard." She yanked against his grip. "Let me go."

"That's it, isn't it? I should have figured, you're running away from a guy." He narrowed his eyes. "Husband or lover?"

She stiffened. "None of this is any of your business. Let me go before I—"

"Not until you tell me." He lowered his voice. "Which was it?"

"Husband." She flung her head back. "Satisfied?"

"No." He tugged her closer, suddenly and irrationally as angry as she. "What happened?"

"Why do you want to know?"

"Because I do, damn it."

"Ask my ex-husband, he'll tell you. I didn't know how good I had it. I was a spoiled, selfish brat. Just like your ex-wife."

"Were you?"

She curled her fingers into the fleece of his jacket so tightly her knuckles whitened. She was done letting other people make judgments about her. She didn't care how it looked, or about the rules of ladylike behavior. She looked dead at him, her eyes narrowing with fury. "To hell with you."

A second of silence tightened between them, then, muttering an oath, he dragged her mouth to his. He took her mouth forcefully, arrogantly, and her neck arched under the pressure of his kiss. He hoped to shock her—at least that's what he told himself. He hoped to send her running back to Houston—or so he assured himself.

But if he wanted her to run, why was he pulling her closer? Why was he winding his fingers in her hair and losing himself in the potent, heady taste of her?

He forced himself to break the contact. Her eyelids fluttered up, and she met his gaze. Her irises had darkened to jade with arousal. Muttering another oath, he took her mouth again.

As Jackson's mouth settled on hers, Bentley shuddered, rivers of heat washing over her. The heat mixed with her fury, and passion exploded inside her. Heady, blinding passion. Opening her mouth, she answered his urgency with her own.

Jackson's kiss wasn't smooth, it wasn't practiced. He neither coaxed nor wooed; he assumed, he took. He plundered. And she relinquished herself to him. Totally.

Tangling her fingers in his hair, she invited him to dive deeper, to take more. And more.

She made a sound of pleasure low in her throat, arching against him, and Jackson went crazy with need. His own response didn't surprise him, not after the garden the night before, but hers did. Gone was any semblance of the woman he'd pegged her to be, the cool, bored princess. The woman who'd had everything handed to her, a woman who was selfish and spoiled and shallow.

The woman in his arms seemed genuine and the tiniest bit vulnerable. There was a sweetness in her kiss, a lack of artifice that he found as endearing as he did exciting. She didn't hold herself back, but instead gave everything and asked for nothing in return.

It couldn't be. But for a moment, he let himself revel in the illusion.

Bentley breathed deeply through her nose, growing dizzy on the scent of the night, the water and Jackson. He tasted wild, like the coast he worked to protect, like his untamed garden. He towered over her, strong, almost overpoweringly masculine. In his arms, against his chest, a woman would never have to worry about falling. She would never have to fear failure or frailty.

But she would never have to stand on her own two feet, either. Bentley lowered her hands to his broad chest, to his thundering heart. Men like Jackson preferred their women that way—feminine and dependent. Under their protection and under their thumbs. And they kept them there by chipping away at their confidence, their self-esteem.

She flattened her hands and pushed against him, a sound of denial wrenching from her as she did. She couldn't be that kind of woman ever again. Not and live with herself.

Jackson didn't resist, and for long moments they stared at one another, both fighting to even their breathing, both working to compose themselves. Bentley read emotions similar to hers in his expression—fading desire, shock, anger, self-directed contempt. It was the emotions she didn't see that made her ache. Ones like humor, tenderness and warmth.

Bentley shook so badly she feared she would fall flat on her face if she stood. She stood anyway and swung away from him. She fought for control and even though it took everything she had, she pulled her armor around her, promising herself she would never allow him to crack her reserve again.

Lifting her chin, she turned to face him. "I hardly think," she murmured coolly, "that was necessary."

"Don't you?" Jackson fought for breath and searched her gaze. "Don't you ever give in to impulse or momentary insanity?"

"No." She dusted sand off her jacket, praying he wouldn't notice how her fingers and voice trembled. Praying he wouldn't see that with him, impulse and insanity ruled her. "Try to restrain yourself in the future. I didn't like it."

"Excuse me?" He narrowed his eyes. She could tell him any number of things right now, and he would take her at her word. But not that. "I'd say you liked it...very much."

She looked haughtily down at him. "Don't presume to tell me what I felt. Not ever. Do not presume to tell me—"

Jackson stood and pulled her into his arms before she could finish the thought. "Then I'll show you," he muttered, and lowered his mouth to hers once more.

She resisted. For a moment. Her hands pressed against his chest. For a split second. Then she curled her fingers into his jacket and tugged him closer. She parted her lips, inviting him inside.

Jackson tangled his hands in her thick, soft curls, satisfaction—and arousal—spiraling through him. He'd won. But lost. For, in proving to her how much he moved her, he had only served to remind himself how dangerously attracted he was to her.

This was a woman who wrapped herself around a man, a woman who could turn him and his world inside out. He'd been gutted once before; it was an experience he wouldn't forget. And one he'd vowed never to repeat.

Jackson released her so quickly she stumbled backward. Swinging away from her, he dragged his hands through his hair and sucked in gulps of the cold, damp air. "That was incredibly stupid," he said, furious with himself, unreasonably angry with her. He looked over his shoulder and met her eyes, his own narrowed with determination. "I'm not going to repeat the mistakes of the past. I'm not going to fall into lust with you."

With trembling fingers, Bentley drew her coat tightly around her. "Just who are you trying to convince, Jackson?" When he didn't answer, she inched her chin up a notch, fighting back tears. "Don't worry about me, I didn't start this. You did. But I am going to end it. Now."

Turning, she walked away.

* * *

It was nearly midnight when her phone rang. Bentley reached for the receiver, catching it before it jangled the second time. "Hello?"

"Did I wake you?"

Bentley squeezed her eyes shut at the sound of Jackson's voice. She hadn't been sleeping; in truth, she wondered if she would ever sleep again. But she would never tell him that.

"Bentley?"

"No."

He paused and a shudder moved over her. She couldn't keep herself from remembering what it had been like in his arms, his mouth on hers. Nor, it seemed, could she keep her body from responding to the memory. Suddenly uncomfortably warm, Bentley pushed the covers aside.

"Why are you calling me?" she asked.

For a long moment he didn't speak, then he said so softly she had to strain to hear, "Being a parent is the hardest thing I've ever done. Loving Chloe's easy, it always has been. Even putting up with the hassles, with the behavior problems, has been easy."

He fell silent for a moment. When he spoke again, the huskiness of his voice made her heart turn over. "But doing the job right, doing what's best for Chloe instead of what's convenient for me, that's hard. I haven't done such a great job."

Bentley fought to keep her voice from betraying her feelings, from betraying the ache of longing in the pit of her stomach. "What are you saying?"

"You were right. About Chloe."

She twisted her fingers around the phone cord. It was a small victory. He wasn't a man who often admitted a mistake. Or one who gave another power. His doing so warmed her more than anything else could have. "I know how hard that was for you to say."

He paused and it was almost as if she could hear him thinking, regretting. Could he hear her own regrets? Or worse, her longings? "Yes," he murmured finally, "it was."

"But you haven't changed your opinion of me?"

"I can't afford to have any affection for you."

"I hardly think we're in danger of that." But they were—at least, she was—in great danger of just that. "A little mutual respect, maybe?"

She could imagine his grin, imagine that impossibly sexy curving of his lips, the flash of his not-quite-straight teeth. The smile colored his voice. "Maybe."

"I can live with that." She'd lived with a lot less; she wanted more . . . much more.

"You'll still take care of Chloe while I'm in Washington?"

"Of course."

"And Bentley?"

"Yes?"

"Don't come to the house this morning. Come to the office. I'm putting you both to work."

Chapter Five

Bentley's elation lasted until she stepped into the Baysafe offices the next morning. And faced Jill Peters.

The other woman looked her over, doubtfully taking in her winter white wool slacks and matching silk blouse, the double strand of matched pearls and low-heeled suede pumps.

"Honey," she said, with a husky Texas twang, "are you sure you have the right address? The Junior League meets down the street."

Heat tinged Bentley's cheeks, and she straightened her spine. "Mr. Reese asked me to come in this morning. Is he here?"

"Nope." A saucy smile spread across Jill's freckled face.

"Oh." Near forty and plain as prairie dirt in both appearance and manner, Jill Peters had a way about her that both intrigued and terrified Bentley. The other woman would not have any patience with airs or incompetence. The two things Bentley did better than anything else. "Do you know when he will be in?"

"Uh-uh. Said something about taking his daughter over to help with the Stewart Beach clean-up. I hear tell she pitched a fit." The office manager clucked her tongue. "He's sure to be in a foul mood when he does get here."

Terrific, Bentley thought. That news really put her at ease. "Did he leave word with you about what I was to do this morning?"

"Nope," Jill said again, then looked Bentley square in the eyes. "This Chloe thing, you partly responsible?"

Getting better and better. Bentley lifted her eyebrows coolly. "And if I am?"

"All I can say is, it's about time." Jill shook her head and her short, sandy hair fluttered around her face. "That child's a regular hellcat. Jackson hasn't had one quiet moment since her mama up and sent her to him."

Uncertain how to respond, Bentley cleared her throat. She didn't know anything about this woman except that she worked for Jackson, and it didn't seem right to stand here and gossip about Jackson's problems. "I'm sure it's been difficult for them both," she said finally.

"Mmm." Jill narrowed her gaze speculatively, eyeing Bentley and her clothes once more. Then, as if making up her mind about something, she smiled and stood. "I tell you what, I've got a stack of news items to clip and file. I've been meaning to get to them for a time now. If you'll watch the phone, I'll get to it. That way both jobs get done and you won't ruin those fancy duds. Ever manned a three-line system?"

She hadn't, but with a minimum of instruction, it proved simple enough. Especially since only a handful of calls came in. The minutes ticked past, the office silent save for the rustle of newspaper and the click of Jill's scissors.

Bentley drummed her fingernails on the desk and wished she was busy. So busy she couldn't think about Jackson and what had happened between them the night before.

Fireworks. Spontaneous combustion. Total insanity.

Her pulse fluttered, and she frowned, annoyed with herself. He was arrogant and narrow-minded and conceited. She barely tolerated his presence.

Then why did he make her feel like a gawky teenager—aware and aching and ready to throw caution to the winds? Still frowning, she dug in her handbag for her nail file.

Bentley paused, remembering the way he'd sounded at midnight, sleepy and the tiniest bit sheepish. Her heart had turned over, and in that moment she'd forgotten all about being angry. She'd forgotten about being smart.

He'd extended the olive branch—just a bit. How could she refuse to take it? A trembling started in the pit of her stomach and spread until her fingers shook so badly she had to put down the nail file. She squeezed her eyes shut. What was she getting herself into?

The door flew open, and Jackson stormed into the office, his expression as dark as a thundercloud. When he saw Bentley he stopped and glared at her. "Where's Jill?"

Bentley glared right back, pushing away the thread of hurt that wound through her. So much for the olive branch. "Well, good morning to you, too."

"Right here, sugar." Jill waved her scissors from the corner by the file cabinets. "And be nice to the girl, she's doing a terrific job with the phones."

"I can see that." He looked pointedly at the nail file.

Bentley counted to ten, then said sweetly, "Got up on the wrong side of our cave, did we?"

Jill giggled, and Jackson shot a withering glance her way. "Any messages?"

"Several." Bentley held them out, and Jackson took them from her, rubbing his temple with his other hand as he did. She noticed the lines of tension around his mouth, the shadow of fatigue in his eyes. He hadn't had a good night; his morning had been worse. Even as she felt—and cursed— the tug of sympathy, she asked softly, "How's Chloe?"

His mouth tightened. "Madder than a cornered coyote. I dragged her kicking and screaming to help with the Stewart Beach clean-up. She had other plans for the day."

Bentley had no doubt what those plans had been— Houston, shopping and lunch. With her.

He smiled grimly. "Last night I called Lee Ellerbee about Chloe's credit cards. After I assured him that he could buy his granddaughter any gift he liked, he agreed to cancel them."

"Oh, dear," Bentley murmured. She knew from experience what credit cards meant to a girl like Chloe. She could imagine how the girl had reacted to having them taken from her. Poor Jackson. "Is there anything I can do?"

"Don't worry about it," Jackson muttered, stuffing the messages into his shirt pocket, "we'll live."

Without you. He didn't say the words but they were there, in his expression, in the way he turned and crossed to Jill, the way he kept his back to her.

Anger curled through her, and Bentley squared her shoulders. If he thought she was just going to sit back and let him shut her out—out of the situation with Chloe, of the workings of Baysafe—he had another think coming.

"Big Earl called me at seven a.m. Seems he got wind of my upcoming trip to D.C. and wants to pay me a call," Jackson told Jill.

"Oh, no," Jill murmured, meeting his eyes. "You think he's going to—"

"Pull his pledge? Why else would he be coming down to take *me* to lunch?" Jackson swore. "We've got problems, Jill."

"You could back off the double-hull issue."

Jackson fisted his fingers. "No way. I'm not going to bow to their pressure. I'll shut down the office and work out of the house first."

"Excuse me," Bentley said, drawing her eyebrows together. "Are you talking about Big Earl Cassidy, king of the Texas Gas 'n Go marts?"

Jackson looked over his shoulder at her, obviously annoyed. "Yes."

"Why, I've known him most of my life. He's just a big old teddy bear."

Jackson scowled. "That's your interpretation, Bentley. Ours is a bit different."

She counted silently to ten, then said sweetly, "I could talk to him."

"No, thanks. Now, if you don't mind, Jill and I have business to—"

"Wait," Jill interrupted, tossing her scissors on top of the newspapers. "Maybe Bentley *should* talk to Big Earl. Maybe she can influence him—"

"No." Jackson looked from one woman to the other. "No," he repeated. "Absolutely not."

"Why?" Bentley hitched up her chin. "I could help. I'm sure of it."

"Let's give it a try." Jill dusted off her hands and stood. "What do we have to lose?"

Jackson gazed at the two women once more, then frowned and faced Bentley. "What do you know about the double-hull bill?"

"Nothing, but—"

"Do you know what a double hull is?"

She narrowed her eyes, offended. "Obviously, it has something to do with a boat. But—"

"Do you know how Baysafe operates? Or what percentage of our budget the Gas 'n Go pledge is?"

Bentley folded her arms across her chest. "No. But I understand charities and the people who support them. I tell you, Jackson, I know how this man operates."

"I already have the meeting planned." When Bentley opened her mouth to argue some more, he held up his hand. "Discussion closed."

"He does have a point," Jill said sadly, smiling at Bentley. "It was a good thought, but you better let him handle it."

The phone rang then and Bentley answered it. It was for Jackson; he took the call in his office. Jill went back to her clippings and Bentley stared at Jackson's closed office door, frowning. His stubbornness came as no surprise, nor did his unwillingness to trust her judgment.

She let her breath out in an annoyed huff. But she could help, she knew she could. Surely he could see that.

Only he didn't want to see. He was determined to discount her.

Fine, she thought. If he didn't want her help, she wouldn't give it. His loss.

Thirty minutes later Big Earl Cassidy strode through the door. With his thatch of thick white hair, florid complexion, cowboy boots and belt buckle that would choke a horse, Big Earl looked every inch the stereotype of a Texas rancher. Bentley knew he'd been born and raised in the city. She also knew his florid complexion had nothing to do with the great outdoors and everything to do with a penchant for Jack Daniel's straight up.

"Earl." Bentley stood and held out her hands to the older man.

He took them. "Bentley, baby, what are you doing here?"

She smiled and offered her cheek. "I work here."

"Work? You?" For a moment he looked stunned, then he grinned. "I know how you gals are about your charities. Why, my own little Bitsy gives up three hours a week to help those stray dogs of hers."

Bentley gritted her teeth at his condescending tone and hoped Jackson hadn't heard. "How is Bitsy?" she asked. Bitsy was Big Earl's fourth wife and had been one of her sorority sisters.

"Fine, just fine. She's out shoppin'." He shook his head, bemused. "That gal can shop more than all my other wives put together. She tells me it's an art."

"Big Earl."

At Jackson's greeting, the other man swung around. "Reese. How are you, my boy?" Earl stepped forward and held out a hand.

Jackson clasped it. "Very well, thank you."

Bentley watched the two men exchange greetings, noticing the subtle hardening of Earl's voice and expression, the determined set of Jackson's jaw. Both were preparing for battle.

She cocked her head. Bentley had always thought Earl Cassidy a big, rugged man, but next to Jackson he seemed like a dime-store cowboy. Even so, Jackson would not win this battle. She knew the outcome from years of watching her father and brothers, from listening to their business associates. And from living with David. Big Earl had made up his mind.

No matter what Jackson had told her about butting out, she had to do something.

She cleared her throat, stood and smiled prettily at Earl. "Are you two gentleman ready to go? I missed breakfast and I'm afraid if I don't eat soon, I'll swoon."

Both men turned and looked at her, Jackson with murder in his eyes, Earl with a gleam of pleasure. In her corner, Jill started to cough.

Undaunted, Bentley tucked her clutch under her arm. Jackson would thank her later, she vowed. This time he would *have* to admit she'd been an asset. "Shall we?"

During the drive to the restaurant and most of the meal, Jackson seethed, his anger barely contained. Big Earl didn't seem to notice, and he spent the entire meal flirting with her and chitchatting about common acquaintances.

Finally, when the waitress had brought their coffee, Big Earl cleared his throat and directed his attention to Jackson. "Came down to talk to you about your upcomin' trip to Washington." He pulled out a cigar and after Bentley nodded, he lit it. "Don't like it, Reese. Don't like it one bit."

"So I gathered." Jackson leaned forward in his chair. "But I don't understand your concern. The double-hull legislation does not directly affect your business, Big Earl."

Earl puffed on the cigar and narrowed his eyes. "Anything that affects Oil and Gas affects me. I want you to lay off. That's not a request."

Jackson tossed his napkin aside. "I can't do that. This is too important an issue. In the long run requiring all tankers to have double hulls will not only save the world another incident like the one in the Prince William Sound, but will save Big Oil millions in clean-up from such a spill. In the end, everybody wins."

"I'm sorry, boy, I just don't see it that way."

"You know, Big Earl," Bentley murmured, laying her hand on the older man's arm, "when you and Bitsy got engaged, there was a lot of talk. There were folks who thought

it just wasn't right because of the difference in your ages."
She squeezed his arm gently to lessen the sting of her words.
"But you and Bitsy, well, you did what you knew was right.
You followed your heart. That's all Jackson's doing. Doing
what he believes is right."

"I'm not arguing with that, gal. But I've got to protect the
people who fuel my business."

"Big Earl," she admonished, fluttering her eyelashes and
leaning a fraction closer to him. "You're a self-made man,
a maverick. Nobody gave you anything, you had to work for
every dime. What would you have done if some big gas
company had come along and told you that you couldn't
pump on Wednesdays?" She didn't wait for his answer.
"The Big Earl I know would have spit in their eye." She
lowered her voice in reverence. "You're a Texan. So am I.
All we're trying to do is save this great state for good Texans
like you and me."

He cracked a smile. "This is the greatest state in the
union. I'd defy any man—or woman—to tell me differently."

"There you are," Bentley murmured as if he'd spoken the
Gospel. "But if we're not careful, Earl, there won't even be
any good fishing left in Texas. Why, if we're not careful,
we'll have to go clear to Arkansas just to catch a fish."

"I do enjoy my fishing trips." The older man studied the
tip of his cigar for a moment, then shifted his gaze to Jackson. "You fish, Reese?"

"Grew up fishing," Jackson murmured. "A lot of those
spots are gone now. The best spots."

Earl narrowed his eyes, then crushed out the stogie. "You
two present a convincing argument. I'm not promising
anything, but I'll think about it."

During the ride to Baysafe, Jackson said little. Bentley kept up a stream of chitchat with Earl, and when he dropped them off, she promised to get together with Bitsy soon.

She and Jackson watched Big Earl's Cadillac drive away, and the moment it was out of sight, Jackson grabbed her arm. She winced at his grip, but met his gaze evenly.

"Don't ever do that again," he said, his voice sharp with fury. "Because if you do, no amount of money will keep me from wringing your beautiful neck."

Without another word, he dropped his hand and strode into the office. She followed him, trembling with outrage. Jill took one look at them and ducked behind a newspaper.

Bentley grabbed his arm, forcing him to face her. "Don't do what?" she demanded. "Save your butt?"

"Misrepresent this agency," he shot back. "You didn't give him one fact. All you did was puff him up and bat your eyelashes. What did you think qualified you to interfere in delicate negotiations with a major donor?"

She narrowed her eyes. "A major donor who was about to pull his pledge. And one who is now, because of me, considering not doing so."

"You don't even know what we do."

She jerked her chin up. "Don't kid yourself, Jackson. It's not that complicated."

A vein throbbed in his neck; his eyes flashed fire. But when he spoke his voice was low and even. Bentley thought of the story Jackson had told her about his mother. If it was a case of like mother like son, she was in deep trouble.

"We're about so much more than a guy being able to go out on the bay and troll for a flounder. So much more than being a patriotic Texan. Our actions have consequences that affect the world...forever." Jackson flexed his fingers. "When Big Earl's blood pressure evens out, do you really think he's going to think any more about his decision?"

"I already considered that. I have a plan."

Jackson's jaw hardened. "No, Bentley. You've done enough. I'll take care of this."

"Jackson." She reached out to touch him, then dropped her hand. "You don't understand. For Big Earl, pledging money to Baysafe isn't about more than fishing." She pushed at the curls that tumbled over her forehead. "This is a form of aggrandizement for many of your donors. Publicity. Public relations. You yourself said that's what Lee Ellerbee used you for. If Big Earl drops you and gives his money to Bitsy's strays, he still gets what he wants."

She lowered her voice and took a step toward him. "I know these people, Jackson. You don't. Charities are a way of life for them, but rarely are their motives completely altruistic."

He raked his gaze contemptuously over her. "You know so much? What the hell are you doing in Galveston? You should be head director at one of those big, swanky charities in Dallas. Hell, in New York."

Bentley caught her breath at his sarcasm, but inched her chin up defiantly. "You can't give me an inch, can you?"

"No." He folded his arms across his chest. "I can't."

"You will," she murmured, narrowing her eyes in determination. "I intend to make you eat crow, Mr. Reese. Just watch me."

The woman was driving him crazy. Jackson sat behind his desk, staring broodingly at the photograph of the whooping crane that had so caught Bentley's attention the day she arrived at Baysafe. A week had passed since their meeting with Big Earl, and in that time she'd hardly looked his way, let alone spoken to him.

He tore his gaze away from the photograph, drawing his eyebrows together in a frown. She pulled at his thoughts, his attention, day and night. He was plagued by the memory of their kiss, by the way she'd made him ache with arousal.

And by the memory of his past mistakes.

His frown deepened. Bentley seemed to be having no such problems. Each day she'd come into the office and had completed any task Jill assigned her, doing so efficiently and with a minimum of fuss. She and his office manager had become big buddies, and periodically he could hear them talking and laughing together in the reception area.

Like now. Jackson tipped his head, listening to Bentley's laugh. The sensual sound washed over him, taking his breath, stealing his good sense until all he wanted, all he could think to do, was to storm into the reception area and drag her into his arms, her mouth to his.

Damn it. Annoyed with himself, Jackson swung his chair around so his back faced the door and Bentley laughing on the other side. This had to stop. The night before he'd sunk to a new and even deeper low. Bentley had called Chloe to see how she was doing, and the two had chatted for thirty minutes. The whole time he had stood brooding at the front window, staring at his garden, his senses swamped with memories of the sweet scent of her hair, the small, breathy sounds she made when he touched her, with the feel of her mouth on his.

He hadn't mooned over a woman since adolescence. Jackson swore and faced the bright, cold day. Why this woman? Why couldn't he do what he had to and put her out of his mind?

Jill buzzed him, announcing Big Earl on line one. Jackson took a deep breath. He'd been waiting for this call, preparing himself for the inevitable. He hadn't had much hope that Bentley's Band-Aid would hold, indeed was surprised it had taken Cassidy this long to get back to him.

Jackson cleared his throat, then picked up the receiver. "Big Earl. Good afternoon. What can I do for you?"

"Reese," the other man said, dispensing with preliminaries, "I've made my decision."

Jackson braced himself, his mind racing ahead to the measures he would have to take should Big Earl say what he expected him to.

"I'm going to continue my pledge to Baysafe."

One moment became several as, stunned, Jackson stared blankly at the view from his window. He cleared his throat. "Could you repeat that?"

The older man chuckled. "Don't act so surprised, boy. Not after having brought in the big guns, so to speak. I've got to hand it to you, getting Bentley to contact Bitsy was a shrewd maneuver. She's in an absolute state about those cute baby birds."

Baby birds? What baby birds? Jackson shook his head to clear it. Bentley had contacted Bitsy—despite his direct orders to butt out?

"We do appreciate your wife's concern," Jackson said finally.

"I'll just bet you do." The older man chuckled again. "I tell you, my boy, at my age—and considering Bitsy's—I'd much rather take the flak in the boardroom than in the bedroom. I can't afford too many missed opportunities."

Jackson laughed. "Whatever your reasons, Big Earl, we're grateful for your support."

After a few more minutes of small talk, Jackson hung up, wrestling with a strange mixture of emotions. Relief that disaster had been headed off at the pass. Surprise at Bentley having pulled it off, admiration at her pluck. And regret—that he could no longer fit her into the neat little niche he'd carved out for her.

That complicated things. Big time.

Jackson squinted against the light tumbling through his window. It would be so much easier to continue to fight the pull between them if he thought her cold and shallow and weak.

But she wasn't any of those things. At least not exclusively. She had guts. And nerve. And there was kindness in Bentley, an ability to feel deeply. Her handling of Chloe was proof of that.

He didn't want her to have any of those qualities. He hated that he'd found one warm, likable thing about her. It scared him senseless that he'd found several.

Jackson frowned, working to focus on what he hadn't learned about her. Things like what her actual motivations for coming to Galveston were. And what her game really was.

He rolled his tight shoulders, acknowledging that the answers to those questions didn't mean nearly as much as they had before. If anything.

Nor did it matter that when she got bored with this, with Galveston and Baysafe, she would move on to something else.

But for now, she'd pulled him—and Baysafe—out of the fire. A little respect, she'd said on the phone. He owed her that . . . he owed her an apology.

Jackson checked his watch and went in search of her.

Bentley said good-night to Jill, then started slowly across the parking lot toward her car. She'd been with Jill when Big Earl's call had come in. She'd held her breath, waiting for Jackson to say something to her or Jill, waiting for a shout of relief or glee, but it had been silent in Jackson's office long after the line's light on the phone had gone out.

Disappointment took her breath. Her ploy hadn't worked.

"Bentley!"

She turned as Jackson called her name, then swore silently. The man was practically swaggering across the parking lot. No doubt he wanted to rub in the fact that she'd been wrong. No doubt he was going to warn her away from all patrons. And enjoy doing both immensely. Blasted man could run after her, she wasn't about to wait around only to be insulted.

Turning, she continued toward her car, this time moving quickly. And just as she knew he would, he caught up with her, anyway.

"Hi," he murmured, matching her gait.

She didn't look at him, but silently cursed his long legs. "Hello."

"Still mad at me?"

She reached her car and stopped beside it. "What do think?"

"I think you are."

"Then, you're more perceptive than I gave you credit for."

Unperturbed, he grinned and leaned against her car. "Nice set of wheels."

"Thanks." She dug in her handbag for her keys. "Want to buy it?"

"Hardly." He folded his arms across his chest. "It's a bit out of my class."

"Mine, too." She found the keys, unlocked the door and started to slip inside.

He stopped her. "I don't get you."

She met his gaze defiantly, immediately furious. "That's your problem, isn't it?"

"My God, you're staying at the Victoria House Hotel, surely you can afford—"

"Cunningham Oil is fifty percent owner of the Victoria House. It's off-season, I'm paying employee rate and only staying until I find an apartment. Satisfied?"

"I didn't know," he said softly.

"You didn't ask."

"I'm asking now."

"Now it's too late. Good day." She pulled at the car door, and again he reached around her and shut it. She faced him, exasperated. "What?"

A grin tugging at his mouth, he held out a single black feather. "For you."

Instead of taking the feather, she crossed her arms over her chest and narrowed her eyes suspiciously. "What is this?"

"You did it, Bentley."

The man was impossible—and impossibly sexy. She gritted her teeth, annoyed with herself as much as with him. "Exactly what did I do?"

"Proved me wrong." He grinned and trailed the feather along the curve of her jaw. "I'm eating crow, Ms. Cunningham."

"Eating..." Bentley let the words trail off, then, realizing what he meant, tipped her head back and laughed. "Bitsy paid off?"

"In aces."

Bentley laughed again and plucked the feather from his fingers. "And just how *does* crow taste, Mr. Reese?"

"It's an unusual flavor. One I'm not accustomed to."

Bentley arched an eyebrow, pleased. "I like that."

"In this instance I have to say that I do, too. Although I don't plan to make a steady diet of it."

"Give me time."

Jackson leaned toward her, amusement sparkling in his eyes. "Exactly what baby bird is Bitsy in such a tither over?"

Bentley ran the feather back and forth between her fingers. "All of them."

Jackson lifted his eyebrows. "Excuse me?"

"I went through the files and found pictures of as many coastal birds as possible. Especially the babies. Then I found literature describing what kind of danger they're in and how our efforts will save them. Then I made a lunch date."

"Damn clever."

"Surprised?"

"Yes." At his response, her eyes flashed fire; angry color stained her cheeks. Jackson reached out and trailed a finger along her elegant cheekbone. Her skin was hot and smooth beneath his fingers. "Surprised this time," he murmured. "I won't be the next."

Warmth speared through her. Warmth and a feeling of satisfaction, of accomplishment. She had *earned* Jackson's respect. No one had helped her; no money or influence had changed hands. She'd done this on her own.

Smiling, she tipped her head back and met his eyes. "Thank you."

Arousal, bittersweet and stunning, hit him in the gut, and Jackson caught his breath. "My God, you are so beautiful."

Bentley stiffened, the satisfaction she'd felt a moment ago racing to a place just beyond her reach. "Stop it."

"What?" Jackson caught one of her dark curls and wrapped it around his finger. It was soft and silky against his skin, and he fought the urge to dig his fingers into the luxuriant strands. "You *are* beautiful. I know you've heard it before."

Too many times to count. To the exclusion of any other trait or quality.

Even so, pleasure curled through her, a feeling of pure feminine satisfaction. The feeling left her weak and warm and wanting. She fought against the sensations, fought against the arousal that flooded through her.

Bentley sucked in a sharp breath. "If there's nothing else, Jackson, I've put in my day. I'm going home."

"But there is something else," he murmured, lowering his eyes to her mouth. "We've got a problem, Princess."

Her heart stopped, then started again with a vengeance. "You're mistaken," she snapped, jerking away from his touch. "Because there is no we. You are arrogant and stubborn and self-important. Whatever happened between us the other night was a mistake. An aberration."

"Are you saying something happened between us?"

The rose in her cheeks became flame. "No."

"Then—" he tugged gently on the curl, inching her toward him "—what *are* you saying?"

Bentley searched for something to say, but found nothing. The blood pounded in her head until all she could think of was the mesmerizing blue of his eyes and her overwhelming need to kiss him.

He drew her closer, so close he could feel her breath against his face. "You've got to stop doing this, Bentley."

"What?" she asked, trying to sound impatient but sounding impossibly aroused instead.

"Getting angry." He gave in to the urge and buried both hands in her hair. "When you're like this, I can't resist you."

And he couldn't. Even though he fought against her effect on him, even as he called himself a dozen different kinds of fool, he couldn't resist touching her.

"Try," she whispered, lifting her face to his.

"I am." He tightened his fingers. "It's not working."

She shuddered and capitulated, bringing her hands to his chest. Beneath her palm, his heart beat heavily. She curled her fingers into the nubby knit of his sweater. "I don't want this."

"Neither do I." Jackson made a sound of frustration. "I want to make love with you. And I despise myself for the want."

"And I despise you. I wish I'd never met you."

"Then go," he said softly. "Do us both a favor. I won't stop you."

Bentley told herself to do just that, told herself to get into her car and drive until she reached Houston, told herself to run and never come back. But she wouldn't run. She couldn't.

So she stood breathless and aching, her face lifted to his. "You go," she whispered, meeting and holding his gaze, challenging him. "*I* won't stop *you.*"

Seconds ticked past; neither moved. The golden light of sunset began to purple; the breeze, which moments before had buffeted them, stilled. Nearby a car door slammed, friends called out greetings, children snickered as they barreled past on skateboards.

"Damn you," Jackson muttered finally and dragged her mouth to his.

She tasted of anger, of determination. And of something rich, potent and womanly. The last had him diving deeper, wanting and taking more. Consequences seemed a far-off threat, promises made to himself farther still. Now his head was filled with Bentley—the way she fit against him, the way she matched his strength with her own, the way her mouth moved hungrily beneath his.

Jackson deepened the kiss.

Bentley didn't resist. Nor did she surrender meekly. She met the furious pressure of his mouth with her own fury, parting her lips and capturing his tongue, lifting her hands, twining her fingers tightly in his hair.

She wanted this no more than—and as much as—he did. Inwardly she cursed herself for the want, for the lack of self-discipline. She was furious with him for his challenge...angrier still that he aroused her so, and with no more than a kiss.

Jackson murmured her name low in his throat. Hearing it spoken that way, as both prayer and epithet, reminded her of her marriage, and Bentley froze. She was breaking every one of her vows about being with someone who didn't respect her.

And how could she ever respect herself if she did that? How could she move forward?

Bentley fought the desire to melt into Jackson's arms. Fought the desire to offer him everything she had and was. For neither would ever be enough for him—he thought too little of her to cherish the offering.

Pain at the truth of that arced through her. How could she want a man who thought so little of her? And how could she want him so desperately?

Self-recriminations washed over her, and with them despair. "What do you want of me?" she asked, struggling for breath, for control. "What do you expect?"

The expression in his eyes told her everything, and making a sound of pain, she jerked out of his grasp. He expected nothing of her. Wanted nothing of them.

"I'm sorry," he murmured, taking a step away from her, waging his own war with regret, his own struggle for control.

"There was a time," she said softly, inching her chin up, "that would have been okay. It would have been enough." She swung her car door open and slipped inside. "It's not anymore. Goodbye, Jackson."

Chapter Six

Jackson lifted his gaze from his half packed suitcase to his daughter. She stood at his bedroom door, glowering at him. "Still mad at me, I see."

She jutted her chin out. "I don't want to go into your stupid office every day. I don't see why I have to."

"Try, because I said so."

She scowled. "It's not fair."

"On the contrary, it's extremely fair." He zipped his garment bag. "You got suspended from school, Chloe. You deserve to be punished. Not coddled. Not pampered."

She folded her arms across her chest. "Mom wouldn't do this."

Even though he wanted to scream out his frustration at the constant comparisons to Victoria, scream out his fatigue at having to fight Chloe every step of the way, Jackson drew in a careful breath and told himself to keep his cool. It wouldn't do any good to yell at Chloe. She would only resist him more.

He tightened his fingers on the bag's zipper pull. Untangling a relationship that had taken thirteen years to snarl would take a while, he reminded himself. Maybe forever.

The truth of that settled on him like a suffocating weight.

"No," he said carefully, "she wouldn't. But I'm not your mother. I never will be."

From below the bell sounded. *Bentley*. He pictured her standing at the door waiting, and a pang of regret rippled over him, a wave of longing. "That'll be Bentley. Could you get it?"

"Fine," Chloe muttered, turning away from him and starting downstairs. "You're the dictator."

A moment later he heard Chloe open the door, heard Bentley's voice, her laugh.

Jackson frowned, steeling himself against the way both made him feel—aching and hungry and . . . alone.

Nonsense. He shook his head against the last and hoisted his bag to his shoulder. Alone was better. He had enough in his life to contend with; the last thing he needed to add to the mix was a relationship—even if only sexual—with a spoiled debutante.

But all the rationalizations in the world didn't change the fact that the days since their meeting in the parking lot had been hell. They had carefully avoided each other. And when avoiding had been impossible because of physical proximity, they had studiously refused to make eye contact.

But their eyes had met. Once. In hers he had read hurt, anger and stubbornness. And need. She wanted him as much as he did her. In that moment, he'd been overcome by the urge to throw everything he knew to be right and smart to the winds, drag her into his arms and kiss her senseless.

Somewhere they'd crossed the invisible line between awareness and arousal, and now they had to pay for it. Hell, they *were* paying for it. At least he was. Dearly.

The taste of wanting and regret bitter against his tongue, Jackson shook his head and picked up his briefcase. Now wasn't the time to be brooding over his rapidly disintegrating relationship with his daughter or his overwhelming feelings for Bentley. A lot rested on this trip to Washington and on his ability to sway key legislators. So much that the next few days would be grueling.

"You're ready to go."

Jackson turned slowly toward the doorway. Bentley stood just outside, her expression at once defiant and heartbreakingly vulnerable. *How had he ever thought this woman cold?* She, too, carried bags.

"Yes," he said, his voice thick. "And you're ready to stay."

She lifted her chin a notch. "Yes."

He shifted the weight of his bags, his gaze still locked with hers. "How was your weekend?"

"Fine." She looked away, then back. "I found an apartment."

"Good." She looked tired. Troubled. He tightened his fingers on the garment bag's strap. "Where?"

"The Strand, actually. It's the place above the flower shop on Market Street. In the morning I can smell the flowers." She colored, and he had the sense that she regretted having told him that.

"I know the shop." He saw her gaze flick from him to his bed, and his pulse scrambled. He imagined her there, naked and wanting; he imagined him with her. He sucked in a sharp, painful breath. "They have the best flowers on the island."

"So they told me." She shifted her travel bag from her right hand to her left. "I went to Houston to get some of my things."

And it had been awful, he thought, studying her expression. But why? Cursing that he'd wondered, let alone cared, Jackson started toward the door. "Why don't you put your things away, then come down. I need to talk to Chloe before I go, and I have instructions and a list of emergency numbers for you."

"Fine." Bentley moved aside. "But first, could you point me toward my room?"

"This is it."

"This?" she repeated, unnerved, looking past him once more. "Your bedroom?"

Jackson followed her gaze. And again he pictured her in his big bed—with him. He swallowed hard. "I've only got two—mine and Chloe's. The third is an office with hardly enough room to walk, let alone sleep. I hope this is okay. I've changed the sheets. The pillow's brand new."

She cleared her throat and forced a smile. "I'm sure it will be . . . fine. Thank you."

"I cleaned out a couple of drawers in the bureau for you."

"Thanks again."

"Okay . . ." Jackson started to back down the hall, loath to let her out of his sight and annoyed with himself for it. "When you come down, I'll fill you in."

Bentley nodded, then ducked quickly into his bedroom, snapping the door shut behind her. Safely inside, she dropped her bags and leaned against the door, squeezing her eyes shut. She'd expected that seeing Jackson again would be difficult, but not gut-wrenching. She'd expected to ache to touch him, but not to be consumed by the ache.

She lifted a trembling hand to her mouth. She wanted the job with Baysafe to work, wanted to be able to say to everyone, "See, I did it." That she liked Jill and Chloe and Galveston was a bonus.

Bentley caught her bottom lip between her teeth. But she didn't know if she could continue working with Jackson. Not the way they had been—without touching or speaking, without acknowledging or giving in to the chemistry between them.

And she couldn't allow herself to give in. A relationship between them would be disastrous.

She took a deep breath, picked up her bags and crossed to the bureau. There she stopped and tipped her head, considering the row of drawers. Jackson hadn't said which he'd emptied. Taking a stab, she pulled open the top one.

It was filled with his briefs. Regulation white BVDs. Bentley stared at the neatly folded briefs, heat flooding her cheeks—not because she'd never seen men's underwear before, but because she had the urge to touch them.

She curled her fingers into fists, remembering overhearing one of her mother's friends complain once that she was certain a workman had gone through her lingerie drawer. Sick, the woman had called him. A pervert.

Was that what she was? Bentley wondered. A pervert?

She slammed the drawer shut, then yanked open another. This one was filled with an assortment of things, including, on top, a daringly brief bathing suit. Bright red and made of clingy spandex.

Her mouth went desert-dry, her pulse berserk, and Bentley shut that drawer, too. The closet, she decided. Carrying her hanging garment bag over, she opened the door. Here she found shirts and sweaters, several suits. His bathrobe hung on a hook on the back of the door.

She stared at the robe a moment, then gave in to the urge and lightly ran her hand over the worn terry cloth. Like everything else about him, the robe was big and masculine and without fuss.

Bentley bunched the fabric in her fingers, enjoying its nubby texture against her skin. She brought it to her nose. It smelled of his soap and shampoo—his person. She breathed deeply, growing dizzy on the combination. It smelled like a man. This man. Like Jackson.

Heart thundering against the wall of her chest and feeling like some sort of voyeur, Bentley released the robe. Quickly, she hung up her bag, then emptied it.

She paused, breathing deeply once more. She ran a hand over one of her silk blouses, rubbed a bit of polished rayon between her fingers. Her things felt sensuously smooth. They smelled sweet, sweetly feminine. Her scents and Jackson's combined, creating another that was earthy and sensual. Exciting. Just as their textures would compliment each other. Man and woman. Rough against smooth. Flesh against flesh.

Bentley pressed her hands to her burning cheeks, acknowledging that her cheeks weren't the only part of her that burned, that her palms weren't the only part of her that was damp.

Dear Lord, how was she going to sleep in Jackson's bed when she couldn't even be in his closet without becoming aroused?

Aware of time passing, Bentley finished unpacking, then patted cold water on her cheeks before heading downstairs. She heard Chloe and Jackson in the kitchen arguing.

"But why can't I?" Chloe demanded. "Bentley will take me."

"Because," Jackson replied evenly, "you have to work." He met Bentley's gaze as she stepped into the kitchen. "And so does Bentley."

"But Christmas is almost here!" Chloe looked at Bentley pleadingly. "I still need to get lots of things, and—"

"We have a couple weeks yet. We'll go together after I get back."

"Oh, goody," Chloe said sarcastically, "shopping with my daddy."

Bentley saw hurt flash in Jackson's eyes and her heart went out to him. She stepped forward, forcing a bright smile. "We have the evenings, kiddo."

"As long as Chloe gets her homework done," Jackson said sternly. "She's behind. It seems she forgot she was given work to do during her suspension."

"Great." Chloe groaned and plopped onto one of the kitchen chairs. "I'm a prisoner."

Jackson met Bentley's eyes once more, his jaw softening. "Did you find everything?" he asked.

Bentley thought of his drawer full of briefs and her cheeks heated. She shifted her gaze. "Yes."

"Good." Jackson cleared his throat. "If you need anything—anything at all—don't hesitate to call."

Did he mean *anything?* Bentley wondered dizzily. If she called him just because she needed to hear his voice, would he laugh? Or if she felt the urge to touch him . . .

She caught her runaway thoughts and clasped her hands in front of her. "I will."

"Good." He motioned to a list posted by the phone. "The numbers where I can be reached and my itinerary are there. Jill has both also. I guess that's it. We're keeping school hours around here. Be sure to eat right and . . ."

He let the thought trail off, meeting and holding Bentley's gaze. In his Bentley read uncertainty, a hesitancy to go and something else, something meant solely for her. Whatever the message, it warmed her.

Jackson dragged his gaze from hers and turned to his daughter. "Chloe...I..."

Chloe glared at him, inching her chin up defiantly. Bentley watched the two, her heart turning over. She saw the pain—and the yearning—in both father and daughter. What would happen, she wondered, if he just hugged Chloe and told her he loved her? Would Chloe relent and hug him in return?

Instead Jackson held himself back, uncertain and obviously aching. "Well, take care. I'll be back Friday." He shook his head and started for the door. "Be good for Bentley."

And then he was gone. Bentley watched him cross the porch, then jog down the stairs. Sadness tugged at her. His leaving this way, without a hug or kiss, without a kind word, seemed so lonely.

Giving in to the impulse, she yanked the door open and leaned out. "Jackson!"

He stopped and looked at her, the breeze lifting his hair, the winter sun turning it to gold. As his eyes met hers, a feeling of propriety rushed over her, as if this man belonged to her. And she to him.

"Yes?"

"Good luck," she said breathlessly, her heart hammering against the wall of her chest.

He smiled. The lifting of his lips was quick but devastating. She felt it to the pit of her stomach—and beyond. "Thanks, Princess. I'll need it."

He climbed into his Blazer, started it up and, after a last look at her, backed out of the drive. Bentley stood at the door for several seconds after his car had disappeared from sight before softly closing it. Turning, she found Chloe standing just behind her, her expression enigmatic.

What was the girl thinking? Bentley didn't know why, but she was certain Chloe would not be pleased with the idea of something going on between her father and her baby-sitter.

Unnerved, Bentley smiled. "We better get ready to go into the office."

"I don't want to go." Chloe tossed her head back. "I don't see why I should have to. I don't care what Daddy says, I'm not one of his *employees.*"

Bentley felt a moment of panic, then scolded herself for it. Jackson had left her in charge; he thought her able to handle Chloe. "No," she said, "but I am. And his instructions to me were clear. We're to go in to Baysafe everyday from nine until five."

"He's good at that," Chloe muttered, folding her arms across her chest. "Giving orders. Be good for Bentley," she mimicked. "Like I was a baby. I don't even need a baby-sitter."

Bentley took a deep breath. She should be angry with Chloe, but she couldn't quite bring herself to be. She saw the brightness in the girl's eyes, saw through the tough behavior to the hurting child. But she could not continue to humor Chloe. It wasn't doing the girl any good.

Acknowledging that her timing probably stank, Bentley murmured, "No, I suppose you shouldn't need one. You're not a baby."

"That's what I told Daddy!" Chloe lifted her chin triumphantly. "I'm going to be fourteen next month."

"Then why do you act like a baby, Chloe?" Bentley asked evenly, holding the youngster's gaze. "Why do you act like you need a sitter?"

Stunned, Chloe's mouth dropped open. A moment later her eyes filled with tears. Chloe tried valiantly to act unaffected, visibly worked to pull her shield of sarcasm around her. Bentley's heart broke for her, and she had to fight the impulse to take the words back, to hold on to her resolve. "You act petulant and sulky. Most of the time you're uncooperative and selfish."

"I thought you were my friend," Chloe managed to say around tears. "I thought you liked me."

"I am your friend. Real friends tell each other the truth." Bentley took a step toward Chloe. "Before, I was just going along with you to get through our time together."

Chloe looked at her toes. "I see," she said, her voice small and broken.

"Do you?" Bentley reached out and touched Chloe's silky golden hair, lightly stroking. "But now, I do like you. A lot. I want you to be happy, Chloe. I want you to realize how really special you are."

"Right," Chloe managed. "Tell me another one."

"Your father loves you."

Tears welled in Chloe's eyes, so many that she could neither force them back nor hide them. "I think...it's you...he loves."

The girl turned and raced up the stairs.

Bentley stared after her, too shocked to call out or stop her. Jackson in love with her? What could have given Chloe that idea? My God, he didn't even like her.

It would even be funny if it didn't make her ache so.

Bentley wrapped her fingers around the ornate old banister. Now wasn't the time to be wondering or worrying about herself. Chloe needed her. Taking a deep breath, she started up the stairs.

Chloe's bedroom door was closed, and Bentley knocked lightly. When the girl didn't answer, she knocked again. "Please let me in, Chloe. Don't shut me out, too."

"Go away."

Bentley opened the door instead. Chloe sat on her bed, clutching a worn teddy bear and staring broodingly at a poster of a teenage rock band on her wall. Her expression was stricken, but her eyes were dry. Bentley crossed the room and sat gingerly on the edge of her bed.

"We need to talk."

"Says who?"

The girl didn't look at her, and Bentley bit back a sigh. "Me. But it's not an order."

Chloe's jaw tightened, and Bentley was reminded of Jackson. Chloe was like her father in so many ways, Bentley realized. The cut of her jaw, the way she carried herself, the streak of pure stubbornness. She wondered if Chloe—or Jackson—saw it.

Bentley tried another tack. "Chloe, downstairs, why did you say that your father loves me? He and I hardly know—"

"The way he looks at you," Chloe interrupted, her voice painfully controlled. "Like you're special." She tightened her grip on the stuffed animal. "He never looks at me that way."

Bentley swallowed, unnerved by the comment and by the way she'd wished, deep in her gut and for more than a moment, that it was true. That Jackson did look at her that way.

Self-destructive foolishness, she told herself. Wishes born from her lack of belief in herself.

Bentley covered Chloe's hand. "You're just not seeing how he looks at you. The love, the yearning ... the wanting to reach out to you. Chloe... Honey..." Bentley forced the girl to meet her eyes. "Your daddy just doesn't know how to love you."

Chloe's eyes filled again, and her throat worked as she tried to control the tears. "But he's my dad. He's supposed to—"

"To know how to love you," Bentley supplied. "He's supposed to know how to show you how much he cares?"

Chloe nodded, a tear slipping down her cheek.

"Oh, Chloe..." Bentley gathered the child into her arms and stroked her hair. "If it was that easy, if it was merely a matter of blood, would there be so many lousy parents? And if it's so natural, why do so many people do it all wrong?"

Chloe shook her head, her shoulders shaking with the effort of holding back her tears. "But you...don't...know."

Bentley drew her eyebrows together and tightened her arms around Chloe. "Know what, honey?"

Chloe shook her head, giving in to the tears until she was sobbing.

For long moments, Bentley held her, making soothing noises and stroking her hair. When the child's tears lessened, she prodded Chloe again. "Tell me, Chloe. What don't I know?"

The youngster met her eyes, and Bentley's heart ached for her. Her face stripped bare by tears, Chloe little resembled the impertinent, sassy and self-confident child she normally presented to the world. In her place was a frightened and hurt child, a child who needed love so desperately that she pushed it away with everything she had.

"They didn't want me," Chloe said softly, averting her gaze and plucking at the lacy pink coverlet. "Mama got...knocked up. Daddy did the right thing by her. But they didn't...want me. I was—" her voice caught on a sob "—a mistake."

No wonder, Bentley thought. No wonder. "Oh, Chloe.... Do you have any idea how many children are conceived that way? A lot, let me tell you. But that doesn't mean your parents didn't want *you*. It only means they weren't ready for you. Once you were born—"

"No!" Chloe shook her head. "I overheard Mama tell Grandmother Ellerbee that...she...should have had—that she wished she'd had an..."

Chloe's words trailed off, and Bentley squeezed her eyes shut. *Please don't say what I think you're going to. Please have it be something else, something—*

"An abortion," Chloe finished, her voice a broken whisper. "She wished she'd had an abortion."

Oh, dear God, Bentley thought, sickened. Victoria Ellerbee couldn't have said that. She couldn't have.'

But she had.

The words—their meaning—slammed into Bentley, ripping and tearing. How could those words ever pass a mother's lips? How could Victoria Ellerbee have looked at this child, her own flesh and blood, and thought them? Bentley tightened her arms around Chloe, aching for her, realizing the pain overhearing such a vile wish must have caused her.

Chloe started to cry again, and Bentley pressed the youngster's face to her shoulder and rocked her. She didn't know how to comfort her. What could she say? She couldn't deny that Chloe had heard her mother, just as she couldn't claim Chloe had misinterpreted her mother's meaning.

Victoria Ellerbee had regretted giving this wonderful being life.

Bentley's stomach turned over. She thought of how she had wished and prayed for a child during her marriage, recalled the emotional debilitation each menstrual cycle had brought. And she recalled the twin expressions of hope and misery that had painted the faces of the other women who had populated the fertility clinic's waiting room.

Bentley squeezed her eyes shut and worked to get a grip on her emotions. This, she reminded herself, was not about her. It was about Chloe. And Jackson.

He had to know. She had to tell him. And it would hurt him. Badly.

"Chloe," she said softly, tipping the girl's chin up so she could look her in the eyes while she spoke. "Listen to me. What your mother said was unforgivable. I won't deny that, and I certainly won't make an excuse for her. There aren't any. But I *know* your father loves you. I know it with my heart. With what I see. With what I hear."

"But he...let me go," Chloe said, hiccuping. "He let her take me."

"Oh, sweetie." Bentley stroked Chloe's hair, tears thickening her own voice. "He didn't know what else to do."

Bentley and Chloe talked quietly for a while after that. Chloe was drained, and although there was much Bentley wanted to say to the girl, she didn't push. There would be time over the next few days, Bentley knew, to talk more.

When Bentley was certain that Chloe felt strong enough, she suggested they head into the office. Chloe went along without a murmur. An hour and a half late, Bentley and Chloe swung open the doors to the Baysafe offices and stepped inside. The reception area was empty.

"Jill," Bentley called out, "sorry we're late." She slipped out of her coat and hung it on the tree. "I hope it wasn't a problem. Chloe and I..."

Bentley's voice trailed off as the other woman, white as a sheet and trembling visibly, emerged from the back of the office. Bentley rushed over to her. "My God, Jill, what's wrong? What's happened?"

"I just..." Jill shook her head and sank into a chair. "I don't feel too well." She tried to smile and grimaced instead. "I'll be fine."

Even as the words passed Jill's lips, she doubled over.

Bentley took a step back, alarmed. "I don't think so. I think you'd better go home."

The other woman brought a shaking hand to her head. "I'll be fine," she repeated. "Ya'll just go on and get busy—"

Making a sound of pain, Jill jumped up and raced to the rest room, barely making it in time. Bentley looked at Chloe. The girl's eyes were huge with worry.

Bentley swallowed nervously. She had to do something. But what?

Jill returned, looking even worse than before. "I've had these cramps in my right side all morning, and they're—" she gasped and clutched her middle "—getting worse."

"Chloe," Bentley said, swiveling to face the girl, "go get Jill a cool, damp towel for her forehead. Jill, what's your husband's number at work?"

Jill shook her head. "He's offshore this week."

"Can you drive?"

The other woman laughed, the sound so weak Bentley wondered how Jill continued to stand. "Truthfully, I don't think I could crawl right now."

Chloe came running into the room with the cloth. "It's paper," she said apologetically. "I didn't know—"

"It's fine." Bentley took the cloth and after easing Jill onto a chair, pressed it to her forehead. "You're burning up. I'm driving you home."

"But the office—"

"Chloe can manage."

"Don't leave me here!" the youngster cried. "I don't know what to do!"

"Then we'll all go," Bentley said, working to keep her voice even, to sound in control. "It'll only take—"

"I'm expecting some calls," Jill whispered, her face ashen. "Jackson's waiting for some—"

Another cramp took the woman, so strong it nearly brought her off her chair.

"Do something, Bentley!" Chloe cried, wringing her hands. "Something's really wrong with her!"

Frightened, Bentley raced for the phone and dialed 911. Heart pounding, she described Jill's symptoms and ordered an ambulance.

It took less than ten minutes for the ambulance to arrive, for the paramedics to get Jill onto the stretcher and on her way to the hospital, but to Bentley they seemed to be the longest minutes of her life.

Bentley and Chloe watched the ambulance speed away, then turned and headed into the now quiet Baysafe office.

"What are we going to do?" Chloe asked, looking around the office as if seeing it for the first time.

Bentley knew exactly how the girl felt. She felt the same way—stunned. "I don't know," she said. "I really don't."

"Let's call Daddy." Chloe tugged on Bentley's sleeve. "He'll know what to do."

Bentley reached for the phone, then dropped her hand. Jackson couldn't do anything from Washington, if he'd even arrived yet. "No. Let's wait until we know for sure what's going on with Jill and how long she'll be out. You heard the paramedic, it might not be as bad as we think. It could just be that nasty flu that's going around."

It wasn't.

An hour and a half later, Bentley thanked the doctor and hung up the phone. Turning, she met Chloe's worried gaze. "It's acute appendicitis. Jill's scheduled for surgery."

"Oh, no."

"She'll be fine," Bentley hurried to add. "But she'll be out for the duration of your father's trip. Longer, really." *And now everything rests on our not-so-capable shoulders.*

"We better call Daddy." Chloe bit her lip. "He'd want to know. He might even come home."

Call Jackson.

Bentley looked longingly at the phone. Maybe they should. She knew shockingly little about the workings of Baysafe and about the duties that filled Jill's day. So far, all she'd done was run errands, answer the phone and file.

She did know there were several projects hanging in the balance right now—a study some marine biologist was knee-deep in, a publicity campaign and several fund-raisers under way, a newsletter to get out this week.

Bentley laced her fingers together and looked longingly at the phone once more. *Call Jackson.*

And what?

Admit that she wasn't competent enough to run Baysafe for four days without help?

"I know!" Chloe said suddenly. "We could call one of those agencies. You know, one of those places that sends out people for jobs."

Even Chloe didn't think she could do it.

Coming to a decision, Bentley squared her shoulders. "No," she said briskly. "We can do it."

"What?"

Bentley smiled at Chloe's shocked expression. "We can do it. You and I."

Chloe shook her head. "I think we better call Daddy."

"Look, your father left a list of the things he wanted Jill to do this week." Bentley picked up the neatly printed list and scanned it. "If we get in trouble, we talk to Jill. Or, if it's really serious, then we call your dad."

Chloe still looked doubtful, and Bentley laughed. "Think of your dad's surprise. Think how happy he'll be. We *can* do it, Chloe."

And they did. The week flew by. Chloe manned the front desk and the phone, buzzing any urgent calls through to Bentley. Bentley got the newsletter written and ready to mail out, and took care of every other item on Jackson's list.

Over the week Chloe blossomed. She'd risen to the occasion and proved herself to be a capable and extremely levelheaded almost-fourteen-year-old. Bentley suspected this was the first time anything had been expected of Chloe. She could relate.

In Bentley's free time she read and studied every piece of literature she could on Baysafe and the plight of Galveston Bay and her wildlife. The more she read, the more intrigued she became. And the more she studied Baysafe, the more she understood Jackson's financial concerns. Baysafe was in trouble. Big trouble.

A great number of sponsors had pulled pledges in the past year. All oil-related.

Each night after Chloe went to bed, Bentley studied and thought about the situation. Baysafe was too dependent on industry donations, especially oil-related industry. She recognized a few names from the social register on his patron list, but only a few.

Jackson had yet to tap a whole market. He needed to diversify.

The more Bentley thought about it, the more excited she became. She thought about Bitsy Cassidy and of how easy it had been to garner her support of Baysafe.

Why not use her influence to benefit their cause? She knew dozens of women who had plenty of money and who loved causes.

Bentley laughed. Wouldn't Jackson be surprised and pleased if she managed to pull Baysafe out of its fiscal trouble without any help from him?

Giddy at the thought, Bentley began to make a list.

Chapter Seven

Light tumbled from the first-floor windows. Jackson pulled his car to a stop in the driveway, gazing for long moments at the warm, welcoming light. He ached. From fatigue and stress, from his large frame being folded into a coach-class seat for too many hours.

His flight had been delayed in D.C. because of bad weather. The airline had finally boarded the passengers, only to make them wait on the runway another three hours. It hadn't helped that small places for long periods of time put him on edge; he hadn't even been able to use the time to catch up on sleep.

Jackson leaned his head against the headrest and closed his eyes. The trip had gone well, although he knew from experience that more often than not, politicians talked out of both sides of their mouths and that their sympathies, in the end, went to the highest bidder.

And Big Oil had very deep pockets, indeed.

Jackson looked at the light spilling into his garden. Considering the sleeping arrangements, he expected Bentley to be waiting up. He hoped that she was ... and prayed she wasn't.

An image of her asleep in his bed, the sheets a tangle around her, her dark hair fanned across the white pillow, played against the back of his eyes. Jackson muttered an oath. Thinking simultaneously of Bentley and of beds was a ridiculously poor idea.

And getting to be a habit.

He shook his head. Several times over the past week he had almost embarrassed himself when he'd let his mind wander to auburn curls against smooth, white skin, eyes the color of jade and small, quick hands.

After a couple of incidents like those, he had put a lot of energy into keeping his mind on business. During the day, anyway. But alone at night, he'd given his mind and imagination the freedom to roam deliciously, allowing himself to linger on one erotic possibility after another.

Jackson groaned as his body protested its confinement. This had to stop. He wasn't a teenager, wasn't an untried boy. And yet, that's exactly what he felt like. That's how he had acted for weeks now.

He looked at the house again, wondering if she would be up, wondering if she'd missed him. The few times he'd been able to break away to call the office, he'd gotten Bentley instead of Jill. Hearing her voice had affected him strangely, had filled him with longing, loneliness and a sense of urgency.

Jackson scowled at his thoughts. Tomorrow, or the day after, when he'd had enough sleep, dozens of lungfuls of fresh island air and had feasted his eyes on the magnificence of the Bay at least once, he would be himself again.

And if he wasn't? Jackson wrapped his fingers around the steering wheel. That wasn't an option. He would be.

He climbed out of the car, took his bags from the backseat and headed up the walk. At the door he took a deep breath, then inserted his key into the lock and turned it.

Jackson stopped just inside the door. Bentley lay curled up on the couch, asleep in the golden light of the lamp. For long moments, he stood and stared at her, his chest tight, his heart pounding as if he'd just run an Olympic mile. Not wanting to wake her, he set his bags down softly, then tiptoed across to the couch, conscious of every creak and protest of the old pine floor.

Stopping beside the couch, he gazed down at her sleeping form. Her lashes made dark crescents against her cheeks; her hair tumbled charmingly across her forehead; her chest rose and fell with her rhythmic breathing.

She was so beautiful, Jackson thought, sitting carefully on the edge of the couch, still studying her. But it was more than her physical beauty that had his breath constricting in his lungs. Much more.

If only he knew what.

Jackson cocked his head. It had been so long since there'd been a woman waiting for him when he returned from a trip—or even at the end of the day. So long that the way it made him feel seemed new, extraordinary.

Had Victoria ever looked like this? he wondered, reaching out and gently touching Bentley's cheek. Had she ever looked so soft and so trusting?

And had looking at her ever made him feel quite this way?

He trailed his finger along the curve of Bentley's jaw, then twined one of her curls around his index finger, rubbing the silky strands between his fingers. Why did this woman make him feel so much?

Bentley murmured something he couldn't make out and stirred; the papers spread out around her crackled in response. Noticing them for the first time, Jackson drew his eyebrows together and eased one out from beneath her elbow.

"Where Will The Whooping Crane Go Now?"

It was an article he'd written for *Conservation Magazine* two years ago. He set it aside and scanned the other papers scattered over the sofa and coffee table—all were about Baysafe and its operation, some written by him, some by other conservation and marine professionals.

Warmth at her interest eased through him, and pleasure followed. Jackson looked at Bentley, working to fight off both emotions. He couldn't afford to care for this woman, he reminded himself sternly. He couldn't afford to forget the lessons of his past.

He was dangerously close to doing just that.

Bentley's eyelids fluttered up. She smiled sleepily. "Hi."

"Hi." He brushed the curls from her cheek, gently tucking them behind her ear.

She yawned. "When did you get home?"

"Just now."

"Mmm." She snuggled into the throw pillow under her head. "What time is it?"

Jackson moved his gaze over her. "Late. I got held up by bad weather." He couldn't resist and touched her hair again, lightly and only with his fingertips. He found her unbelievably sexy with her sleep-tangled hair and heavy eyes. "Go on up. I'll take the couch."

Bentley shook her head. "You're twice as big as this piece of furniture." She pulled herself into a sitting position. "I'll go."

"I'd rather you stayed."

The words hovered between them for a moment, then she met his eyes. "Would you?"

"Yes."

She touched his cheek, caressing lightly. "You look tired."

He smiled. "Exhausted. And hungry."

"We saved you dinner."

His heart stopped for just a fraction of a second, and in that time he wondered how he had gone so long without hearing those words. He called himself a fool even as he searched Bentley's gaze. "What did we have?"

"Tuna noodle surprise." She yawned again. "Chloe made it."

He lifted his eyebrows. "Chloe? That *is* a surprise."

"She really missed you."

"Did she?" Jackson looked away, then back, a muscle working in his jaw. "Considering the way it was between us when I left, I find that hard to believe. Although there was a time when she..."

He let the words trail off, then began again. "I wanted to call...I wanted to talk to her." His mouth twisted in self-derision. "But I was afraid. Isn't that something? Afraid of calling my own daughter."

Bentley laid a hand on his arm and squeezed reassuringly. He looked at her again, then away once more. "I just couldn't face the thought of going another round with her. Not when I was so far away."

"It's going to be okay," Bentley murmured, lifting her gaze to his.

"Is it?"

"Yes." Bentley smiled. "No doubts."

He wished he could say the same, wished he could believe her words, her reassuring smile. He couldn't, but neither could he openly discount or question them. Because tonight he needed words like those, needed warmth and re-assurance and company.

Bentley's company.

Only hesitating a moment, Jackson sat back and eased her into the curve of his arm. She made a sleepy sound of pleasure, and he squeezed his eyes shut for a moment, al-lowing himself to question what he was doing.

Living dangerously. Following his urges rather than his intellect. Giving in to his need for her.

If she weren't so warm and pliant and sweet, maybe he would have the self-discipline to be smarter, stronger. Maybe, if he weren't so fatigued, so beaten down from a week alone with the enemy, he could tell her good-night and walk away.

Maybe. But right now smart and good-night weren't even possibilities.

"You never said," she murmured, tilting her head against his shoulder. "Was the trip a success?"

"I don't know." He frowned in thought. "It's difficult to accurately judge. The environment is a popular topic right now—to talk about. Everybody's giving it lip service. But will any real action be taken?" He shook his head. "I don't know."

"I'm sorry."

He tangled his fingers in her hair. "I often wonder how everybody's values got all screwed up. Mandatory double hulls on all tankers is such a simple step, but it could save so much. If the *Valdez* had had one, the Prince William Sound would have been saved."

He made a sound of frustration. "I went there, you know. I was one of the specialists called in to help assess the dam-age, help plan the clean-up. I couldn't sleep at night. I had nightmares about the destruction I was seeing...and

nightmares about it happening to our Bay. We've had so
many close calls."

Reaching up, Bentley stroked his cheek. She knew if he
hadn't been so fatigued, he wouldn't be talking to her so
openly and emotionally, knew he wouldn't have let down his
guard. But she didn't care. Being with him like this felt too
good to question or worry over the reasons.

Jackson tipped his head into her caress, his expression
sad. "With all the money Exxon spent, they hardly made a
dent. After days of high-pressure hosing the beach, all we
had to do was dig our fingers into the gravel and sand to
come up with oil. The truth is, only nature has the power to
clean up that spill. And we don't know how few or how
many years that will take. It could take ten, it could take five
hundred. Nor do we know exactly how the ecosystem's been
permanently changed by the spill. We can only guess."

"Oh, Jackson."

He looked at her, his eyes full of doubt. "And sometimes, especially after a week like this one, I wonder if
maybe I'm not the one whose values are screwed up. If I'm
not the dinosaur standing in the way of progress. Victoria
thought so. Chloe probably does, too."

"You're not," Bentley murmured, twisting to look at
him, tenderness wrapping around and enveloping her. She'd
never known a man who cared so deeply about life, only
men who cared about their careers and money. The kind of
men who truly didn't care who or what they destroyed in
their pursuit of both.

He smiled at her. "No?"

"No." Reaching up, she touched the laugh lines that radiated from his eyes. So often she'd yearned for Jackson to
look at her with warmth and tenderness, with an understanding of her, a silent communication—the way he was
looking at her now.

Her heart turned over, and she realized she was dangerously close to feeling too much for this man. And that it was already too late to do a thing about it.

Bentley took a deep, shuddering breath. She tried to recall their last argument, tried to remember the reasons she loathed him. She couldn't think of one. Even as she told herself it was madness, she moved her hand higher until she tangled her fingers in his hair.

"What am I, then?" he asked, his voice thick.

"Sexy and stubborn," she murmured. "Arrogant, yet somehow sweet." She lowered her voice to a throaty whisper. "Driving me crazy."

"I like that," he said, lowering his mouth. "Because you're driving me crazy, too."

As his mouth took hers, Bentley sighed. It seemed years since he'd touched her, decades since his mouth had been on hers. Searching. Heating. Exploring.

And she responded like a starving woman, opening her mouth to his, too greedy to savor, too hungry to do more than devour. When he lifted her so she straddled his lap, all she could do was murmur her appreciation.

Jackson dragged his mouth from hers to taste the shell of her ear, the fragrant and milky skin of her throat. A small and rational part of him acknowledged that Chloe slept upstairs and that this was madness. That part was small indeed.

He'd denied himself the pleasure of touching her for too long.

He yanked her soft chambray shirt from the waistband of her jeans, then slid his hands beneath. A shudder moved through him as he felt her skin for the first time. Warm as sunlight and smooth as silk, the sensation against his palms was pure luxury. He could only imagine how her skin would feel against other, even more sensitive parts of his anatomy.

His imaginings were unbearably exciting.

Although it cost him, Jackson moved his hands slowly, taking his time, exploring and savoring. Beneath his touch, Bentley quivered, goose bumps racing ahead of his hands. He eased his hands over her rib cage to the curve of her breasts. He cupped her, sucking in a sharp breath as her flesh molded to his palms, as the peaks pressed against him.

Bentley made a sound of pleasure and arched against him, trapping his hands on her breasts. She was still straddling his lap, and his arousal pressed against her. She moved against him, delighting in the feel of him against her womanhood and the way he muttered her name, deep in his throat, before capturing her mouth in a hungry kiss.

As they strained against each other, the events of the week tumbled through her head, kaleidoscope fashion. With them came satisfaction and pride. A feeling that, for once, she was good enough for anybody. She wanted to share the feeling with him, just as she wanted to share her body.

Bentley broke away from him, breathing heavily. She smiled and touched his lower lip with her thumb. "There's so much I have to tell you...so much happened this week."

"Tell me first that you want to make love," Jackson murmured, sliding his hands from her breasts to her bottom. Cupping her, he fitted her against his arousal. "Tell me that, Bentley."

Her mind emptied of everything but the thrum of blood in her head and the sensations skittering through her. She curled her fingers into his shirt, crumpling it, holding on to the fabric as if it were her only anchor to the real world.

"Tell me, Bentley," he said again, raining kisses over her face and neck. "Do you want to make love? We could go away for the day." He smiled against her throat. "I have a sailboat...we could spend the day out on the Gulf. Making love with the breeze on our backs, the sun warming our faces."

Bentley arched against him. "What about work?"

He laughed low in his throat, the sound husky and amused. "You've become so diligent. Jill can take care of the office and Chloe for another day without me."

"But—"

"Uh-uh." He nipped at her full bottom lip. "No buts. Only yes...and yes...and yes."

Each word he uttered was punctuated with a kiss, and Bentley had to fight to concentrate on what she needed to say. She caught his hands and arched away from him. "Wait...Jackson..." She drew in a deep, steadying breath. "Jill won't be there."

Jackson froze. "What?"

"That's one of the things I had to tell you." Her voice trembled so badly, she had to pause to collect herself. "She's in the hospital. She had to have an emergency appendectomy."

Concerned, he searched Bentley's expression. "My God, when did this happen? Is she all right?"

"The day you left. And she's fine."

It took a moment for her words to register. When they did, Jackson loosened his hold on her. "The day I left?" he asked quietly.

"Mmm." Bentley rested her forehead on his shoulder. "When we came into the office that first morning, Jill was so sick. We were so frightened for her. I thought—"

"Whoa." He drew his eyebrows together. "Why didn't you call? Why haven't you mentioned this before now?"

He hadn't raised his voice; if anything it had become deeper, softer. Outwardly he gave no indication of anger. But his eyes had changed, cooled, his facial muscles had tightened. In a matter of moments, he had taken on the look of a predator.

A sinking sensation in the pit of her stomach, Bentley dropped her hands from his shoulders. "I thought we could take care of Baysafe by ourselves. I didn't think it necessary to bother you."

"We as in you and Chloe?"

"Yes." Bentley drew her eyebrows together confused and hurt by his sarcasm. She scooted off his lap, then self-consciously straightened her skirt. When she looked at him she was shocked to see the anger seething in his expression.

She folded her arms across her chest and jerked her chin up. "I . . . did some research, and I . . . think I've found one of your problems."

"One of my problems?" he repeated furiously, standing.

"Yes." Bentley followed him to his feet, nervously twisting her fingers in front of her. When she spoke, she worked to keep the hesitation from her voice. "I think . . . I mean, it looks to me, like you're too industry dependent. Especially the oil industry. And, as you're finding out, that's a dangerous position to be in. One unpopular issue, you lose your funding."

He raked his gaze over her. "And you've found a solution to this problem?"

"Yes." She narrowed her eyes at his tone, vacillating between the urge to hit him and convince him. "You've hardly tapped the social set. These people give tens of thousands of dollars to charities each year. There is no reason Baysafe shouldn't be getting a big piece of that pie. I made some calls and set up some lunches."

For a full ten seconds, Jackson stared at her. Then he took a step toward her, something akin to violence in his eyes. "Baysafe is mine," he said, his voice tightly controlled. "It's a living, breathing company. That company supports me and Chloe, it supports Jill. It's not a toy... it's not your toy."

Bentley stiffened at the blow. "I never thought of it as a toy. Never. Why would you think that?"

Jackson turned and crossed to the window. For a moment he stood and stared out at the night, then he swung around, pinning her with his furious gaze. "I can't believe this. You know nothing about my business. Nothing. And yet you decide you're qualified not only to make a week's worth of decisions, but to evaluate my shortcomings, as well."

"If you'd just listen." Bentley clenched her hands into fists at her sides, suddenly so angry she shook with it. "Doesn't the accused get a trial around here? You haven't even bothered to ask *what* we accomplished. Or doesn't it matter?"

His expression told her everything, and she made a sound of pain and frustration. Swinging away from him, she started to gather up the articles spread over the couch.

"I don't care what you're trying to prove," Jackson said softly from behind her. "I don't care who you're trying to prove it to. Baysafe is not a game. It's not some sort of test."

The urge to hit him charged through her until she trembled with holding it back. Even after what they'd just shared, even after all she'd done for Chloe and Baysafe, he thought no more of her than the day she'd walked through his door. He still thought her worthless and spoiled.

What had happened between them a moment ago had been strictly sexual. Strictly physical. It had to do with how she looked, not who she was.

Hurt mingled with fury, just as the urge to run warred with the desire to stand her ground. Pushing away the hurt, the lifetime of self-doubts, Bentley turned slowly to face him. She lifted her chin. "I'm not a worthless princess,

Jackson. And I won't let you, or anybody, treat me like one. Never again."

She took a step closer to him, never taking her eyes from his. "Chloe and I did a great job. Not good—*great*. We...*I* expected your thanks. Your appreciation and respect. I deserve them."

Bentley hiked her chin up a notch more as she realized she meant every word she said. "You know, what I did this week I did to impress you. To prove to you that I'm serious about working and that I am capable. But don't worry, I'll never try to prove anything to you again. Because it doesn't matter. Your opinion of me doesn't matter. Because, for once, I believe in myself."

"Thanks?" he murmured, outraged. "Appreciation? That's rich. You involved my daughter—"

"Involved her in something that gave her a feeling of self-worth, of accomplishment." Bentley took another step closer. Tears stung the backs of her eyes, and she fought against them. Jackson Reese, she told herself fiercely, was not worth crying over. His opinion was not worth a single one of her tears. And yet a part of her wished so desperately she could go back a matter of minutes, to the moment when he had looked at her as if she was everything wonderful.

Closing that part of herself off, she narrowed her eyes. "And as for your daughter, she blossomed this week. If you'd talked to her, you would know that."

Blanching, Jackson took a step away from her. Instead of satisfaction, Bentley felt regret. "Jackson, I—"

She reached her hand out in apology. He looked at her hand, her offering, as if it was something loathsome, and her regret vanished.

She swept her hair away from her forehead with a quick, jerky motion. "You're so damn quick to point fingers. You couldn't wait to discredit me, could you? You've been wait-ing for an opportunity."

"That's ridiculous."

"Is it?" She snatched up her handbag. "I'm not so sure. I think maybe you feel more in control when you're con-vinced I'm the enemy. The problem is, it's getting harder for you to believe that. Isn't that right? Maybe I should even be flattered by all this."

He was silent, and she crossed to the entryway closet and took out her coat. Not bothering to put it on, she turned to him. "When was the last time you told Chloe you loved her, Jackson? Don't you think maybe she needs to hear it once in a while?"

Jackson swore. "So, we're back to my parenting. Pretty clever way to shift the heat from yourself, Bentley. But then, I never said you weren't clever."

"Damn you, Jackson Reese." She drew in a sharp, angry breath and faced him as haughtily as the princess he ac-cused her of being. "You know something? I can't wait for tomorrow morning, because you're going to feel like a first-class jerk. I almost wish I was going to see it. My bag's al-ready in the car. Good night."

The next morning Jackson stared out at the tangle of his garden. He'd showered, shaved and dressed, he'd had his first cup of coffee hours ago. He'd seen the sun creep over the horizon and into the sky, creating a day that was bril-liant and mild. He wished he could feel as bright, as warmed. Instead, he felt dazed, still felt punch-drunk and raw.

He brought his coffee cup to his mouth, but didn't drink. He couldn't put the scene he'd had with Bentley out of his head. Not the passion they'd shared . . . or the anger. He lowered his cup, frowning. And he couldn't shake off the niggling sense that he'd overreacted. That his fury had had more to do with himself than with Bentley or anything she'd done.

He'd wanted to pick a fight. He'd wanted to push her as far away from him as fast as he could.

Ridiculous. He lifted the cup to his lips once more and downed the coffee, wincing at its heat. The issue was Baysafe. Not his feelings. Not his need for distance—

"Daddy!"

Jackson swung around, stared as his daughter came barreling down the stairs. His mouth dropped. Not only was she up and dressed, but she was smiling at him as if she was happy to see him. A sense of déjà vu, at once bitter and sweet, washed over him in a wave.

"Chloe, baby." He swallowed past the lump in his throat and smiled. "I was getting ready to come up and wake you."

She stopped in front of him and clasped her hands together, looking at him almost shyly. "I set the alarm."

Set her alarm? Chloe? Jackson wasn't quite sure what to say—since coming to live with him, she hadn't done that even once. He smiled again, awkwardly, and hugged her. "I . . . brought you something."

"You did?" She beamed at him.

"Uh-huh. It's upstairs."

"What is it?"

"Go get it and find out. It's on my dresser."

Chloe raced up the stairs, then a moment later, raced down, ripping the gift open as she did. "Oh, Daddy," she said, holding up the crystal, heart-shaped box. "It's so pretty."

"Look inside." She did, then squealed as she found the dainty porcelain earrings, also shaped like hearts. Hearts because she had his, he thought, watching as she slipped them into her ears.

He opened his mouth to tell her, then swallowed the words, feeling vulnerable and uncertain. "Do you like them?" he asked instead.

"Oh, yes." She stood on tiptoe and kissed his cheek. "Thank you, Daddy."

"You're welcome—" Jackson realized he was about to call her princess and bit back the word.

Chloe didn't seem to notice. "Did you talk to Bentley?" she asked excitedly. "Did she tell you what we did?"

Several emotions hit him at once—anger, envy at the way his daughter glowed as she said Bentley's name, longing. It was the last that bothered him most. He worked to keep all of them from his voice.

"Yes. She told me."

Chloe's face fell, and she took a step back from him. "Oh."

Jackson muttered an oath. Strike number ten thousand and ten. How many did he get before he was out for good?

Pushing away panic, he put his arm around Chloe. "I hear you're becoming quite a little cook."

Chloe tipped her head, excited again. "I really am. Did you try it? It was good."

"No, but I—" Her smile faded, and Jackson kicked himself for his honesty—and his stupidity. "It was after two a.m. when I got in, sweetie. I'll eat some tonight."

"Sure." She stepped out of the curve of his arm. "If you want."

"I do. I wouldn't miss it." She didn't look at him, and Jackson flexed his fingers in frustration. *Couldn't he say anything right?* "How about breakfast out? My treat."

Chloe shrugged, indifference firmly in place. "Whatever."

They barely spoke through breakfast. Chloe picked at her food, refusing to be drawn out. Finally, on their way out of the diner, he brought up Jill.

Chloe looked up at him, eyes wide. "It was so scary! I've never seen anybody who was that sick. I thought she was dying or something." Chloe scooped up a handful of the complimentary mints by the cash register. "Bentley took care of everything, though. She was real calm." Chloe giggled. "Well, pretty calm. She had me get Jill a cloth for her forehead, then she called 911."

Jackson held open the diner door for Chloe, once again fighting a wave of jealousy at his daughter's affection for Bentley. Holding his daughter's elbow, he steered her across the street to the building that housed Baysafe's offices.

"You should have seen those ambulance guys run in with a stretcher," Chloe continued. "I was worried about Jill and all, but it was so neat. Just like that TV show—you know, *Call 911*."

"Chloe," Jackson asked quietly, "why didn't you call me?"

Even though he tried to sound nonjudgmental, Chloe paused and drew her eyebrows together in worried thought. "I wanted to," she said finally, cautiously, giving her allegiance to Bentley. "But Bentley said we should surprise you. She said it would make you . . . happy."

Fresh anger at Bentley surged through him, and he dug his keys from his pocket. That she'd involved Chloe in her recklessness was unforgivable.

He jammed the key into the lock, but before he could twist it, Chloe caught his arm. He met her eyes. "I'm sorry," she whispered.

His chest tightened at the dampness in her blue eyes. "Why are you apologizing?"

"Because I can tell it didn't make you happy."

Jackson's heart turned over, and he gave his daughter a quick, fierce hug. "Thank you."

She sniffed. "For what?"

"Being so sweet." He unlocked the office door, then held it open for Chloe.

She ducked inside, rushed over to the front desk and grabbed a handful of message slips, then raced back with them. "I took every one of these," she said proudly, holding them out to him. "Look, I even noted the times. This guy wanted you to call him first thing today." Speechless, Jackson took the messages. "It's about the study results."

Chloe raced to the desk again, bursting with pride. "All the donation reminders went out, right on time." She swiveled and pointed to some boxes stacked beside her. "We got the newsletter ready to go." She lifted her chin proudly. "I was a big help with that. Bentley said she couldn't have done it without me. And—" she paused for breath "—we only had to call Jill twice!"

Stunned, Jackson looked around the reception area, noting that not one article was out of place. Far from the chaos he had expected to find last night. He settled his gaze on Chloe. *What had happened while he was gone? This was not the same child he had left.*

As his daughter raced around the office, showing him this and that, describing her week, the more foolish—the more ridiculous—he felt. He'd acted like a total...ass. Everything Bentley had said to him was true.

He had to apologize.

No. Jackson frowned. He had to beg her forgiveness. And even after begging he wouldn't blame her if she told him to take a flying leap.

The morning ticked by, minute after agonizing minute. He waited for Bentley, practicing what he would say to her, rehearsing his apology so many times he could have recited it in his sleep.

No Bentley.

Finally, at noon, Jackson had to accept the fact that she wasn't going to show.

He'd blown it.

Frustrated, he turned away from the door, only to find Chloe watching him. He forced a smile and crossed to her. "Quiet day."

"She's not coming, is she?" Chloe asked quietly.

"No. I don't think so."

"Oh." Chloe bit her bottom lip and cocked her head. "What are you going to do about it?"

Jackson gazed at his daughter a moment, then shook his head. "I haven't figured that out yet."

Chloe opened her mouth, then looked away, stubbing her toe into the carpet.

He drew his eyebrows together. "You have an idea?"

Chloe lifted her head, a bright flush climbing her cheeks. She shrugged. "Well, you might try—" She shook her head. "Never mind."

"What?"

"You promise you won't get mad?"

He held up two fingers. "Let me have it."

Chloe twisted her fingers together. "You get kinda crabby sometimes, Daddy. She might not understand that's . . . just the way you are. Maybe if you explained that to her, and told her you were sorry . . ."

His daughter let her words trail off, then bit her lip. His heart swelled. For the first time since she'd come to live with him, he felt that they were really communicating. "Crabby?" he repeated, arching his eyebrows, amused.

"Kinda. Sometimes." She lifted one shoulder. "Demanding, too."

Jackson gazed at her a moment, then tumbled her into his arms for a bear hug. For a moment Chloe resisted, standing stiffly in his arms, her own arms at her sides. His heart broke. Then she shuddered, snaked her arms around him and hugged him back. Hard.

Squeezing his eyes shut, Jackson decided he owed Bentley a lot more than an apology.

Chapter Eight

Bentley threw open her living room window to the unexpectedly warm winter day and leaned out. From the shop below the rich, sweet scent of flowers wafted up to her. She breathed deeply and wished the balmy, scented air could cleanse her of the turbulent emotions churning inside her.

Jackson hadn't called. He hadn't come by to apologize. She felt as if she had been holding her breath since she'd walked out his door the night before. Bentley tipped her face toward the sky, squinting against the brilliant sunlight. She had wanted him to come after her. Wanted it so badly it hurt. She had waited for his call, his knock on her door.

The time had come to stop waiting and wishing. The time had come to face the truth. For whatever reasons, she was susceptible to Jackson. An inexplicable chemistry crackled between them despite their differences, despite the fact that he loathed her.

Bentley closed her fingers around the windowsill. She should stay as far away from him as possible. He had hurt her; he would hurt her again.

Even facing that truth, she wasn't certain she had the strength of will.

Leaving the window up, Bentley ducked inside. Turning, she faced her apartment, faced the first concrete evidence of her independence, her growth. This was hers, she reminded herself. She had taken big steps to get here, and she wasn't about to throw everything she'd gained away. Not on something as insubstantial and fleeting as chemistry. And certainly not on a man who cared so little for her, a man who continued to judge her by someone else's sins.

She'd set her music box on a pedestal by the bed. Crossing the room, Bentley picked it up. She trailed her fingers lightly over the filigree, thinking back, as she had so often in the last hours, to her and Jackson's fight.

He hadn't been completely wrong. She should have called him. Baysafe was his. He'd had the right to know of any changes that might affect his business. She'd known that even as she'd made the decision not to. But she'd also known that if she called, he would come racing back to Galveston. No matter what she said, no matter how she would have tried to convince him, he wouldn't have believed in her ability to handle Baysafe even for a few days.

She'd wanted her chance. She'd taken it.

Bentley gazed at her porcelain look-alike, pride warring with despair inside her. She had done it. She'd proven herself to herself. Her satisfaction would have been complete if he had been happy for her, if he had been able to admit she'd done a good job. Instead, he had lashed out at her. His accusations had been unforgivable in light of what they had shared only a moment before. He had shown her, once and for all, how little he thought of her.

Bentley inched her chin up. She would survive without his approval, without him. She had lived through much worse and gone on.

Tears stung her eyes, and she cursed them. She had a decision to make. Could she stay on at Baysafe? Or should she throw in the towel and admit defeat? Her chest tightened at the thought of leaving. She wanted to stay and continue what she'd begun this last week. Baysafe needed her; she could make a difference there.

But not without Jackson's cooperation. Not without his belief in her.

And she would never have either.

Bentley set the music box on the pedestal, her hands trembling so badly she feared she might drop it. The truth of that shouldn't hurt so much. It shouldn't make her feel alone and torn in two. But it did, she acknowledged, her eyes filling, brimming over. What was wrong with her that it mattered so much what he thought of her?

She was falling in love with him.

Bentley shook her head against the thought, denial racing through her. No. Impossible. She couldn't afford to love him. She couldn't afford to give her heart—or her burgeoning self-esteem—to someone who would crush it.

And he would crush it, just as David had done.

She had to get out of here, Bentley thought, looking around her nearly empty apartment. She had to go someplace there were people talking and laughing, somewhere she couldn't hear her own thoughts.

Grabbing her handbag, she raced to the door and jerked it open. Jackson stood on the other side, his arms filled with yellow roses arranged in a beautiful vase, his expression uncertain.

Bentley stared at him, nonplussed and aching, her heart a freight train in her chest. He'd come.

They gazed at one another, one second becoming two becoming a dozen. He looked tired. And worried. His light eyes seemed shadowed by some deeply felt emotion. Her heart went out to him, and she called herself a softhearted ninny.

"Why have you come here, Jackson?" she asked, finding her voice, reminding herself that anger was her best defense against him.

He cleared his throat. "These are for you."

She longed to take the flowers, to touch one of the butter-colored blossoms, to bury her face in their sweetness. But to do so would be to give him more than she could allow herself to.

She folded her arms across her chest and forced herself to keep her eyes on his. "And we both know that doesn't answer my question."

"Why do you think I've come, Bentley?"

His voice, soft and thick, moved hypnotically over her. She shook off its affect, shook off the urge to forgive him anything and everything for the pittance of a bouquet of flowers and one of his smiles.

Nothing had changed. He was unwilling to admit he was wrong about her, unwilling to give her credit.

Anger jumped to life inside her, and she lifted her chin. "I don't have time for games, Jackson. Excuse me."

"I was wrong," he said quickly, stepping forward, stopping the door with his hand. "I'm sorry."

Her heart stopped, then started again with a jerk. Still, she didn't move away from the door, didn't make a move to take the flowers. "Sorry isn't enough."

"Give me a chance, Bentley. Please. Let me in."

"I don't think so." She gripped the edge of the door more tightly, her knuckles whitening. "I don't think it's a good idea."

She was a liar—she *knew* it was a bad idea. Risky. Dangerous. Already, she could feel herself weakening, giving in to the way he made her feel, the way he made her ache to touch him.

He took another step closer. She could smell the roses then, their subtle potency going straight to her head, weakening her resolve even further.

"I don't blame you if you don't want to listen to one thing I have to say." He lowered his voice. "I'm asking you to listen anyway."

Suspecting that she was making the mistake of her life, Bentley stepped aside to allow him in, then shut the door behind him. But she didn't take the flowers, didn't offer a place for him to set them.

Jackson stood just inside her living area, filling it with his size, his presence. The air seemed to become his, crackling with his energy, his magnetism.

Needing space, hoping to clear her head, Bentley took a step away from him. It didn't help.

Jackson moved his gaze around the large, sparsely furnished space, then met her gaze again. "This isn't what I expected."

She stiffened her spine. "I don't own much. I—" She shook her head, cursing herself for her need to justify herself to him. "You have something to say to me?"

"Many somethings. But first, I was wrong, Bentley. I behaved like an idiot, like an unforgivable ass." After plucking one flower from the bouquet, he set the vase of roses on the floor. "You and Chloe did do a great job. And you were right. When it comes to you, it seems I can't admit how capable you are. Until now."

She didn't move, didn't comment. She hoped he couldn't see the hope in her eyes or the way her chest rose and fell like a marathon runner's.

"You've changed my life." He took a step closer to her. "You're changing it still. The difference you made in Chloe—in Chloe's and my relationship—is like a miracle."

He took another step. "And you were right, what you said about Baysafe being too industry dependent. I'm not a good salesman. I naively believe that people should give us money because it's the right thing to do, because the Bay needs us. Arrogantly, I think everyone should feel as zealously as I do about this cause.

"I didn't want to admit any of those things," he continued, softly. "Not last night, not ten minutes ago. Humility doesn't come easily to me. Neither does self-awareness. Because when I look at myself and my life, I see a flawed man who's made a lot of mistakes."

Bentley drew in a deep breath, fighting for reason, for control. "And now?" she asked.

"Now, I'm trying to undo one of those mistakes." He moved a step closer. "I was deliberately pushing you away. Last night and from the moment we first met. Because everything about you pulls at me. I was afraid. Of being hurt. Of making a mess of my life. Again.

"But I'm more afraid of losing you. You've brought something special, something warm to my life." He held out the rose. "Tell me it's not too late."

Bentley searched his gaze. How could she not forgive him? He spoke from his heart. To hers. The too-proud man who had once told her he never apologized had just humbled himself to her.

She took the rose from his outstretched hand. Holding it to her nose, she breathed in the delicate scent, then trailed it lightly across her mouth. How could she be angry with him for not believing in her when until recently she hadn't believed in herself?

Over the delicate bloom she met his eyes. "It's not too late."

Jackson smiled. The curving of his mouth was as spontaneous and pleased as a boy's. It affected her in ways and places only a woman would know. Turning, he scooped up the vase and handed it to her.

Bentley took the flowers carefully, almost reverently. Once they were in her hands, she gave in to the urge and lowered her face to the velvety blossoms and breathed in the light but heady scent. She knew she would never again be able to smell roses and not think of this moment and of Jackson.

"They're beautiful," she whispered, meeting his eyes once more.

"No thorns." He reached out and touched her hair. "I once likened you to a rose, an exquisite blossom that needed to be coaxed and pampered, a cultivated beauty. But like the rose, I thought there was a catch attached to your incredible beauty. I thought you had thorns."

He moved his hand to the curve of her cheek. "I know now there's no catch, no thorns." He cupped her face in his palm. "You haven't any meanness or cruelty in you, Bentley. I know that now. I misjudged you."

The breath caught in her lungs, then shuddered out. She tipped her face into his caress. How could she not respond to his words? And what could she give him besides everything?

She wasn't beginning to fall in love with him.

She had already fallen. Deeply and passionately. Irrevocably.

As frightened as she was exhilarated, Bentley swung away from him. She set the vase of flowers on the bed stand, then crossed to the open window. For long moments, she stared at the busy street, at the flower vendor's baskets of blossoms below.

Love? she thought dizzily, sucking in a lungful of the scented air. How had she let herself get in so deep? How had he gotten by every one of her defenses without even trying?

She squeezed her eyes shut. Jackson wasn't in love with her. Not now. Maybe he would never be. Panicked laughter bubbled to her lips. She was thinking love and he'd just realized he didn't despise her.

Could she take the chance and make herself vulnerable to him?

She already had.

Jackson came up behind her, stopping so close she could feel the heat that radiated from him, feel his breath stir against her hair. But he didn't touch her, and it was all she could do to keep from swinging around and clutching him to her.

"What are you thinking?" he asked quietly, rubbing some of her soft, dark curls between his fingers. "Don't shut me out, Princess."

She caught her bottom lip between her teeth. If only she could tell him. If only she wasn't so certain that words of love would have him running. She took another deep, healing breath. If onlys sapped dreams and peace of mind. Wishing and worrying about the future and the impossible did nothing but rob the here and now.

And she wanted the now. She wanted Jackson.

She turned. Heart racing, she met his gaze. "I was wondering where we go from here."

"You tell me."

"I'd like to stay on at Baysafe."

"I'd like that, too."

"But if I do stay, I'll need your cooperation. I intend to pursue what I started last week."

"You've got it." He cupped her face in his palms. "Where else, Bentley? Where else do we go from here?"

The expression in his eyes was hot and dark. It melted her. "The decision's not only mine."

"But it is." He tightened his fingers, lowering his eyes to her mouth for a moment before lifting them back to hers. "I want us to be lovers. That hasn't changed since last night. It won't change." He dragged his thumbs across her bottom lip, smiling as it trembled under the caress. "What we both need to know is, what do you want?"

Lovers. Not I love you. The truth of that ripped through her, and she lifted her hands to his chest, the rose still clutched in her fingers. He offered no promises, no declarations of affection. But hadn't she had both once? And hadn't they turned out to mean less than nothing?

Bentley searched his gaze. He offered her more; he offered honesty, respect and trust. He desired her, but he also liked her. Those were things she'd never had before, special and wonderful, and she would cherish them later, when she was regretting and wishing for everything. Wishing for love.

Bentley curled her fingers into his shirt. Outwardly he looked in control, even cool. But beneath her hand and the flower, his heart beat wildly. Almost out of control. He wanted her badly.

She tossed the rose on the bed. "Where's Chloe?" she whispered, flattening her hands against his chest and leaning into him.

Jackson drew in a shuddering breath. "Home. A neighbor's looking in on her. The answering machine's on at Baysafe." He searched her gaze. "Why?"

Bentley smiled wickedly and moved her hands to the waistband of his denims, then jerked his shirt free. "Just making sure you wouldn't have to rush." Slowly, deliberately, she slipped one button through its hole, then another. "It would be a shame to wait so long for something only to hurry through it."

Jackson linked his arms loosely around her, his heart beating heavily against the wall of his chest. "Are you sure you know what you're doing?"

Not answering, she pushed the shirt from his shoulders, then pressed her mouth to his chest, tasting, then nipping. He tasted and smelled like a man, of fresh air and sweat. Intoxicated on both, she tasted him again. And again.

He was hard beneath her hands, muscular and fit. The hair on his chest was blond, and crisp against her fingers. Liking the sensation, she tunneled her fingers through the hazing of fur.

Jackson caught her hands, forcing her to meet his eyes. "Are you sure?" he asked again, his voice thick with arousal, tight with control.

"No," she whispered. "I'm not. I'm afraid I'm going to have to feel my way."

In her gaze Jackson read desire and laughter. And vulnerability. The combination tugged at him more than it should have, more than he should have allowed it to.

Some things were beyond his control.

Even as he called himself a fool, Jackson eased her shirt from her slacks, and began working the tiny pearl buttons through their loops. " 'Feel your way,' " he murmured. "I like the sound of that."

"Feel free to follow my example."

"I think I will." The last button released, Jackson slipped the silky shirt off her shoulders. It slithered to the floor, a shimmering puddle at their feet.

For long moments Jackson gazed at her. Her skin was as white as fresh cream and as flawless. But warm. And yielding. Jackson trailed his fingers lightly across her collarbone and down the sides of her breasts. Beneath his touch her flesh quivered and goose bumps raced after his fingers. He lowered his mouth to her shoulder, tasting her. "You're perfection."

She tipped her head, making a sound of pleasure deep in her throat. "I don't want to be perfect. Perfect is lonely."

"Not today, it's not." Jackson traveled, tasting and teasing, to the vulnerable curve between her neck and shoulder, then to her breasts. "You're the most beautiful, the most exciting woman I've ever known. And I've never wanted anyone more."

Bentley shuddered and arched her back, closing her fingers around his shoulders, holding on for dear life. Through the sheer lace of her bra, he caught the hard peak of one breast, sucking, nipping, then moved on to the other. Her flesh strained against the lacy fabric, as if begging for his touch, and she moaned as he unfastened the garment and tossed it aside.

The breeze from the open window was cold against her fevered flesh, and Bentley caught Jackson's hands. "Come," she whispered, lacing his fingers with hers and leading him to the bed.

Antique white iron, delicately scrolled and draped in filmy muslin, the bed was one of the few things she owned. After her divorce she'd seen it in a magazine and had fallen in love with it. She was glad that this first time with Jackson would be on this bed, on this sea of white, in this place that had no memories.

The slate would never be so clean, so pure, again. Today the memories began.

Bentley stopped beside the bed and, not taking her eyes from Jackson's, she unfastened his jeans and pushed them over his hips. He stepped out of them, then slipped her slacks off. Lacing their fingers again, she drew him onto the bed.

Jackson caught his breath at the sweetness of her offering. This woman turned him upside down and inside out, jumbled his senses and left him aching and out of breath. She had from the first. Only now, he was done fighting. Only now, that fact didn't frighten him. In an odd way, he trusted her now.

Pressing her against the mattress, Jackson caught her mouth, diving deeply into her. She met his assault with her own, twining her tongue with his, her fingers in his hair. She strained against him, he against her. She arched and sighed as he stroked, then returned the favor, delighting in his sounds of pleasure. Moments ago the breeze had felt cold, now it hadn't even the power to chill.

She moved against him, against his arousal. "Jackson," she murmured. "Jackson..."

He tore his mouth away from hers, the act almost painful. "Wait... Bentley... sweetheart, I need..." Groaning, he caught her mouth again. A moment later he wrenched himself away and rolled to the side of the bed. Reaching over the side for his jeans, he fumbled with the denims, then his wallet.

He swore and fumbled again. *It couldn't be. But it was— or, more to the point—wasn't.*

Jackson rolled onto the bed and threw his arm over his eyes. *How could he have been so stupid? How could he have started this without making sure he had protection?* Breathing deeply, he struggled to contain his desire.

"Jackson?" Bentley whispered, her voice trembling. She laid a hand on his heaving chest. Her eyes filled with tears when he flinched. "What's wrong? Did I do something... wrong?"

He lifted his arm, just enough to see her eyes. He tried to smile. And failed. "Not you. Me. I didn't bring... anything. I didn't expect... so I didn't check..."

Jackson groaned again and pulled himself into a sitting position. He dragged his hands through his hair. "Since Victoria," he said, not trusting himself to look at Bentley, "I have never gone without protection. Never." He did look at her then. "Chloe wasn't planned."

"I know." Bentley saw shock in his eyes, followed by dismay and guilt. She touched his arm, hoping to soften the blow of her words. "Chloe told me. She overheard Victoria talking about it one day."

Jackson swore again, this time viciously. "I never wanted her to know that. I never wanted her to think that she wasn't wanted."

In that moment Bentley knew the sin Jackson punished himself for—the circumstances of Chloe's birth. Sitting up, she wrapped her arms around his waist and fitted herself to his back. She couldn't tell him that was exactly what Chloe thought, not now, anyway. It would hurt him more than she could bear.

"I've messed this up," he murmured, bringing her hands to his mouth, then extricating himself from her arms. "I'm sorry."

"Don't go."

"I can't stay," he said, his voice thick with regret. "I can't take the chance, and I can't not touch you."

He moved to climb off the bed. Bentley caught his hand. "I can't conceive, Jackson."

He stopped and met her eyes. "What?"

She drew in a deep breath, fighting the tears that threatened, feeling exposed and ridiculous and alarmingly lacking. "You don't have to worry about getting me pregnant. I'm...barren."

She said the last flatly, or tried to, but Jackson heard the whisper of grief beneath the matter-of-fact words and tone.

He reached down and cupped her face with gentle fingers. "I'm sorry."

Bentley covered his hand with her own and tipped her face into the caress. "I spent a good bit of my short marriage trying to get pregnant, thinking a baby would make things okay between me and David. Stupid, I know." She tried to laugh; she choked on the sound instead. "And I thought a baby would make me whole."

"Ah, Bentley..." Jackson eased her into his arms, against his chest. "I don't know what to say."

"Don't say anything." Beneath her cheek his heart beat sure but not quite steadily. She slipped her arms around him and stroked his back, fingers of desire beginning to lick at her again. She wanted this man as she'd never wanted before. Enough to lay her soul bare. "The fertility clinic was a wrenching and humiliating experience. I hated it, every moment." She tilted her head, meeting his eyes. "I had blood tests almost monthly. And I haven't been with anyone since my marriage."

Jackson's heart turned over and he lowered his mouth to hers. He brushed his lips against hers, nuzzling them open, dipping his tongue inside to taste hers. "I wasn't worried about that."

She slid her hands up to cup his neck. "But you're not foolhardy, either. You're not a reckless man."

"No?" Jackson lifted his eyebrows, amused and charmed. "When I'm with you I feel quite reckless. When I'm with you, all I can think of is the unmentionable and delicious things I want to do to your body. It scares me senseless."

Bentley laughed and pulled him down to the mattress. "Show me, Jackson. Show me just how reckless you can be."

So he did. Recklessly, he explored her body. Daringly, he tasted and caressed. With his hands and mouth he showed her until she writhed beneath him, until she called his name and begged him to end the exquisite torture.

But still he held himself back. So Bentley showed him how reckless *she* could be, exciting and arousing him, bringing him to a point where he had no more control.

He rolled her onto her back. The single rose she'd tossed on the bed was crushed beneath her shoulder, and for one moment the scent was almost overpowering. At that precise instant, he slipped into her, and the sweetness of the flower intermingled with the sweetness of sensation. And possession. He was hers. She loved him. It had never been so good—so special—before. The future would take care of itself.

Bentley wrapped her legs around his, moving her hips in time with his until frenzy took them both. As they reached the peak and crested it, Bentley called out his name. He caught it with his kiss, murmuring his own words of passion and pleasure.

For a long time they lay twined together as their flesh cooled and breathing evened. Totally relaxed, Bentley let herself float, thinking of nothing in particular, clueing in to sensations rather than thoughts.

Jackson shifted his weight, smiling as she murmured a protest. "I'll crush you," he said, drawing her to his side.

"Mmm." She pressed her mouth to his chest, tasting the salt of his sweat, their passion. "But what a way to go."

Jackson laughed and tangled his fingers in her soft curls, brushing them away from her face. "Bentley...tell me about your marriage. Tell me about...David."

Bentley stiffened, unpleasant memories flooding her mind, memories of moments like these with her husband. But ones without the softness, without the trust. She snuggled closer to Jackson's side, forcing those memories aside, focusing instead on this moment. "What do you want to know?"

Jackson heard the pain in her voice, felt the change in her at his question, and he kicked himself for it. "Never mind. It's none of my business."

Bentley laced their fingers. "No...actually, I think I'd like to talk about it." She tipped her head and met his eyes. "Nobody else knows the truth. They just think they do."

"What do you mean?"

"That I didn't care what people thought," she said simply. "I only cared about escaping."

Her words slammed into him, taking his breath and his peace of mind. David had hurt her. Badly. Unnaturally. Jackson forced himself to stay relaxed, to continue to gently stroke her hair when all his instincts had him wanting to howl with rage.

"I married David because I wanted to please my parents," she began softly. "I told myself I loved him. I didn't. I couldn't. The David I thought I knew didn't exist."

Bentley heard the bitterness in her voice and despised it. Someday, she vowed, it wouldn't matter any more. It wouldn't hurt any more.

"David was quite a catch," she continued. "Rich, successful. A family name as old and respected as my mother's. I sometimes think Mama was more excited about having David in the family than having me for a daughter."

Jackson kissed her. "I can't imagine that. You're quite a catch yourself."

She smiled, pleased with his words, but shook her head in denial of them. "It's true. Mama went slumming when she married Daddy. *New money,*" Bentley whispered in a mimicry of her mother. "Problem was, the Bartons didn't have any money. So she married Daddy for his bank balance and he married her for her name and social connections."

"True love," Jackson said, not bothering to hide his contempt. "So, what happened to your fairy tale?"

"Mine was a nightmare in disguise." She laughed without humor. "How clichéd that sounds. But it didn't feel that way. It felt . . . unique. Extraordinary."

Unable to lie still, unable to feign calm any longer, Bentley sat up, bringing the sheet with her. She clutched it to her breasts and stared at the patterns of sunlight on the wall. "I didn't think it possible that other people lived that way. It was incomprehensible to me."

Jackson watched her, his every muscle quivering with the effort of control. "What did he do to you?"

"David had a streak of cruelty in him. In public he was charming. The loving and devoted husband, the gallant gentleman. But in private . . . he did his best to destroy me."

Jackson sucked in a sharp, angry breath, wishing there was something he could do with the violence raging in him, some place he could put it. He flexed his fingers. "If I ever get my hands on him, I'll—"

"Don't." Bentley covered Jackson's clenched hand with her own. "He didn't hit me," she said softly. "Not with his fists, anyway. Although by the end of our marriage, I was practically begging him to. If I'd had physical evidence of his abuse, I would have known it wasn't *me,* I would have known I wasn't going crazy. And maybe if I'd had bruises I would have left sooner. Maybe I would have had the guts to tell the world what a creep he really was.

"Words," she said simply. "His words bruised me in places fists couldn't. In places that couldn't be seen and wouldn't heal. David's quite intelligent, a master manipulator. He started on me subtly at first, undermining my confidence, questioning my every decision. I couldn't do anything right or well, including sex. I couldn't even get pregnant." She plucked absently at the white sheet. "A blessing, I realize now. I can only imagine what he would have done to a child."

Bentley looked at Jackson, her heart twisting at his expression. *Did he think less of her now, knowing how weak she'd been?* She shifted her gaze to the window. She was who she was, Bentley told herself. If he couldn't accept all of her, including her past, he wasn't worth having.

"Before I married David, I worried I was nothing. When he was finished with me, I knew it with every fiber of my being. It got to the point that I was afraid to pick out my own clothes for fear of making a mistake."

Muttering an oath, Jackson hauled her into his arms and against his chest. "Bentley...baby, it's not true. He's a sick, sick man."

"I know that now." She cleared her throat of the tears clogging it. "But when you're in a relationship like that, it's hard to see the truth. When you're a woman, and particularly a southern woman, things are expected of you. Essentially, I was raised to be David's wife. Nothing more, but certainly not less. The outside world, including my family, believed me to be the problem. 'Make the marriage work,' they said. 'You're not trying hard enough, you're letting us down.' So I tried harder. I wanted to please them. That's all I ever wanted."

Jackson tangled his fingers in her hair, softly stroking. "What happened?"

She paused, wanting to look at Jackson but afraid of what she might read in his eyes. "The longer we were married, the more abusive he became. One day he would take my car keys and forbid me to leave the house. He took my credit cards, telling me that without them, I was nothing. A pretty, empty shell, he called me so often."

She looked at Jackson, then away. "I think his abuse worked so well on me because, deep down, I feared the same things about myself.

"Finally, I couldn't take any more. I made some mistake, served the wrong tea, wore the wrong dress...I don't remember, I made so many mistakes. He locked me in the closet and left. I was in there all night. The maid found me the next morning. I made up a lie, but she knew the truth."

Bentley drew in a shaky breath. "You can't imagine how humiliating that was. But in a way, the look in her eyes was the physical proof I needed. I left. I took nothing of his— even left things that were ours. I didn't want one reminder of David, or of the person I had become while married to him."

She twisted her fingers together in her lap. "That's why I'm in Galveston. I gave up my family credit cards, my place to live, I got this job. I had to find out if he was right. I fully expected to fail."

"Bentley, look at me." When she wouldn't, he tipped her chin up gently. "You didn't fail. And you won't. You're made of tough stuff, Bentley Cunningham. Tougher than you think."

She smiled, pride flowing through her. "You really think so?"

"Yeah, I do."

She leaned into him, her muscles beginning to loosen, the knot of tension at the back of her neck easing. "Thank you, Jackson. You helped me."

Jackson gave a hoot of laughter. "I find that hard to believe."

"You did. You made me so damn mad. You refused to cut me a break, you refused to give me an inch." She smiled at him. "So I stood up to you in a way I never had to anyone. Ever."

"Felt good, didn't it?"

"Yeah." She cocked her head, her smile fading. "You accused me of trying to prove myself, of using Baysafe, this job, as a way to prove myself. You were right. I had to know if I could stand on my own two feet, I had to know if I was anything more than a decoration."

She met his eyes, hers swimming with tears. "I am, Jackson. I am more."

"Bentley—"

She placed her fingers over his mouth, stopping his words. "Does having done that make me selfish and shallow? Maybe you were right, Jackson. Maybe it does. And I'll understand if you want—"

Jackson tumbled her to her back and rained kisses over her face. "I'm sorry...so sorry, Bentley." He pressed his mouth to her throat, then the shell of her ear. "You're not selfish...not shallow." He caught her bottom lip between his teeth and nipped.

Bentley brought his mouth to hers in a deep kiss. She didn't want to talk any more, and neither did he. They clutched at one another, each wrestling with their own demons. In moments, tenderness was replaced by a kind of desperation, a need to forget the past and avoid the future.

Bentley cried out as Jackson thrust into her for the second time, crying out with her almost immediate release. Jackson caught her cry with his mouth, then offered his own for hers.

For a long while after they didn't speak. The pattern of light on the wall shifted and changed, becoming longer and softer. The sounds from the street below mellowed.

Jackson pressed his lips to Bentley's head. "It's getting late."

"Yes."

"I should call Chloe. She'll be worried."

"Yes," Bentley said again, nuzzling his shoulder. "Phone's right there."

Jackson reached for it, then stopped. "My God. This is you."

Bentley opened her eyes. Jackson had seen her music box and was propped up on an elbow, staring at it. She smiled. "Not really. I found it in a curio shop. Marla's Small Miracles."

Jackson sat up and lifted the box from the pedestal. For long moments he studied the figurine inside. "No relation at all?"

"No. It's from a Mississippi plantation." She cocked her head, studying the piece. "But it's odd, I do feel like I know her."

"It's the resemblance," Jackson said, setting the music box down.

Bentley sat up. "You're right, I'm sure. But it feels like more." She smiled at her own whimsy and motioned to the phone. "Chloe."

"Right."

Bentley watched as he reached for the phone and dialed. Chloe must have answered right away, because he began talking almost immediately.

"I'm here at Bentley's." He paused. "Yes, everything's fine." He angled a glance at Bentley. "Don't sound so surprised, I'm not a total brute."

Bentley raised an eyebrow, amused. That was the first teasing exchange she'd ever heard between father and daughter.

"I know, I know. We had a lot of... talking to do."

He blushed—everywhere—and Bentley put a hand over her mouth to stifle a giggle.

"I need to go into the office. You want me to pick you up? Okay...see you in fifteen minutes." He looked at Bentley again; she blew him a kiss. "Maybe a little longer."

As he hung up the phone, Bentley gave in to the urge and laughed. "You blush deliciously, Mr. Reese." Jackson looked at her crossly, and she laughed again. "How was she?"

"Worried about you. I think she was afraid she'd never see you again."

"My, my, Mr. Reese," Bentley drawled, drawing him against her, "the lengths you will go to keep your daughter...and your employees...happy."

He wiggled his eyebrows and lowered his mouth to hers. "I aim to please."

She ducked away. "Oh, no, you don't. I need to get ready."

"You seem ready to me."

She climbed off the bed, then tossed one of the pillows at him. "Wipe that lecherous leer off your face. I'm talking about the office."

"Stay here. I can handle it."

"No way." She looked at him archly, fists on hips. "I'm a working woman. Working women have to work. Got that?"

Jackson grinned. "Yes, ma'am."

Then he tumbled her onto the bed.

Chapter Nine

They all went to dinner together. Jackson and Chloe were more relaxed with each other than Bentley had ever seen them. And Chloe chattered, talking about the approaching Christmas holiday and the ski vacation she was taking with her mother and grandparents.

Bentley pushed her food around her plate, only half listening to Chloe, unable to concentrate on anything but Jackson. Sitting next to him, so close she could feel his heat, not being able to touch him, was agony. All she could think about was their earlier lovemaking; all she wanted was to make love again.

Jackson's thigh brushed against hers, and she caught her breath as fire flashed through her. When her world righted itself again, Bentley peeked at him from the corners of her eyes and found his heated gaze on her.

Wait, his eyes seemed to say. *Soon we'll be alone.*

But the wait seemed interminable.

Chloe cleared her throat, and Jackson jerked his gaze away from hers. Suddenly cold, Bentley shivered and slipped her sweater around her shoulders.

Jackson smiled at his daughter. "Sorry, sweetie, what did you say?"

Chloe looked from her father to Bentley, then back. "That I still have a couple of Christmas presents to buy." The girl sighed. "Do I *have* to get one for Jacques?"

"What do you think?" Jackson asked.

She sighed again, this time more dramatically. "That I do."

Jackson glanced at Bentley, then cleared his throat. "Would you like to go to the mall tonight? You could call and see if Randa or Billie could go."

Chloe lifted her gaze, surprised. "Really?"

"Sure. I'll drive."

Chloe drew her eyebrows together, looking once again from Bentley to Jackson. "It's a school night," she said.

"But it's early. And I'd expect you home by nine." Still Chloe said nothing, and Jackson shrugged. "I just thought you'd enjoy being with your friends. You worked so hard this week."

Chloe paused only a moment more, then grinned. "Cool," she said, jumping up. "Can I call now?"

"Sure." Jackson fished in his pocket for a couple of quarters, then handed them to his daughter. After she'd taken them, she flashed him another smile then trotted off in the direction of the restaurant's foyer and the pay phone.

When she'd disappeared from sight, Jackson turned to Bentley. "If I don't touch you soon, I'm going to explode."

"I know," she whispered, shifting her gaze to the entryway, then to him. "This is torture."

"I can't stop thinking about making love. I keep remembering how you were this afternoon, how you felt in my arms and under my hands."

Bentley sucked in a sharp breath, uncomfortable from wanting. "Stop, Jackson."

"I can't. God, I feel like a teenager." He caught her hand under the tablecloth and brought it to him. Under her fingers he was hard, ready. She pressed her hand against him, then, shocked at her own daring, jerked her hand away.

"You're blushing," he murmured, amused and obviously pleased. "No one can see."

"They don't need to," she whispered, trembling. "I'm afraid they've only to look at me and know."

"Know what?" He leaned toward her, lowering his voice to a thick whisper. "That we're playing touchy-feely under the table?"

"No." She met his eyes. "That I'm making love to you already. That I'm so aroused I can't sit still, so aroused I'm afraid to stand."

This time it was Jackson who sucked in a sharp breath. "This was an incredibly stupid idea."

"Yes."

"Let's change the subject."

"Yes. Let's." Bentley fidgeted with her teaspoon, searching for something to say. The only thoughts that jumped to her mind and tongue had to do with the two of them. Alone and naked. She swallowed. "This isn't working so well."

"No." He checked his watch. "If Randa or Billie can't go to the mall—"

"Don't even think it."

He met her eyes. "I have to think of something besides—"

"Yes. Me, too." She picked up her teaspoon once more, then set it down again. "When are you going to tell Chloe about us?"

"I don't know. Not yet." Jackson shook his head. "I'm not sure what I'm going to tell her. Or how. I just...I guess I'm not ready to admit to my daughter that I have a sex drive." He looked at his hands, his mouth lifting in self-directed amusement. "Stupid. But I've never had to face this with her before."

"Not stupid," Bentley murmured. "Understandable. But I think—" She shook her head. "Never mind."

"Please." He motioned with his right hand. "Say what's on your mind. So far your instincts have been a hell of a lot better than mine when it's come to Chloe."

"Okay. I think she's going to suspect that something's going on between us. In fact, I think she does already. And knowing Chloe, I don't believe it's a good idea to try to keep a secret from her."

"You're right." Jackson covered her hand with his, trailing his fingers sensually over hers, dipping into the junctures between her fingers, then out. "I know you are. But I'm not ready. Play along?"

"Of course. You're Chloe's father."

He lowered his eyes to her mouth. "And your lover."

Arousal was back, washing over her in a hot, breath-stealing wave. "Jackson—"

"When we're alone..." He moved his fingers over hers in an imitation of lovemaking. "I'm going to undress you. Slowly." He dipped his index finger to the juncture between her thumb and first finger and rubbed it slowly back and forth. "And as I do, I'm going to touch you and taste you and do my best to drive you crazy. I want to hear you cry out my name just the way you did this afternoon."

"Jackson...stop it." Bentley tried to jerk her hand away, and Jackson laughed low in his throat, tightening his grasp.

"Randa's got a test," Chloe said, bopping up to the table. "But Billie can go as...long...as..." The girl let her words trail and looked at them, a frown creasing her forehead.

Jackson eased his hand from Bentley's. He cleared his throat. "As long as what, Chloe?"

"She's home by nine," Chloe finished, cocking her head, her frown deepening. "What are you guys doing?"

"Talking," Jackson said quickly.

"Right," Bentley murmured, knowing she sounded as guilty as Jackson looked.

Chloe frowned again. "I told her we'd pick her up right away. Is that okay?"

"You bet." Not even waiting for the check, Jackson tossed some bills on the table and stood. "Let's go."

They picked up Billie and dropped the two girls at the mall in record time. As soon as the giggling girls had slammed the car door behind them, Jackson turned to Bentley. "Your place or mine?"

"Yours is closer." She clasped her fingers in her lap. "Hurry, Jackson."

Without another word, he started toward his house. He drove just short of recklessly, and every time they caught a red light, he swore under his breath and flexed his fingers on the steering wheel.

Finally, they reached Jackson's house. He swung the car into the drive, and they both slammed out of it and raced for the front door. Inside the dark house, they flew into each other's arms.

"Oh, God..." Jackson rained kisses over her face. "I thought I would die waiting."

"Me, too..." Bentley tangled her fingers in his hair and arched against him. "Me, too..."

As their mouths mated, they began to push at each other's clothing. Bentley kicked off her shoes even as she frantically tugged at Jackson's shirt, then sweater. Threads groaned, then gave; a button popped, sailing to the floor.

"Thank you," he muttered against her mouth. "Thank you."

"For... what?"

"Wearing this dress." He tugged on the zipper pull, and the back of the dress parted. He pushed the soft knit from her shoulders. It puddled on the floor at their feet.

They parted long enough to remove the rest of their clothing. Jackson pushed at his denims; Bentley shimmied out of her clinging hosiery and silky undergarments. Nude, they came together again, urgency clawing at them both.

Jackson moved his hands desperately over her, molding, stroking. He found the warm, wet center of her, and she cried out as sensation after sensation rocked her. He followed his hands with his mouth, until finally her legs gave and together they sank to the stairs.

They made love impatiently. Engulfed by passion, caught in the frenzy of need, Jackson thrust into her. Bentley gripped a baluster for support and let herself be sucked into the maelstrom, stunned at her wanton behavior, shocked that sex could be like this. She'd never lost herself before. Never forgotten who and where she was, never been willing to let go of fears and inhibitions to give herself totally to another person.

Until now.

And yet, doing so didn't frighten her as it would have only days before. But then, she wasn't the same woman she'd been only days before.

And when it came to Jackson, her body—and her heart—had a mind of its own.

She cried out his name as release shattered her into a billion perfect pieces. Jackson caught the last of it with his mouth, with his own release, and all her pieces fit back together, perfectly matched and melding with his.

The trip to reality was fast. The cold licked at their passion-warmed flesh, and the stairs proved an uncomfortable and unyielding mattress.

Without preamble Jackson scooped her into his arms and carried her up the stairs to his big, soft bed. He laid her gently on the mattress, then followed her down. He searched her gaze, his soft with remorse. "I'm sorry."

"No." She moved her fingers lovingly over his face, tracing the craggy features she had come to love so much. "Don't be sorry."

"I don't want you to think I'm like that bastard you were married to."

"You're not like him," she said quickly. "I know that. I never thought—"

"The stairs." He ran his hands tenderly over her body. "You'll have bruises."

Heat flew to her cheeks as she thought of what they'd done, then she smiled. "We were impatient."

"Is that what you call it?" He made a sound that was a cross between a laugh and a groan. "I think I could make love again."

She lifted her eyebrows teasingly. "Already?"

He brought her hand to him. "See what you do to me."

Bentley curled her fingers around him, giddy with her own power. "Come here, Jackson."

* * *

A short time later Bentley stretched sinuously. "I love this bed," she murmured, running the flat of her hand across the rumpled bedding.

Jackson trailed his fingertips lightly over the smooth curve of her abdomen. "Mmm."

"I hate this bed."

Jackson paused, looking at her. He raised an eyebrow, amused. "And what has this poor bed done to inspire such a wild range of emotion?"

"When I stayed here, while you were gone—" She arched when he momentarily dipped his fingers between her thighs, continuing when her world righted itself again. "I couldn't sleep. I kept imagining you here. With me."

"Amazing." Jackson moved slowly up her body to nip her ear. "I was hundreds of miles away, having the same fantasy. Experiencing the same inability to sleep."

She laughed, the sound husky and satisfied. "It smells like you. This whole place smells like you."

"Not any more." He nuzzled her neck, breathing deeply of her. "Now it smells like us."

Us. Bentley hung onto that word—its meaning—during the following days and weeks when she and Jackson were together but unable to be together. Unable to be *us.*

The worst times were the ones at Baysafe with Chloe. There they would go through the day, interacting as colleagues and uneasy friends. Except for the heated glances they exchanged when they thought no one was looking, the secret touching of hands, the whispered words they thought no one else could hear.

Chloe suspected. Bentley was certain of it. Often she found the girl's questioning gaze upon her and Jackson, and lately, when Bentley had smiled, Chloe had snubbed her.

Chloe was feeling shut out.

Unsettled, Bentley tapped her pencil against the desktop. Chloe needed to be told what was going on. Bentley felt it strongly and in her gut, but Jackson kept resisting. Every time she brought it up, Jackson asked her to wait.

Bentley frowned. Why didn't Jackson want to tell Chloe that they were having a relationship? It made her feel dishonest. It made her feel as if what they were doing was wrong—as if Jackson thought what he was doing was wrong.

And that hurt. Bentley pushed the question, and her hurt, away. He'd explained why, and she understood. She did. Shifting her gaze to Chloe and Jackson, she watched as father and daughter laughed together. She tipped her head. Maybe she was imagining things. Maybe it was she who was feeling shut out. Jackson and Chloe were getting along so well. They talked and laughed, they even ribbed each other occasionally. Gone was the sullen and petulant teen that Bentley had met only weeks ago.

Bentley drew her eyebrows together, noticing not for the first time the way Chloe turned her back to her these days, noticing how she seemed to be competing for Jackson's attention.

Nonsense. Bentley shook her head. The girl was simply basking in her father's love.

Love. As she had many times over the last few weeks, Bentley thought of what Chloe had told her about her mother and what she'd overheard her say. It had been bothering her, but she hadn't yet told Jackson about the conversation. The time hadn't seemed right. Things were going so well—between him and Chloe, between the two of them. She hadn't wanted to upset him. And it would. Badly.

Love, she thought again, melancholy slipping over her. She loved Jackson so much she couldn't imagine a day without him, let alone a lifetime.

Yet it would probably come to that—a lifetime without Jackson.

Determined not to dwell on that aspect of her and Jackson's relationship, Bentley shook her head and flipped open her appointment book. She smiled as she read the notations, the number of meetings she had already attended, the number she had scheduled for the coming week. She was enjoying fund-raising; she was good at it. She had already garnered financial commitments from almost everyone she had met with, and those who hadn't committed yet, would.

She picked up the phone, fixed on snagging a particularly elusive friend of her mother's.

"Bentley, could you come into my office for a moment?"

Bentley looked up at Jackson, heat rushing over her until she was sure she must glow with it. *So much for nonchalance.* She set the receiver in its cradle and stood. "Sure."

"Chloe, you have the phones?"

For a split second the girl looked defiant, then she smiled prettily at Jackson. "Yes, Daddy."

He smiled back and Bentley's heart turned over at the adoration in his eyes. It was as it should be. She just wished there was room in there for her.

She followed Jackson into his office, shutting the door behind her. "What's up?"

"This." He tumbled her into his arms and took her mouth in a fierce and possessive kiss.

Bentley curled her fingers into his soft flannel shirt, clinging to him. When he lifted his head, she looked at him, dazed. Was it always going to be like this? she wondered. So cataclysmic? So breath-stealing?

Jackson rested his forehead against hers, breathing heavily. "I've wanted to do that all morning."

"And I've wanted you to." She relaxed her fingers. "I missed you last night. The bed seemed so big and cold."

Jackson slid his hands down her back to cup her bottom. He pressed her to him; he was hard with arousal. "This is insane. I wasn't this randy in my twenties."

She drew away from him a fraction so she could look him in the eyes. "What are we going to do about this, Jackson?"

He laughed huskily. "I have about a dozen ideas."

When he tried to tug her into his arms, she resisted. "No, I'm serious. We need to talk."

He frowned and loosened his hold on her. "You've got my attention."

She drew in a deep breath, readying for a fight. "We need to tell Chloe about us."

"I agree."

Her mouth dropped. "You do?"

He laughed. "Yeah. I'll tell her before she goes back to school."

"Why the—" Bentley caught her bottom lip between her teeth. "What's the point in waiting?"

"It's only a couple of weeks. And she leaves for Colorado Saturday." Jackson drew her into his arms. "Why so worried? Everything's going great."

"I know...but—"

"Uh-uh. No buts." Jackson caught her mouth again. "God, I can't wait until Saturday. We're going to be alone. Just you and me. Let's stay in bed all day."

"Mmm." She melted in his arms, dizzy at the prospect of having Jackson all to herself. "Sounds glorious."

He kissed her again. And again. Finally, regretfully, he released her. As he did he smiled. "Although by Sunday morning I'll probably be missing Chloe so much that I'll mope around and call her a dozen times. This last week and a half has been so good. I wish she didn't have to go back to school. I wish she wanted to stay and go to school here."

"Maybe she does. Ask her."

He smiled. "I think I will."

"You've got to go."

Jackson checked his watch. "No kidding."

Bentley rested her forehead on his chest and sighed. "I wish you didn't have that appointment in Austin this afternoon. I'm going to miss you."

"And I, you." He cupped her face in his palms, searching her gaze for long moments. Something in his expression had her chest tightening, had the breath catching in her lungs. Then it was gone, and he smiled. "Maybe I should make that guy from the EPA wait?"

She returned his teasing smile. "I don't think so."

"You and Chloe going to be all right?"

"Of course. I'll drop her at Randa's before I meet Bebe McKay for dinner, you'll pick her up when you get back from Austin. It's all set."

"Good luck with Bebe. I hear she's pretty tightfisted."

"She is. But I'm pretty persuasive."

Jackson laughed and kissed her. "That you are."

And then he was gone. She stood in the doorway to his office and watched as he said goodbye to Chloe, then walked out the door. She ached to race after him, to tell him she loved him, ached so badly she had to grip the edge of the door to keep herself from doing just that.

When the double-glass doors had clicked shut behind him, Bentley sighed, turned to Chloe and forced an easy smile. "Well, kiddo, it's just you and me."

"Not quite the way you like it, is it?"

Bentley lifted her eyebrows at the antagonism in the girl's voice. "Excuse me?"

Chloe jutted her chin out. "No, I don't think I will."

"Did I do something to upset you?"

"You tell me."

She hadn't been wrong; she hadn't been imagining things. Chloe knew. She was angry. And hurt. Chloe had deliberately waited until Jackson was gone to confront her, because, obviously, she blamed Bentley.

Dismayed, Bentley drew in a deep, careful breath. "I think we need to talk. I understand why you're—"

"Save it." Chloe glowered at her. "I don't need another one of your lies."

Bentley stiffened her spine. "I'm not a liar, Chloe. When you want to talk, when you have something to ask me and can do it nicely, we'll talk."

Bentley turned and started to walk away. Chloe stopped her. "I thought you didn't want to get into my dad's pants. Looks like that's all you wanted all along."

Several emotions hit Bentley at once, shock, embarrassment, regret. And hurt. Chloe was young, Bentley rationalized. She was insecure with her place in her father's heart. She was vulnerable. But still, she'd thought Chloe had come to know her, she'd thought they were friends.

Slowly, Bentley turned to face the youngster, not bothering to hide the way she felt. "I don't deserve that, Chloe. I think you know it. Your father and I are having a relationship. We didn't mean to hurt you."

"No?" she flung back, a hysterical edge in her voice. "Then why did you keep it a secret from me?"

What could she say? Bentley wondered. That her father hadn't wanted to tell her because it was only sex for him? That on some level their affair embarrassed him?

As she allowed the thought to take form in her head, she acknowledged it was the one she had been denying all week, the one she had not wanted to face. Why else wouldn't he have told Chloe?

Bentley worked to quell her own fears, concentrating instead on Chloe's. "Your father wanted to wait to tell you until—"

"I was going back to school," Chloe supplied bitterly. "Until right before I was getting out of your hair."

"That's not true."

"You're lying again. You're good at that, aren't you?" Chloe jutted her chin out, battling tears. "It is true. I listened. Daddy can't wait for me to leave so you two can be alone. Just like Mama and Jacques."

"It's not like that. Not at all. Your father loves you. And I care for you very much. If you'd listened longer—"

"You used me!"

"He wanted to tell you," Bentley continued softly, working to keep the panic out of her voice. "But in his own way. When he was ready. It's difficult to know—"

"Yeah, right. It's always so difficult for adults."

"It's difficult for kids, too. I know that. So does he. Chloe, please, before you judge him—us—too harshly, talk to him."

But Chloe had tuned her out. The girl refused to even look at her for the rest of the afternoon, and it passed with agonizing slowness. Bentley left several messages for Jackson, but by the end of the day he still hadn't called her back.

Everything would be all right, she told herself as she drove Chloe to Randa's house. Chloe would be safe and happy with her friend; in a matter of hours Jackson would be back and he and Chloe would work things out. Bentley caught her bottom lip between her teeth and angled a glance at the silent girl. She hated having Chloe so angry at her. It hurt to think that Chloe might never trust her again.

Bentley stopped the car in front of Randa's house and turned to Chloe. "I really want us to talk." She caught the girl's hand. "After you see your father, please come to me."

Without acknowledging her plea with so much as a blink, Chloe snatched her hand back, alighted from the car and walked away.

Thunder awakened her. Bentley jerked up in bed and looked around the room, chilled and disoriented. A violent storm raged outside, and every few seconds lightning eerily illuminated her apartment.

Thunder crashed again, followed by a brilliant flash of light.

"Bentley, it's me. Open up!"

Jackson? She turned toward the door, not quite believing her ears. The pounding came again, more audible this time, and she grabbed her robe and ran to the front of her apartment.

She unlocked the door and he burst through. He was soaked to the skin, and water ran down his neck and under the collar of his shirt and puddled at his feet.

What concerned her more was the panic in his eyes. "Jackson, what's—"

"Is she here?"

"Chloe?"

"Yes, damn it. Is she here?"

"No." Bentley hugged herself, shivering. "She's at Randa's."

Jackson swore and dragged his hands through his dripping hair. "No, she's not."

"But I dropped her off," Bentley said, a sinking sensation in the pit of her stomach. "I watched her go in."

"She didn't stay." Jackson pressed the heels of his hands to his eyes. "Randa said she was upset about something. She wanted to go home."

"But surely Randa's mother—"

"Was at the grocery. When she returned, Chloe was gone. Her mother didn't think anything of it."

Bentley pressed a hand to her chest, to her racing heart. Stay calm, she told herself. For Chloe, for Jackson. But after the words she and Chloe had exchanged that afternoon it was difficult. "You tried the house?"

"Yes." He flexed his fingers and swung his gaze over the dark, empty apartment, then met hers again. "What happened? When I left, everything was fine. Great, I thought."

Bentley clasped her hands in front of her. "I'll get you a towel. Sit down and—"

"I don't want a towel and I don't want to sit down." He glowered at her. "Damn it, I just want to know where my daughter is."

"Don't yell at me! I don't know where she is!" Bentley took a deep, calming breath, fighting panic. "This afternoon, after you left, Chloe confronted me about your and my...relationship. She accused me of lying to her. She was really angry. And hurt."

At the guilt that twisted his features, Bentley reached out to him. "Don't," she said quickly. "You did what you thought was best."

He shrugged off her hand. "You mean, I screwed up again."

That he didn't want her comfort hurt. Bentley bit back a sound of pain at his rejection, even as she told herself she was being too sensitive.

She folded her arms across her chest to keep from reaching out to him again. "I thought it would be okay. I thought being with a girlfriend would be the best place for her until the two of you could talk. I tried to reach you and left several messages. Obviously, you didn't get them."

"The trip was a nightmare. Fuller put me off, pushing me onto a lackey—" Jackson shook his head. "I'm going to the house. Maybe she's there now. Or maybe there's a message."

"I'm coming, too."

"No. You wait here. She might show up—"

"She won't, Jackson. Trust me on this. I'm the last one she would be running to." At the questions in his eyes, she shook her head. "We'll talk more in the car. It'll only take me a minute to throw on some clothes."

While Bentley dressed, Jackson paced, trying to harness both his runaway heart and imagination. And the debilitating fears that clawed at him.

Where was she?

Everything had been going so well. For the first time in what seemed like forever, he'd had his daughter back.

Now she was gone. Only this time she could be hurt. Or in danger.

A brilliant flash of lightning rent the sky, and he shuddered. *She had to be home. And safe. If anything had happened to her, he would never forgive himself.*

"I'm ready."

Jackson turned to Bentley. "Let's go."

The storm was at its peak, and Bentley's umbrella provided little protection against the fierce wind and driving rain. By the time they were both in the Blazer, Bentley was nearly as wet as he.

Jackson started the vehicle, maneuvering carefully through the flooding streets. "Why, Bentley?" he asked after a moment, not taking his eyes from the road. "She seemed happy. We were getting along."

Bentley twisted her fingers together in her lap. "She suspected something was going on, so when we went into your office this afternoon she eavesdropped."

"So, she heard us making out."

"And she heard you say how much you were looking forward to her trip, how much you wanted us to be alone."

"But I also said how much I would miss her." Guilt stabbed at him, and he gripped the steering wheel tighter. He swung his gaze to Bentley's. "Didn't I say that?"

"She didn't hear that part. And she wouldn't believe me when I told her."

"I can't believe this. Just when we were starting to—"

"There's more, Jackson."

At the anguished tone of her voice, Jackson took his gaze from the road, but only for a second. "More?"

"Yes." Bentley took a deep breath. "While you were in D.C. Chloe and I talked. That's when I learned about the circumstances of her birth. She *does* think she wasn't wanted."

"But—"

Bentley held up a hand. Jackson saw that it trembled, and he clenched his jaw. He knew he wouldn't like what was coming next.

"She overheard Victoria say she wished she'd had an abortion."

Jackson slammed on the brakes and the car skidded to the side of the road. For long moments he rested his forehead on the steering wheel, fighting the violence that raged through him. He lifted his head and met Bentley's ravaged gaze. "That bitch. That selfish, conniving—"

Jackson bit back the epithets that jumped to his tongue, struggling for control. Losing it wouldn't do Chloe any good.

"She thinks you feel the same way. I assured her that wasn't true. But..."

Bentley's words ricocheted through him like buckshot, ripping and tearing, destroying the fragile security he had built up over the last days. The daughter he loved with all his heart thought he wished she had never been born.

Bentley pressed her face to his shoulder. "I'm sorry, Jackson. So sorry."

Jackson turned to her, needing and accepting her comfort.

"I told her," Bentley whispered, "that it wasn't true. I told her you loved her, that you wanted her. She didn't believe me."

"Why?" Jackson asked, even though in his gut he already knew the answer. He lifted his head, forcing Bentley to lift hers and meet his gaze. "What have I done to make her think this?"

"You let Victoria take her."

Silently Jackson started the car again, this time driving with precise care. He had known the answer before he'd even uttered the question. The same sin he punished himself for was the one she hated him for.

"I planned to tell you," she said softly. "But it seemed to be going so well. I knew how upset you'd be."

Upset? What an understatement, Jackson thought bitterly. Dear Lord, he felt as if he were being ripped in two. His daughter thought he wished she'd never been born. And the truth was, he couldn't imagine a world without her.

Bentley touched his arm. "I'm sorry."

He met her eyes, touched by the concern, the understanding, he saw there. "I know. I am, too. Damn sorry."

They rode the last couple of minutes to Jackson's house in silence. When they reached it, they both ran from the car and into the house.

"Chloe!" Jackson called, hoping, praying for a response. Nothing. Even though he knew in his gut she wasn't there, they searched the house. Bentley took the upstairs, he the downstairs.

"Jackson?"

He turned. Bentley stood at the top of the stairs, her expression stricken. Fear won the battle raging inside him, and he sucked in a sharp breath. "What?"

"She's run away. Her drawers look like they've been rifled through, and there's hangers strewn across her closet floor."

"Anything else?"

"The pictures from her bed table."

"The one of her and I?" he asked, swallowing past the lump in his throat.

"Gone."

She didn't totally hate him. It wasn't too late. Jackson squeezed his eyes shut and said a silent prayer of thanks.

Bentley descended the stairs. "Did you call Billie's? Chloe's grandparent's?"

Jackson was already heading for the phone. "No, I was so certain she'd be at your place. I—" He shook his head. "I'll make the calls."

No one had seen her or heard from her. The Ellerbees were frantic and promised to start a search from that end, calling anyone they thought Chloe might feel she knew well enough to run to. Including her mother.

Jackson hung up the phone and turned to Bentley. "I guess it's time for the police."

"Wait..." Bentley drew her eyebrows together, something plucking at her memory. "Jackson, does Chloe have a boyfriend?"

"No." He shook his head, then frowned. "At least... I don't think so."

"There was a boy. We saw him at the Galleria. Chloe said he was a family friend."

"Yes?"

"He was older and—" Bentley searched her memory. "There's something . . . Oh, God." Her eyes widened. "He was at the beach party at Tony's! He was with that group of boys that scattered when we came up. I recognized him, but at the time couldn't remember why he looked familiar."

"What was his name?" Jackson took a step toward her, a headache beginning to throb behind his eyes. "Think, Bentley."

"I don't remember." Bentley pressed the heels of her hands to her eyes. "It's a Texas name . . . I recognized it, I was reassured . . ." She snapped her fingers. "Able. That's right! Rick Able."

Jackson was immediately on the phone to Lee Ellerbee. The Ables were indeed family friends and they did have a son named Rick. In a matter of moments Jackson had the Ables's number, then their son Rick's at school.

And there they met a dead end. They awakened the boy from a sound sleep and, disoriented, he swore he hadn't heard from Chloe.

Jackson believed him. Hanging up the phone, he made a sound of rage, frustration and fear. As each minute passed, Chloe slipped farther out of his grasp.

"Rich girls don't hitch," Bentley said suddenly.

Jackson turned to her. "What?"

"Rich girls don't hitch. And they don't rough it." She looked at Jackson. "Did she have any money?"

"Not much." He drew his eyebrows together, searching his memory. "That I know of, anyway."

"Credit cards?"

"I took them away . . ." Jackson let the words trail off. *Her credit cards. Of course.* He tore upstairs, to the bureau drawer he'd tossed the cards into. *Gone. They were all gone.*

Bentley had followed him. He turned and met her eyes. "Let's call the bus and train station, then the Houston airports. I don't know where she's going, but I think I know how she's getting there."

Chapter Ten

After a series of frantic calls and lucky hunches, Jackson learned where Chloe was headed and on what airline. Airport security agreed to pick her up and hold her until he arrived.

By the time Jackson did, his nerves were stretched to the snapping point. He had no idea what he was going to say to his daughter, no idea whether he should be angry or relieved, whether he should play it hard or soft.

He'd decided he would just have to go with his gut. And his heart.

After pausing to collect his thoughts, Jackson pushed through the glass doors marked Security. He introduced himself to the officer behind the desk, who assured him his daughter was fine and directed him to an adjoining room.

Jackson followed the man's directions, stopping when he reached the open doorway and had a first look at his daughter. Thank God, he thought, taking his first real breath in hours. She was here. She was safe. Soon she would be home, in her own room and within his reach.

He moved his gaze over her, reassuring himself that except for looking lost and more than a little bit frightened, she was unharmed. Relief rushed over him. Muscles he hadn't consciously realized were bunched began to ease and loosen. As they did he experienced the overwhelming and ridiculous urge to laugh.

Chloe lifted her head, her eyes widening when she saw him. She opened her mouth to speak, then closed it again. Folding her arms across her middle, she jutted her chin out defiantly.

Jackson did his best to look stern, but all he wanted to do was haul her into his arms and against his chest. How could he stay angry when her eyes glistened with tears and that defiant little chin of hers wobbled with the effort of holding them back? He crossed to stand in front of her, forcing her to look up at him.

"Chloe."

Silence stretched between them for a long moment, then she cleared her throat. "I guess you're mad at me."

He let out a long, slow breath. "I'm a lot of things right now. Relieved. Frightened." He squatted in front of her so their eyes were level. "And yeah, I'm mad as hell."

She twisted her fingers in her lap.

"What did you expect me to be?"

She peeked at him. "I thought you might be happy."

"Happy?" he repeated incredulously. "Chloe, I had no idea where you'd gone or why. You could have been hurt. You could have been in real danger. Terrible things happen to kids on the street." With his forefinger, he tipped up her chin, forcing her to look at him. "And all I could think was, what would I do if something happened to you? How could I go on?"

"I'm sure Bentley could have helped."

"Baby, Bentley could never take your place. Nobody could."

Tears filled her eyes and she jerked her chin from his grasp. "Right."

"You don't believe me?" he murmured.

She shook her head again, her throat working with the effort of holding back her tears.

Torn between pushing the issue and letting her compose herself, Jackson allowed the silence to stretch between them once more. After a moment, Jackson said, "I hear you were going to Colorado."

She nodded. "To find Mama. I decided to go and live with her."

Her words hurt, but he fought to keep the emotion from affecting his reasoning. "Why?"

Chloe's chin began to wobble again, but she met his gaze evenly. "At least she's honest about not wanting me around."

"I see."

"Why did you stop me?" she continued brokenly. A tear rolled down her cheek, and she brushed impatiently at it. "I'd be out of your and Bentley's hair. You could do whatever you liked without having to worry about me."

Jackson sat back on his heels. He didn't know what to do, didn't know what to say first. He decided to start with the most important thing of all. "I love you, Chloe," he said, covering her small hands with his larger ones. "I love you so much."

"Sure."

"It's true." He smiled softly. "You've owned my heart from the first moment I saw you. Did you know that when you were a baby I used to come home during the middle of the day just to look you? If you were sleeping, I'd stand by your crib and watch as you slept. When your mother took you away, I thought I was going to die. I felt like the sun had been stolen from me."

"Then why—" She cleared her throat. "Why did you let her?"

He brought her hands to his mouth. "Baby, I didn't know what else to do. I was young. I'd grown up believing that a child's place was with her mother. And I had a fledgling business to run..."

Jackson let the words trail off, finding his reasons weak even to his own ears. "None of those excuse me, and if I had to do it over again, I would fight for you."

He smiled tenderly. "I used to look so forward to our weekends together, our holidays. I don't know if I ever told you that. I should have, I realize that now."

"Then what happened?" Chloe's eyes flooded with tears again. "What did I do to... How did I change so you didn't want me any more?"

"Oh, baby, nothing happened." Reaching up, he cupped her face in his palms. "You didn't change and neither did my feelings for you. I do want you. I want you to live with me. I was happy when your mother sent you to me." At her disbelieving look, he laughed. "It's true. I was scared as hell. But happy. I thought it would be a new beginning for us."

With his thumbs, he brushed tenderly at the tears that spilled down her cheeks. "Bentley told me what Victoria said. Your mother can be selfish and spiteful, she's spoiled and immature, but I can't believe she meant what she said. She was probably in some sort of snit with Grandma Ellerbee and said it to upset her.

"But in any case," he murmured, his voice thickening, "she doesn't speak for me. She never has. Your mother and

I are two very different people. That's why we couldn't live together."

"You only got married because of me."

"That's correct. But you know what? I wouldn't change a thing. Chloe, I can't imagine what my life would be like if you hadn't been born."

"Really?"

She looked at him with such hope that his heart wrenched. "Oh, sweetheart . . ." In a second Jackson was beside her, his arm around her shoulders. He hugged her to him tightly, but she didn't protest. "For so long I've been stumbling around in the dark, wanting to be the kind of father you needed and deserved, but not knowing how. I felt so bad about losing you . . . about letting you go, that I kept trying to make up to you for it." He took a deep breath, thinking of Bentley. "Finally, a friend suggested that I stop trying to make up for what I did wrong and start doing what was right."

"Bentley?" Chloe asked, meeting his eyes.

"How did you know?"

"Because everything started to change when she came," Chloe said simply.

Jackson realized she was right. Everything had begun to change when Bentley had entered their lives. The realization made him uncomfortable, and he shook his head. "You're really something, you know that?"

She blushed with pleasure, and he felt her happiness clear to the bone. It touched him in places and ways that hadn't seen warmth in a very long time.

"I don't want you to go back to boarding school. I want you to stay here in Galveston and live with me full-time, Chloe. Like a real family. But I want us to be happy. I want us to love each other. We can't go on the way we have been." He stroked her silky hair. "What do you say, sweetie? I'm willing to work on this, I want to work on it. What about you?''

"I want to," she whispered, her face still pressed to his shoulder. "I haven't been a very good daughter. And I shouldn't have run away. But when I heard you and Bentley together.... I felt so left out. I felt like I was just...in your way. Like with Mama and Jacques."

Jackson set her away from him so he could look her in the eyes. "If you had listened a little longer, you would have heard me say how much I was going to miss you while you were gone. You would have heard me say how happy I was. Because of you and me and how well we were getting along."

Doubt still clouded her expression. "Then why didn't you tell me about you and Bentley?" She sucked in a deep, shaky breath. "Why did you try to hide it from me?"

Jackson paused at the question. It was a tough one to answer honestly, because he wasn't certain of all the answers. Because some things were too private—too adult—for her to know.

"I should have told you," he began hesitantly. "Bentley wanted to. She urged me to. I wasn't trying to keep a secret from you..." He paused. "I guess I wasn't ready to...admit Bentley and I were a couple."

"Are you a couple?"

Jackson's chest tightened; his palms began to sweat. "Kind of. I guess.... Yes."

Chloe searched his expression, her own confused. "So, she's your girlfriend?"

Jackson smiled. How simple that made it. If only it was that simple, that easy. "Yes. You could call her that."

"Are you going to marry her?"

He swallowed past the knot in his throat. Marriage? His daughter wasn't wasting any time. "I don't know.... It's complicated for adults, Chloe. Marriage is a big step. A lot of men and women date but don't get married.''

Chloe thought a moment. "So are you just going to live together?''

Jackson caught his breath, taken aback. "We haven't discussed it. We . . . I—''

"You don't want to make another mistake like you made with Mama.''

There she went again, astounding him with her insight. "No, I don't. But it's more than that. And Bentley has to be considered here, too. I have no idea what she wants.''

"That's easy.''

Jackson arched his eyebrows at his daughter's very adult grin. "Is it?''

"Uh-huh. She wants you. She's in love with you.''

Her words settled like a fist in his chest. He didn't want Bentley to love him; he didn't want the responsibility, the complication.

As panic licked at him, he told himself that Chloe was only thirteen and looking at them with the naïveté of the very young. "Chloe, it's not that simple.''

"Yeah, it is. She's in love with you. And I guess it would be okay if you loved her, too. I really like her and...'' Chloe let her words trail off and ducked her head. "I said some pretty rotten things to her. Did she tell you?''

"Not what you said, only that you were angry and blamed her.''

"I wasn't very nice.''

"No, you weren't.''

She bit her lip. "You think she'll forgive me?''

"I think so. But you'll have to ask her that question yourself.''

Chloe sighed. "I suppose I've been a real pain.''

Jackson kissed the top of her head. A moment ago his daughter had astounded him with her adult grasp of a situation, and now she sounded so much like a child. No wonder hers was such an awkward and difficult age.

"Sometimes, yes," he murmured.

She paused. "I'm sorry, Daddy. I didn't mean to upset you or hurt Bentley, but I felt so sad, so left out."

His heart broke and he pulled her closer to him, trailing his fingers through her silky blond hair. He didn't want her to be sad or unhappy ever again. Even as he made the wish, he acknowledged that he didn't have that kind of power.

But he did have the power to try to guide her toward choices that would make her happy. He did have the power to comfort her when she was sad. "What do you say? Want to give it a try? Would you like to stay in Galveston? Go to school on the island?"

For several seconds she said nothing. She didn't move, didn't seem to breathe. And neither did he. If she said no, his heart would really break.

Finally, she looked at him. Her eyes swam with tears. She nodded, her throat working with the effort of holding them back. "I . . . would like that. More than . . . anything."

She gave up the battle then and started to cry. Jackson wrapped his arms around her and comforted her, never wanting to let her go, feeling so much like a father he wanted to shout with it. It was going to be okay.

One of the security officers looked in on them and smiled. "Glad to see everything's all right. Just thought I'd let you know, we've got a group of protestors coming in. Just in case you're ready to move along."

Jackson looked at Chloe. "What do you say we go home?"

She wiped her eyes and stood. "I'd like that."

Jackson followed her to her feet. "As soon as I give Bentley a call to let her know you're safe, we're out of here."

Bentley gazed out her living room window, shut today against the cold December breeze, waiting for Jackson and Chloe to pick her up on their way to the airport. The days since Chloe had run away had flown by. Jackson had filled her in on his and Chloe's talk, but even if he hadn't, she would have seen the difference it had made in their relationship. She was delighted for them both.

She moved closer to the glass, peering down at the street and the vendor's baskets of flowers. She wished she could throw the window wide open and breathe in their scent. She needed their sweetness, needed something to stave off the melancholy that had gripped her and wouldn't let her go.

Chloe hadn't talked to her about their argument, and it hurt that the child was reluctant to open up to her. Or maybe, despite what Jackson had told her to the contrary, Chloe meant the things she'd said. Could the girl still be worried about Bentley and Jackson's relationship?

She had no reason to. Bentley wasn't even sure there was a relationship to be worried over. A cloud moved across the sun, and Bentley frowned. Over the past few days, she'd told herself she was being silly. She'd told herself she was being paranoid. But she hadn't believed her own assurances.

She still didn't.

Something had changed between her and Jackson. Since the night Chloe had run away, their relationship had been different. Less intense. Less emotional. They hadn't spoken of it, and she was uncertain whether the change had been brought about by Chloe's act or by altered feelings on Jackson's part. Or both.

She did know, however, that her feelings for him hadn't changed. She ached for his arms and warmth, for what they'd had for those few weeks. She'd never felt this alone before.

Bentley trailed her finger across the cold glass. She and Jackson had been lovers just over three weeks. Hardly enough time to really know each other, let alone tire of one another.

Had he tired of her? she wondered, a thread of panic curling through her. What would she do if he had? She loved him. She would never tire of him.

She dropped her hand. After they left Chloe at the airport, they would talk. She had to know how he felt; she had to know where she stood. She couldn't go on the way she had been.

Jackson pulled up on the street below. Chloe jumped out of the Blazer, and the sun turned her hair to gold. Just like it sometimes did Jackson's.

Chloe looked up at her window and waved. Aching, Bentley waved back. How wonderful it must be to see yourself in another person. How wonderful to know there was a part of you out there, a part that would continue on after you'd gone. She would love to call Chloe her daughter, would love to look at Chloe and see something of herself in the child, one of her own mannerisms or habits. She would love to be called Mama.

Bentley turned away from the window and picked up her coat and handbag. Since David, she hadn't experienced the bitter disappointment, the stinging sadness, she had once felt at her inability to conceive. She'd thought, maybe, that she'd left them behind with David and the woman she had been then.

She hadn't. Looking at Chloe just now, she felt the disappointment and sadness keenly. And she felt like crying.

Forcing a bright smile, she let herself out and went to meet Chloe and Jackson. Neither of them seemed to see beyond her bright facade, and they kept up a constant flow of conversation all the way to the airport.

They arrived with plenty of time to spare before Chloe's flight, and after checking her bags, they stopped for a snack. Through it all, Chloe and Jackson talked, and as the minutes ticked by, Bentley felt more and more left out. More alone.

What was wrong with her? she wondered. It wasn't like her to be so melancholy. So emotional. She really was feeling strange.

As the time of Chloe's flight drew closer, her state of mind seemed to rub off on the others, and by the time they reached the gate, even Chloe had become subdued. They stood together, hardly talking, watching the clock inch closer and closer to flight time.

Chloe touched her arm lightly. "Bentley," she said, her cheeks pink, "could I talk to you a moment?"

"Sure."

"Over there?" She motioned with her head to an unoccupied corner of the waiting area. Bentley nodded and together they crossed to it.

"I just wanted to say... I'm sorry." Chloe's eyes welled with tears. "I was mean to you. I took stuff out on you that wasn't your fault. It wasn't fair. You were my friend."

Chloe started to cry softly, and Bentley hugged her. "I hope," Bentley murmured, "that I still am?"

Chloe nodded and sniffled. "I'm going to miss you guys. I wish we were spending Christmas together."

"I know." Bentley brushed the tears from the youngster's cheeks, moisture stinging her own eyes. "Me, too." Cupping Chloe's face, she gazed at her. "But I want you to have fun. And Chloe, despite how she acts, I'm sure your mother loves you. Try to remember that. Okay?"

"I'll try." Chloe grinned through her tears, looking suddenly mischievous. "I'll even *try* to be nice to Jacques."

"Baby, your flight's boarding."

Chloe turned to Jackson, who had come up behind them. "Okay, Daddy." She turned to Bentley. "I have something for you." She pulled a festively wrapped package out of her knapsack and handed it to Bentley.

"Oh, Chloe. Thank you." Bentley took the present, touched beyond words. "Would you like me to open it now?"

"No. Save it for Christmas morning. That way—" Her throat closed over the words and she fought to clear it. "It'll be like me being there with you."

"Chloe," Jackson called. "Time to go."

Standing on tiptoe, Chloe kissed her cheek, then ran toward Jackson, who waited with her ticket at the gate. After hugging her dad and giving Bentley a final wave, she disappeared down the ramp.

Bentley joined Jackson at the window and together they watched Chloe's plane back away from the terminal, then taxi down the runway. When she'd disappeared from sight, they turned and started to the parking area.

They didn't talk much, not on the trip to the car, nor after they were on the highway heading to Galveston. And as each silent second passed by, it seemed like another tiny piece of her was being ripped away.

What would she do if she'd lost him?

Jackson took her home, and without discussing it walked with her up to her apartment. Once inside, Bentley was unable to take the silence, the not knowing how he felt, one more moment. She whirled to face him. Curling her hands into fists, she met his eyes unflinchingly. "Has something changed, Jackson? If so, tell me now. I can't go on this way."

For one unbearably long moment he stared at her. "What do you mean?"

"Our affair." She trembled so badly she wondered how her legs continued to support her, but she jerked her chin up boldly, almost arrogantly. "Is it over?"

"Over?" he repeated, taking a step toward her. "Where did you get that idea?"

"It hasn't been the same between us since the night Chloe ran away. If you've changed your mind, if you're having second thoughts—"

"I'm not." He reached out and stroked his thumb lightly over her jaw. "I haven't."

She inched her chin up, not believing him though she wanted to so desperately. "Then why have you been acting differently toward me?"

"Have I?"

"Yes. You've been distant. Cool."

He turned away from her and crossed to the window. He stared out at the day for a moment before turning and meeting her eyes once more. "I don't know what to tell you. The night Chloe ran away took so much out of me. I was so afraid I'd lost her. I guess, knowing that she was leaving today, I focused on her."

Relief moved over Bentley, warring with the doubt that lingered, refusing to be shaken. Something glimmered at the back of his eyes, something that made her wonder if he was being completely honest with her. If he was holding something back. "There's nothing... wrong?"

"No." He shook his head. "Nothing."

This time it was she who turned away. Tears stung her eyes, and she blinked furiously, trying to keep them at bay. They slipped down her cheeks, anyway.

"Hey..." Jackson came up behind her and eased her against his chest. He buried his face in her hair. "Don't cry."

Squeezing her eyes shut, she leaned into him. If only she could believe everything was fine. But she had this horrible, sick feeling in the pit of her stomach, a sense that something was very wrong.

But she didn't tell him that. Instead, she tried to pretend that everything was okay. She turned in his arms and linked her hands around his neck. "I'm being silly. I've been so emotional lately. And I've been having these funny little pains."

He drew his eyebrows together. "Pains?"

"More like twinges." She rubbed her cheek against the soft flannel of his shirt. "Next week I have to go see my parents before they leave for the Caribbean. I'm going to see my doctor while I'm there."

Jackson drew back so he could look in her eyes. In his she read concern. It warmed her more than she could ever have imagined. She smiled. "I'm fine. Really."

He touched her cheek lightly with his fingertips. "You're sure?"

"Yes." She straightened, pulling completely out of his arms. "Truthfully, I wouldn't even go if Jill wasn't returning and I wasn't way overdue for a checkup. I haven't been since the fertility clinic a year and a half ago." When he still looked doubtful, she laughed. "Sometimes the holidays give me the blues."

"I have the cure for that."

"You do?"

"Mmm-hmm." He grinned wickedly. "I thought we'd go and pick out a tree this afternoon. And tonight, I'll make some spiked eggnog and we can decorate the tree. Ever strung popcorn while under the influence of eggnog, Bing Crosby and me?"

She tapped her chin with her index finger. "I don't recall."

He drew her closer, fitting his hips to hers. "Oh, you'd recall if you had. Especially the 'me' part."

"Well," she teased, moving suggestively against him. "It has been a long time. Maybe my memory needs to be refreshed."

With a hoot of laughter, Jackson picked her up, tossed her over his shoulder and carried her to the bed.

Chapter Eleven

Something *was* wrong. Very wrong. Or very right, depending on one's perspective.

She was pregnant.

Nude, Bentley stood before her bathroom mirror, studying her reflection, looking for even the tiniest change in her body. She saw none. But then she was barely pregnant, only three weeks along.

Just in time for holiday gift giving, Bentley thought, a hysterical giggle bubbling to her lips. Wouldn't Jackson be surprised?

Wasn't she?

Three weeks, she thought, touching her abdomen lightly with only her fingertips. She and Jackson had made love so many times, she couldn't determine exactly which time had been the lucky one.

Lucky? She caught her bottom lip between her teeth. She hardly thought that particular adjective the one Jackson would use to describe this situation.

She squeezed her eyes shut for a moment. He was going to be furious—especially considering the way she'd assured him this couldn't happen.

Bentley cocked her head. How had this happened? The doctor had been amused by that question. "The usual way," he'd answered, grinning. "It's not uncommon for women who have been unable to conceive to suddenly become pregnant at forty, or for couples who are finally able to adopt to turn up the same way." He'd smiled and patted her hand. "Don't quote me to any of my esteemed colleagues, but nature is a mysterious and miraculous thing. And one that often defies science. Now," he'd finished, "I can add you to my list of miracle stories."

It sounded logical to her. Believable. But she wasn't Jackson. An unexpected present hadn't altered her life once already.

Pushing thoughts of Jackson's reaction away, Bentley turned to the mirror, focusing on her own. She tilted her head. She didn't look any different, but she felt worlds different. She felt full and lush; she felt complete.

She touched her still-flat abdomen again, caressing it ever so softly. "Hello there," she whispered, heat blooming in her cheeks. "I'm your mama."

The words, the way they sounded, the way they made her feel, flowed sweetly over and through her. And with them flowed contentment. A kind of rich joy, a different kind of happiness than she'd ever known.

She smiled and hugged herself. The doctor was right, it was a miracle. She wanted to shout her happiness from the rooftops, she wanted to tell the world about her miracle.

But first she had to give Jackson the news. She dreaded telling him. But she had to. And soon. The longer she waited the more difficult it would be.

Her smile faded, her legs turned to Jell-O, and she called herself a coward. She was pregnant. It was a fact, one she had to deal with. Logically. Unemotionally. Immediately.

She brought a trembling hand to her mouth. Only logic didn't have a thing to do with this situation, and unemotional was an impossibility. And immediately? Her every instinct told her to run to the bed and hide under the covers for nine months. Or until nature forced the issue.

Turning away from the mirror, Bentley slipped into her robe. Crossing to the bed, she sank onto it. She would tell Jackson. Then her parents and Chloe and . . .

And Jackson was going to be mad as hell. He might very well tell her to take a hike. And then what would she do?

He wouldn't. He couldn't.

Her heart began to thrum in her chest. True, Chloe had been an accident, but he loved his daughter. And hadn't he said many times that he wouldn't change one thing about the past if he had it to do over again?

But that was then. He was a different man now, and she a different woman. He could abandon her.

What would she do then?

Bentley plucked the music box from its stand and sat cross-legged on the bed with it in her lap. She gazed at her look-alike. "This is some mess, isn't it?" She touched the glass with her fingertips. "Did you know this was going to happen?"

Sighing, Bentley returned the dome to its pedestal, then flopped back against the mattress. She stared at the ceiling. Things had been so good between her and Jackson the past few weeks. They'd readied for the holidays together, decorating and shopping, doing a round of parties.

They'd even strung that impossible popcorn. Bentley smiled, remembering. They'd ended up laughing and flinging the corn at one another, then had made love on the mattress of crunchy kernels. The stuff had been everywhere, and for a day after she could have sworn she still smelled of it. Bentley breathed deeply now, imagining the scent of the corn, the feel of it beneath her as she and Jackson made love.

Bentley gazed dreamily at the patterns of light above her head. Their hunger for one another had been insatiable, their passion boundless. And they'd laughed. Lord, how they'd laughed.

She drew her eyebrows together. Then why did she have this sinking feeling that something was not as it should be? Why did it feel like Jackson held a part of himself back?

Because he held his heart from her. Because he didn't love her. The truth hurt, and tears stung her eyes. He hadn't spoken of it—not once—and she'd been afraid to.

Just as she'd been afraid to face the fact that there was more wrong between them than that. She had this awful sense that he wasn't being honest with her.

And now this.

Bentley rolled onto her side, curling around her big feather pillow. Regardless of how Jackson felt, she wanted this baby. But, she admitted, she was terrified of doing it alone. She didn't know if she could, didn't know if she was strong enough. Her eyes filled. She wanted him to marry her.

There, she'd admitted it. She was terrified of ending up alone and pregnant, terrified of not being capable enough to take care of a child without help. She hugged the pillow tighter, David's brutal assessments of her character filling her head, pummeling at her security, her self-esteem.

She wasn't that woman anymore, Bentley told herself. She'd proven David wrong. She wouldn't go to her mother and father. No matter what. If Jackson abandoned her, she would make it on her own.

Bentley squeezed her eyes shut, her doubts stronger than her belief in herself. She felt so weak and frightened.

So happy.

Tears slid from the corners of her eyes and rolled down her cheeks, pooling on her soft white bedspread. She had wanted to be a mother so badly. And now she would be. For her, it *was* a miracle.

She might lose Jackson. Her chest tightened. In all probability she would.

Panic coursing through her, Bentley lifted her gaze. It landed on her porcelain look-alike. Something about the figure calmed her. Reassured her. For long moments, she stared at the miniature's enigmatic expression and smile, letting it soothe her.

Pulling herself into a sitting position, she wiped the moisture from her cheeks. She loved Jackson. It would be all right. She would *make* it all right, she vowed, looking at the music box.

But how?

It didn't take Bentley long to come up with a plan of action. She decided on one as old as time.

Seduction.

Bentley surveyed herself in her bedroom mirror, her stomach fluttering like a field of butterflies. Everything was in place—the gourmet dinner she'd ordered, the soft music and candlelight, the dress that was at once too revealing and not revealing enough.

She studied her reflection. Emerald green, strapless and made of touchable velvet and shimmery taffeta, the dress hugged her body to below the hips, then flared out to inches above her knees. She'd chosen hose that were sheer and dark, and glittery earrings that called attention to her bare throat.

She'd never looked better. Or been more nervous. It would be a Christmas Eve to remember.

Or to forget.

Bentley swallowed, her mouth suddenly desert dry. The two days since she'd been to the doctor had passed with alarming swiftness. A dozen times she'd almost blurted her news to Jackson, but she'd held back, wanting the timing to be just right.

And for two days, she'd alternated between feeling like a little girl with a delicious secret and a grown woman consumed by fear and guilt. Every time the guilt had plucked at her, she had reminded herself that she hadn't planned this pregnancy. She had been as surprised, as shocked, as Jackson was going to be.

Bentley closed her eyes tightly and said a quick, silent prayer. Then she opened them again and resolutely pushed away the what ifs scrambling around in her head. Even if Jackson didn't love her, he did care for her on some level. Of that she was certain. This would work, and everything would be all right.

Bentley managed to hold on to her calm until Jackson knocked precisely at eight. She lit the last candle, blew out the match, then took a deep, steadying breath. She *could* do this.

Crossing to the door, she paused, then swung it open. "Merry Christmas," she murmured, smiling alluringly.

Jackson moved his eyes slowly over her, then lifted them to hers. His lips tipped up in a devilish smile. "It certainly is. You look sensational."

Bentley flushed and drew him inside. "I have a surprise for you," she murmured seductively, then winced to herself as she thought of the other surprise she had waiting for him. "Oysters on the half shell, chateaubriand for two, your favorite wine."

"Mmm." Jackson drew her against his chest. "I like this surprise best of all." He pressed his mouth to her throat, her collarbone, then the swell of her breast revealed by the dress's daring décolleté.

Heat rushed over her, as did panic. She wasn't ready for this, the scene wasn't set, she . . .

She sucked in a quick, shaky breath and ducked out of his arms. "Come." She caught his hand and led him to the table. She sank onto one of the big throw pillows she'd arranged around the coffee table.

He followed her down. "Very romantic."

"I hope so."

"Do you?" He turned toward her, his eyes gleaming with heat, with wicked amusement. He trailed his fingers over the curve of her jaw, across her shoulders, then lower, again to the swell of her breasts. "Do you have romance on your mind, Princess?"

She shuddered and tipped her head back. Her nipples hardened, pressing boldly against the the dress's bodice. "Yes," she murmured, her eyes fluttering shut.

He laughed low in his throat and cupped her. "I hope that's not all you have on your mind."

Her eyes snapped open, and she stared at him. Oh, Lord, if he only knew. And he would know. Soon.

The butterflies were back, only it felt as if they'd grown to the size of hummingbirds. She eased out of his arms as unobtrusively as she could, fighting to control her fluttering nerves, her runaway heart. "Why don't you open the wine."

Jackson arched his eyebrows. "You're acting strangely tonight."

"Am I?"

"Yes." He smiled and reached for the wine bottle and corkscrew. "You seem nervous. And just the tiniest bit winded. Can't you catch your breath, Princess?"

She'd heard that women in their ninth month of pregnancy were often unable to catch their breaths. The thought popped into her head, and with it guilty laughter. What would Jackson say if she spilled out that particular pearl of wisdom?

"Bentley?"

She blinked. "What? Oh, no, I can't."

He poured a glass of wine and held it out to her. She looked at it for a moment, her mouth dry. Then she lifted her eyes to his and forced a smile. "Thank you, but I'm not... I'll have the mineral water instead."

His eyebrows lowered in question even as he complied, and guilt rushed over her in a wave of heat. She didn't drink much but Jackson knew she adored a glass of wine in the evening.

She felt dishonest. Like a fraud, a cheat. She'd always been honest with him. Always.

Until now.

"Shall we make a toast?" he asked.

"I'd like that."

"To the coming year."

He tapped his glass against hers and her heart wrenched. *Not "To us." Not "To our baby."* It hurt so badly she wanted to wrap her arms around herself and sob. "The coming year," she repeated hollowly and took a sip of the water.

For long moments silence stretched between them. Bentley glanced at him over the rim of her glass. She didn't want him to think of her as a liar or a manipulator. And she didn't want to have their lovemaking sullied by deception. Or machinations.

Tell him, she thought. Tell him now.

Panic, real and debilitating, hit her as she faced the prospect of telling him. A whimper escaped her and she set her glass down sharply on the tabletop.

"Bentley?" Jackson set down his own glass and caught her hands. "Your fingers are like ice." He rubbed them between his. "Are you all right? You never mentioned what the docto—"

"I'm pregnant."

The words spilled plainly, baldly, from her lips. They landed between them the same way. Jackson forced a laugh. "Not one of your more humorous jokes. What's the punch line?"

That was the punch line. A hysterical laugh flew to her lips; she bit it back. "I'm pregnant," she repeated as calmly as she could.

For several excruciating seconds, Jackson held her gaze. Then he dropped her hands. "I thought," he said softly, "that you were unable to conceive."

Bentley cringed at his tone. "I thought I couldn't. The doctor said that miracles sometimes happen. He said—"

"Miracles?" Jackson looked at her, his eyes glacial. "I'd hardly put this in that category."

She clasped her hands together, fighting a wave of hurt, of self-doubt. "Even under treatments I was unable to get pregnant, but they never pinpointed exactly why."

He swore and stood, turning his back toward her. "Terrific," he muttered. "Fabulous."

"Jackson, I—"

He looked over his shoulder at her, his expression deadly. "Don't say anything, Bentley. Just don't say anything."

He began to pace, visibly fighting for control. Bentley watched him, her heart hammering. She'd never seen him this angry, she realized, swallowing hard. He'd always had his emotions leashed. The too-quiet voice she'd always associated with his fury was actually the result of tremendous control.

Finally, Jackson turned to her. "When did you find out?"

"When I went to Houston . . . to my doctor."

"And you're just telling me now?"

She nodded. "I wanted the . . . timing to be right."

"Timing," he repeated, laughing tightly. "Interesting word choice, considering the topic of discussion."

As if something had just occurred to him, he swept his gaze over the the carefully prepared table, over her. When he met her eyes once again, the cynicism in his tore at her. He shook his head. "That's what this is all about, isn't it? Timing?"

Thinking of honesty, she took a deep breath and met his eyes. "Yes."

He swore viciously.

Bentley stood and held out a hand to him. "But I couldn't go through with it. I—"

"How long have you suspected?"

"I didn't." She shook her head. "It was a complete surprise."

"'A complete surprise,'" he mimicked her. "How convenient."

"Jackson, I didn't plan this!"

"You didn't?"

"No!" Fury chased away fear and hurt, and she clenched her hands at her sides. "How could I? I thought I'd never have a baby. If you knew how much that hurt, you wouldn't be able to stand there and accuse me of trying to . . . to trap you."

The words were between them. The ones she hadn't even allowed herself to think. All along she'd known that was how he was going to feel, what he was going to think. She had wished for a different reaction; she had been fooling herself.

At his expression, Bentley instinctively backed up. But she didn't avert her gaze, and she jerked her chin up defiantly. "I didn't try to trap you. I'm still not."

He took a step closer to her. "So, what do you want, Bentley? What is it you expect of me?"

She opened her mouth, then shut it, knowing how damning the truth would sound.

He took another step. "Do you want me to marry you?"

Her eyes filled and her heart beat so heavily against the wall of her chest that she thought she might faint. "Yes," she whispered. "I do."

He sucked in a slow, careful breath. "And can you deny you thought about the fact that I'd married for this same reason before?"

She wished she could. Lord, how she wished it. She wrapped her arms around her middle. "No...I can't."

His lips twisted. "You probably figured if I'd done it once, I'd do it again."

"No, it wasn't like that." She moved her head in denial, her tears brimming, then spilling over. "You make it sound so—"

"Conniving?" he supplied. "Dishonest?"

"It wasn't like that. It wasn't."

"You're happy about this," he said, as if the thought had just occurred to him. "The last few days you've been walking around on air. I wondered what—" He choked back the words. "I thought it was me. The holidays." He laughed, the sound hard and self-mocking. "Dear God, what is it about me and women? How can one man be the same fool twice?''

"Don't, Jackson.'' Bentley closed the distance between them. "I am happy I'm pregnant. I'm ecstatic.'' She caught his hands. "I thought I'd never be a mother. I wanted to be one so badly.''

He made a move to turn away from her and she tightened her fingers on his. "I wish the circumstances were better, Jackson. I wish you wanted this. I wish you loved me.'' She drew in a deep, shuddering breath. "I love you, Jackson.''

"Love?'' he repeated incredulously. "Don't try to confuse what's going on here. Just don't—'' Swearing, Jackson dragged his hands from hers. "I've got to get out of here. I've got to think.''

Wheeling around, he strode across the room, grabbed his coat and slammed out of her apartment.

Bentley stared after him, tears sliding down her cheeks. A Christmas Eve to remember, she thought, pain twisting inside her. One she would never forget.

Wrapping her arms around her middle, she sank to the floor and cried.

Jackson drove. Without destination, too fast for safety, he hoped only to outrun the emotions churning inside him.

How could he have allowed this to happen to him again? he wondered, taking a corner at a speed that should have left him breathless. And with two women who were so much alike? It was too unbelievable for coincidence. It was as if life had dished up one of its perverse little tests.

And he'd failed.

Swearing, Jackson flexed his fingers on the steering wheel. Unlike Victoria, who had admitted to having gotten pregnant on purpose, Bentley hadn't planned to trap him. He believed her—with his gut—even though he didn't want to. He wanted to think of her as dishonest and manipulative. He wanted to be angry.

He felt cornered instead. Trapped. Because whether she'd planned to or not, that's what he was.

Jackson realized he was in front of St. Mary's Hospital, that he had driven there on instinct. He paused a moment, then gave in to the impulse and turned into the parking lot. Shutting off the Blazer's engine, he stared at the building's brightly lit facade.

Red and green lights twinkled around the entryway, and in front a nativity had been set up. Jackson stared at the softly lit manger scene, at the silent figures, a strange sensation in the pit of his stomach.

The night Chloe had been born had been one very much like this. He could recall it as if it had been yesterday, could recall every nuance of the way he had felt. The knowledge that in a matter of hours he would be a father had thrummed in his head, turning him inside out and sideways. Along with the adrenaline of fear, and excitement. He'd been the stereotypical first-time father.

Without a conscious plan, Jackson opened his door and climbed out. With long strides, he closed the distance to the hospital's welcoming doors and let himself in.

Carollers sang in the lobby, and a group of hospital personnel were gathered around them. Jackson stopped to listen. The words of the song, ones about the birth of a child, about the gift of that child, moved him as they never had before.

He didn't want to be moved. He didn't want to feel soft and achy, or to be reminded of Chloe's first hours of life.

Life didn't always offer options.

Jackson turned away from the carollers' glowing faces and started for the elevator. He remembered which floor obstetrics was on. He could have found the nursery blind-folded. Letting his memory guide him, within moments he stood before the big window used to present all the new little people to the world.

Jackson gazed at the sleeping babies, at their wrinkly, red faces, his heart turning over. Would it be a boy this time? Or another girl? It mattered not at all to him, either would be perfect.

And this time, Jackson vowed, perfectly loved. He would see to it. This time he would do everything right.

Everything right. He thought of Bentley. And of Victoria. He hadn't been fair when he'd likened the two women. For just as there were many things about them that were alike, there were many that were different.

Bentley was kind. Bentley was soft, vulnerable. Bentley cared about others, she cared about life.

But he and Bentley were from two very different worlds. Even worse, they were from polar perspectives. She was here in Galveston, at Baysafe, testing herself, learning what she was made of.

He respected her for it. But he also believed, with everything he was, that she would grow tired of this quiet island and his quiet life. And then she would leave, go back to Houston, to society and a life-style he could never tolerate.

Panic tightened in his chest. Then she would leave. And she would take his child.

A baby in the nursery began to howl, and Jackson touched the nursery glass lightly, wishing he could comfort the infant.

He sucked in a deep, determined breath and thought of Chloe, of what he'd said to her. Not this time, he vowed again. This time he would fight. He wouldn't just let go. This time he wouldn't make mistakes.

Bentley. She'd said she loved him. Maybe she did, or maybe she just believed she did. Either way, a marriage between them wouldn't last. He frowned. It seemed wrong going into a marriage knowing it would end.

But he couldn't not go into it. He touched his fingertips to the nursery glass once more. Maybe he was old-fashioned, but he thought it was important that this baby—*his* baby—have a legitimate father, that the baby have his name.

He wanted this child. Looking at the rows of infants, his breath lodged in his chest. His hesitation had nothing to do with not wanting another child, but with the circumstances. He didn't want to feel forced into getting married.

And without the baby, he wouldn't marry Bentley.

And no matter what she said about love, Bentley wouldn't choose to marry him. Not in the long run.

The nurse who had come in to soothe the crying infant turned to the window, wondering which baby he wanted to see, thinking him one of the proud new daddies. Not yet, he thought, shaking his head. Not for eight long months.

The nurse smiled, her eyes moving to his ring finger, then back up to his eyes. Her smile brightened.

Jackson lifted a hand in goodbye, turned and walked away from the window. Funny, he felt married to Bentley already. When the woman had glanced at his hand, he'd felt odd. Naked without his wedding ring.

Jackson left the hospital, suddenly eager to share his decision with Bentley. Suddenly aching to see her, to hold her.

But first, if he was going to do it right, there was something he had to get.

It was the middle of the night before Jackson made it back to Bentley's. The streets were silent, the houses dark.

All of Galveston slept, awaiting Santa Claus and the dawn of a new Christmas.

Jackson pulled up in front of Bentley's apartment building and climbed out. Tipping his head, he looked at her dark windows. He'd considered waiting out the day and letting Bentley sleep, but only for a moment. He felt as if he would burst if he didn't see her immediately, if he didn't cradle her and their unborn child in his arms.

He entered the building and instead of waiting for the elevator, took the stairs. He ran up them and within moments was pounding on her door.

Bentley answered just as he started to panic. She swung it open, and his breath caught at her appearance. She'd been crying. Her eyes were red and swollen, the expression in them heartbreakingly sad. She held on to the door frame so tightly her knuckles were white; she looked as if she might pass out.

Tenderness moved over him like the scent of roses, slowly but potently. Without a word Jackson stepped into her apartment and closed the door behind him. He swept her into his arms and carried her to the bed.

After laying her gently on it, he shrugged out of his coat and eased down beside her. She started to cry and he cradled her in his arms. "Shh...it's okay." He stroked her hair. "We're going to get married...it's going to be all right."

Bentley shuddered. "I was so scared I'd lost you." She tipped her head to meet his eyes. "I never thought this could happen, Jackson. I didn't. You have to believe me, I wouldn't—"

"I do believe you." He pressed his lips to the top of her head, breathing in her light, sweet scent. "I was shocked. I lashed out at you. I shouldn't have."

"I love you."

"Shh...it's going to be all right."

Bentley pressed her face against his chest, tears filling her eyes once again. *He didn't love her. He might never love her.*

"I would have been here sooner, but I had to drive to Port Arthur."

"Your parents?" she asked, tilting her head, searching his expression. "Why?"

"Wait here." He rolled off the bed and went to his coat. Out of one of the pockets, he pulled a folded tissue. Crossing to the bed, he knelt on the edge and handed it to her.

Bentley looked at him in question, then unwrapped the tissue. Inside was a ring. Small. Simple. Two delicate strands of rose gold, braided together and set with three tiny diamonds.

Jackson took it from her trembling hands and slid it on her third finger. "It was my grandmother's. Mama meant for me to have it, and I didn't want to do this without a ring. It didn't seem right."

"Oh, Jackson."

"I know it's not much, but until I can get you something that's grander—"

"No," she whispered, not taking her eyes from the ring. "It's perfect. I don't want anything else."

"You need to sleep," he said, his voice thick. "You're exhausted."

"Make love to me."

"Bentley...honey..." He brushed the curls away from her face. "You need sleep."

"I need you more." She cupped his face in her palms, his cheeks rough with his morning beard. "Please love me."

So he did. Gently, tenderly, he stroked her body. Carefully he fondled her, exciting her with caresses no louder than whispers, but no less cataclysmic for being so.

As he moved his hands and mouth over her body, he paused almost reverently on her abdomen. Their eyes met and in his she read all the things he'd never said to her, all the things she longed so desperately to hear.

Drawing him to her—and inside her—she arched and cried out her love. Jackson caught her words, but didn't return them.

His silence tore at her.

As Bentley drifted off to sleep, she wondered if she had imagined the things she'd seen in his eyes. And she wondered if she could go on if she had.

Chapter Twelve

Bentley slept, deeply and until late. When she awakened, Jackson had already showered, dressed and made himself coffee. She opened her eyes and found him sitting on the edge of the bed, watching her.

"Morning," she mumbled, burrowing a little more deeply into her pillow.

Jackson leaned over and kissed her. "Merry Christmas, sleepyhead."

"Nice." She smiled, then yawned. "What time is it?"

"Almost noon."

It took a moment for the words to register, and when they did she dragged herself up. "Noon! But your parents—"

"Know we're going to be late," he said, grinning. "I already called them."

Bentley sagged against the pillows and groaned. "I'm making a great first impression—knocked up and sleeps until noon. Terrific in-law material."

"Hey..." Jackson tipped her face to his, gazing deeply into her eyes. "They're not going to judge you. That's not the way they are."

Jackson hadn't been merely placating her, Bentley discovered later. His family was genuinely nice and seemed to accept her not only warmly, but with open arms. The Reese clan was like no family she'd ever known, loud, boisterous and without a bashful bone among them. She took plenty of ribbing about shotgun weddings, just as Jackson took plenty over his prowess.

Every time she began to feel a little overwhelmed, she looked up to find Jackson's eyes upon her. He smiled as if to say, "You're doing great," and her balance returned, along with an incredible warmth and feeling of acceptance.

They'd called Chloe and talked to her from Jackson's mother's bright kitchen so that everyone could get in a hello and a Merry Christmas. She and Jackson had agreed beforehand to wait until Chloe returned at the end of the week to tell her their news.

When they did tell her, Jackson's worries, for the most part, proved unfounded. Chloe sat quietly for several moments, before looking from her father to Bentley. She inched her chin up. "So," she said, her tone cocky, "do you still want me to hang around? I mean, now that you're getting married and are going to have a new baby maybe I'd just be in the way."

For all her bravado, her throat closed over the last words, betraying her. Jackson must have heard it, too, because he hugged her so tightly Chloe squeaked in protest.

"Of course I want you to stay. *We* want you to stay," he amended. "A baby isn't going to change how I feel about you. Nothing could change that."

Chloe searched both their expressions, her own hesitant. She opened her mouth, then closed it again and shook her head. "Never mind."

"Tell us what you're thinking, Chloe," Bentley said, touching the girl's hand lightly. "We want honesty all around. That's the way we're playing it." Chloe bit her lip and eyed her warily. Bentley smiled her encouragement. "Go ahead. Say whatever's on your mind."

"Well," Chloe began, "if you guys get divorced, who would...it live with?"

Bentley's heart stopped, then started again with a vengeance. Chloe was a sophisticated child; she knew the circumstances of her own birth, she knew these were similar. She had to be worrying that the end result would be the same. Bentley opened her mouth to reassure Chloe; Jackson beat her to it.

"Try not to think about that, sweetie. I'm going to do everything in my power to keep this family together, and no matter what the future brings, this baby will always be your little brother or sister."

Bentley stared at Jackson, her mouth dry, her pulse fast. His words, their meaning, ricocheted through her.

Jackson expected this marriage to fail.

He was, truly, only marrying her for the baby.

Through the following weeks, Bentley held that painful realization to herself. It ate at her contentment, her happiness. She found herself watching Jackson, studying the expression in his eyes, listening to his words, hoping to hear something other than what she knew in her heart was true.

She didn't broach the subject with Jackson, although it was at the front of her mind all the time. She was afraid to. It was as simple—and as complicated—as that. She couldn't imagine confronting him and hearing him speak the words.

Because, if he said the words aloud, she would have to deal with them. She would have to make a choice. It was so much easier—and more difficult—to pretend everything was as it should be.

Three weeks after their talk with Chloe, Bentley drove to Houston to have lunch with her mother. She and Jackson had made their announcement to her parents almost immediately, but this was the first time she'd been able to break away to see her mother since. Bentley's legs shook as she stepped out of her car and handed her keys to the valet.

Both her parents had been nonplussed by her engagement and pregnancy, but particularly her mother. And she wanted her mother to be happy for her. She wanted the two of them to have, finally, a comfortable and accepting relationship.

Bentley entered the restaurant, scanning the diners for her mother's familiar platinum head. As she spotted her, at a table at the very center of the dining room, she indicated to the maître d' that she could find her way on her own. Taking a deep breath, she started across the room.

"Mother," Bentley said, reaching the table. "Sorry I'm late. I got stuck in traffic." She bent and kissed her mother's cheeks, then slid into the chair opposite hers.

Trixy waved aside her apology. "Between your daddy and brothers, I'm used to sitting alone and waiting in restaurants. Last week I'd been waiting an hour before your daddy called the restaurant to make excuses." She swept her gaze critically over Bentley, taking in every detail of her appearance. "You look a bit tired."

Not so long ago, that glance and tone from her mother would have sent Bentley scrambling for her compact and brush. Not today. The realization made her smile. "I am, a little. It's the pregnancy. But you look wonderful, as always."

Trixy fluffed her hair. "Thank you, darling. I work very hard at my appearance."

The waiter came with their menus and took their drink orders. When he'd left the table, Bentley turned to her mother. "This is a new place." Bentley looked around the lushly appointed dining room. "It's lovely."

Her mother followed her gaze. "Yes, it is. I keep forgetting you've been away."

Bentley laughed. "Galveston is hardly another country."

Trixy's expression suggested that it might as well be. "This is *the* place to go right now. Were it not for the Cunningham name, we never could have gotten reservations on such short notice."

"Sorry about that, but now that I'm working it's harder to get away. Besides, anywhere would have been fine. The important thing is that we're getting a chance to visit. It's been so long."

"It has," Trixy murmured, a shadow crossing her expression. "Since before you took that job."

Bentley laughed. "And I have you to thank for finding it for me. Although your methods..." She shook her head. "I was mad as hell at you."

"Bentley!"

She laughed again. "Well, I was. Who would have thought it would have turned out like this?"

"Who indeed?" Trixy picked up her menu and scanned it.

Bentley leaned toward her. "I love fund-raising. And I'm really good at it. I've gotten a tremendous amount of support for our cause in a very short time. Jackson says my success has been phenomenal."

"I'm sure he does." Trixy looked at her daughter over the top of the menu. "But you are planning to retire when you and Jackson get married."

"Why would I?" Bentley picked up her own menu. "I love the work. It's challenging, it's fun. In fact, I hope to continue after the baby comes."

"Oh, honey, I'm so sorry."

At her mother's words and tone, Bentley looked up from her menu questioningly.

"Maybe this will help." Trixy reached into her pocketbook and pulled out a small, square envelope. She held it out.

"What's this?"

"Your credit cards. I thought you'd want them back now."

Bentley stared at the envelope a moment, then lifted her gaze to her mother's. "But why would you think that?"

"Well, I just thought, with the wedding and then the baby coming..."

Her mother meant well. She did. Bentley understood that to Trixy Cunningham, existing on an average person's salary was inconceivable. Bentley shook her head. "Mama," she said gently, "Jackson and I can live quite comfortably without Cunningham Oil's help."

Confused, Trixy tried again. "But that's not necessary. We have the means, take them, the cards are here."

Bentley shook her head. She closed her mother's fingers over the envelope. "Yes, it is necessary. Jackson and I would rather do it our way. But thank you for thinking of us. And be sure to thank Daddy, too."

Her mother couldn't understand or totally approve of her actions. But it didn't hurt the way it used to; it didn't make her doubt herself. She and her mother would never agree on this subject or on many others. But that was okay, Bentley realized, looking at her mother as if for the first time. It was okay to be different. People could love and respect each other without being clones.

The waiter arrived with their water and a basket of warm, soft bread, then took their lunch orders. Bentley broke off a piece of the bread. "Jackson and I have decided on a date," she murmured, looking longingly at the butter for a moment before giving in and spreading a bit on the bread. "March tenth."

"March tenth," her mother repeated. "We need to start making plans."

"We've been through this before, Mama. Jackson and I want immediate family only. It's the second time for both of us and—"

"And the circumstances are less than ideal." Trixy held up her hand. "I know. But there are many people you simply *must* invite." She lowered her voice. "This isn't at all like your first wedding. Jackson's name isn't what your daddy and I would have hoped for, but proper arrangements must be made, anyway."

Anger surged through Bentley. She drew in a deep, calming breath, attempting to shrug it off and finding she couldn't. "But David did have the kind of name you'd hoped for."

Trixy made the tiniest sound of annoyance. "Now, don't get peeved, darling. Jackson is a perfectly... nice choice. And it's not that we're displeased. He does have a certain... stature because of Baysafe. And—"

"And nothing, Mother," Bentley snapped. "I love Jackson. He's a good man. He's real and he's kind." She took a deep breath. "I don't care about his name or lineage or portfolio. He may be a shrimper's son, but he's going to be my husband and I expect you to show him the same respect you would the governor."

"Of course I will, darling." Trixy glanced around them, then lowered her voice even more. "I didn't mean to suggest I wouldn't. And I didn't mean to upset you."

"Why don't you be honest with me, Mama? You're disappointed."

Unnerved, Trixy brought a hand to her throat, then dropped it to her lap. "It's not that I dislike Jackson, it's just that I ..."

"What, Mama?" Bentley prodded. "I think we're both grown up enough to tell each other the truth."

Trixy met her eyes, then looked away. "I wish you and David's marriage had lasted."

Bentley swore silently. She wasn't surprised. And the blame for her mother's wish rested squarely on her own shoulders, because she'd never told her the truth about her marriage. Because she'd been afraid her mother wouldn't believe her, afraid her mother would side with David.

She wouldn't have, Bentley realized, noting her mother's concerned expression. Her mother loved her. The realization sent happiness and confidence soaring through her.

It was time she told her mother the truth. It was time she stopped hiding and pretending. She was done being afraid.

"Mama," Bentley said gently, "I need to tell you about my and David's marriage, explain to you why it didn't work. Why it would never work. And after I do, I hope you'll understand why I never again want you to toss David's name up to me as if he was some sort of saint."

Bentley fisted her fingers in her lap. "The David you saw in public was not the man I married. The real David is sick and cruel and twisted. From the day we were married he did everything he could to destroy my self-esteem. He verbally abused and tormented me. He told me I was nothing, that I was useless, an embarrassment to him and the entire family."

Bentley's eyes swam with tears, and she fought to control them. She wouldn't cry over David, she vowed. Never again. "He took everything away from me, hoping to break me. He *almost* did. I thank God every day that I was strong enough to escape him.''

Trixy stared at her daughter, her throat working. When she finally spoke, her voice shook. ''But...you can't mean... our David?''

''Our David got off on manipulating and crushing people. The less he made me think of myself, the more powerful he felt.''

Trixy brought a hand to her chest. ''But I don't understand. Why didn't you... I didn't have a clue that something was wrong.''

There were plenty of clues, Bentley thought, searching her mother's expression. She just hadn't wanted to see them. But sometimes people didn't want to see, Bentley reminded herself, sometimes you had to force them to.

''I should have told you. I know that now. But at the time, I didn't believe in myself enough to stand up for myself.'' Bentley reached across the table and caught her mother's hand. ''Someday I'll tell you everything, but not today. Today I want to talk about the future, not the past.''

''Well, if it isn't my beautiful ex-wife.''

At the sound of David's voice, Bentley's blood ran cold. She looked slowly up at him, her stomach twisting into a dozen different knots.

This was the first time she and David had been face to face since the day she'd left, and as she met his eyes a wild mix of emotions raced over her. Fear and vulnerability, revulsion, panic. She wanted to run, she wanted to drop to her knees and, as she had done more than once during their marriage, beg him to leave her alone.

In her lap she flexed her ice-cold fingers. She wasn't a victim anymore. David had no control over her. She was done letting him, or anyone else, have the power to hurt her without reason.

She recognized him for what he was. And, more important, she recognized what she was.

In that moment her fear disappeared, as did her panic. In that moment, the terrible feeling of being cornered evaporated, leaving in its place a feeling of power, of strength.

As he had done so often to her, she swept her gaze tauntingly over him. "David," she murmured, smiling coolly. "What brings you out from under your rock?"

Bentley heard her mother's quickly indrawn breath and when she darted a glance at the other woman, she saw that her face had drained of color.

David laughed smoothly. "My little kitten has grown claws."

Bentley narrowed her eyes. "A lot more about me than that has grown. But that's no concern of yours." *How could she have ever been married to this man? How could she have not seen that his eyes were as flat and lifeless as a shark's?*

He raked his gaze insultingly over her, telling her without words that she was nothing, hoping to intimidate. His mouth tightened almost imperceptibly when Bentley smiled, unperturbed, and tipped up her chin.

"I hear through the grapevine," he said, "that you're taking another stab at marriage."

"Stab implies uncertainty. Sorry to disappoint you, David, but that's not the case. There's nothing in my life that's uncertain any more."

He lowered his eyes to her ring. "I can't quite remember. What does this fellow *do?*"

"Jackson runs an organization designed to protect Galveston Bay and the Texas coast. Perhaps you'd like to contribute something to our cause?"

"Perhaps. Why don't you call my secretary about it." He turned to her mother and smiled warmly. "Trixy, it's so nice to see you again. You look lovely, as always."

Actually, her mother looked as if she might swoon, but she still managed a gracious smile. "Thank you . . . David."

He turned. "I wish you well, Bentley."

"Do you really?" She arched her eyebrows. "Then perhaps you should be one of the first to know. I'm pregnant, David."

He paled. "What?"

"Pregnant." She smiled. "Without benefit of doctors, drugs or technology. Interesting, don't you think? Considering that you and I . . ." She let the thought trail off and smiled again, this time sweetly. "But I'm sure it's for the best. You would have been a horrible father. But you know what? I'm going to be a good mother, David. I don't have any doubts about that."

His face mottled with color, and he opened his mouth to say something, then closed it again. Turning on his heel, he walked away.

Bentley watched him go, a feeling of elation charging through her. A feeling of freedom. She'd done it! She'd stood up to him. She hadn't allowed him to hurt or bully her, and he hadn't the power to do either ever again.

With her elation came thoughts of Jackson. Thoughts of how much she loved him and of how desperately she wished that he returned her love.

Bentley gazed at Jackson's ring, tears springing to her eyes. She deserved his heart as well as his name. She deserved a man who believed in her. In them. She'd evaded facing the truth about Jackson's real feelings because she'd been afraid of the truth.

Only a fool or a coward feared truth. She was neither.

"Honey . . . I'm so sorry."

Bentley looked at her mother's stricken face. "Why, Mama?"

Trixy folded her hands in front of her, visibly working to calm herself. "I ran into David a couple days ago. I mentioned your engagement and that we were...having lunch today. Here. He seemed to still care for you and I thought... I'd hoped—"

"It's okay. You didn't know." Bentley covered her mother's hand once more, squeezing her fingers. "David didn't hurt me today. And he never will again."

Jackson strode to his picture window and stared out at the empty drive and wintry garden.

Where was Bentley?

He checked his watch again. She'd left before eleven to meet her mother for lunch in Houston. It was nearly five now and he hadn't heard from her.

What if she didn't return? What if she'd decided to leave him?

Jackson spun away from the window, too keyed up to stand still. He paced the length of the living room, struggling to get hold of his runaway imagination.

Get a grip, Reese, he chided himself. Bentley had simply gone to the city to have lunch with her mother. They had visited longer than she'd expected. Maybe they had decided to catch a show, or go to a museum, or—

A car swung into the drive, and Jackson's heart tipped over. A moment later he saw that it wasn't Bentley's BMW, but Randa's mother's white station wagon. Randa jumped out and waved excitedly. Jackson returned the smile and wave, then turned. "Chloe," he called. "Randa's here."

Chloe barreled down the stairs, her overnight bag clutched in one hand, her pillow and sleeping bag in the other. Billie was having a slumber party, and Chloe had been beside herself with excitement all week. "Bye, Daddy." She yanked the door open.

"Hey...haven't you forgotten something?" He tapped his cheek.

"Oh, yeah." Leaving the door ajar, she raced over to him and planted a kiss on his cheek.

He wrapped his arms around her and hugged her tightly. The difference in her, in their relationship, continued to astound him. "Have fun. But be good. And get some sleep."

Laughing, she pried herself free. "Tell Bentley I borrowed her crimping iron." At his look, she added, backing toward the door, "She said I could."

"I'll be here if you need me."

"Right, Daddy." Chloe rolled her eyes, then ducked out the door.

Jackson watched as his daughter raced down the steps and across the drive. With a final wave, she hopped into the waiting car, and Randa's mother backed down the drive.

When the station wagon had disappeared from sight, he glanced at his watch, his thoughts returning to Bentley. The last few weeks had been strained between them. She'd been on edge and uncommunicative. A half dozen times he'd looked up to find her watching him, the saddest expression in her eyes.

Jackson swung away from the window, unreasonable panic tightening in his gut. Bentley felt trapped, too. He recognized the signs, felt them himself. She'd begun to have second thoughts. And they weren't even married yet.

Jackson swore. This was great. Just great. If they did go through with the marriage, how long would it last? A month? Three? Until the baby was born?

If they went through with it. *If* she came home.

Where the hell was she?

Jackson dragged his hands through his hair. This was insane. He had to get a grip on his emotions. Ever since she'd told him about the baby, he'd been acting—feeling—strangely. On edge and possessive. Illogical and sentimental.

Like a lovesick fool.

Ridiculous. Impossible. He wasn't in love.

Furious with himself for his thoughts, Jackson turned toward the window. He hardened his jaw. No, it was the baby that had him acting so out of character. The upcoming wedding. In love with Bentley Cunningham was one thing he wasn't. And never would be. He wouldn't allow it.

The sun had made its final dip below the horizon when Bentley's headlights cut across the driveway. Even as he said a silent prayer of thanks, he acknowledged a simmering anger. Jackson crossed to the front door, opened it and stepped into the cold evening air.

He descended the steps to the drive, stopping at its edge. At his first sight of her his knees went weak with relief. The baby, he told himself for what seemed like the millionth time. He'd been concerned about the baby.

Bentley turned off the car's engine. She looked anxious, on edge. She smiled, but the curving of her lips looked forced.

Tension settled like a fist between his shoulder blades, and Jackson swore. This had to stop.

What was wrong with him?

"Hi." Bentley swung open the car door and stepped out.

"Hi." He shoved his hands into his pockets, moving his gaze over her, looking for something, anything, about her that was different from this morning. He found nothing. And yet, something about her *had* changed.

He leaned down to kiss her, and she averted her head, motioning to the trunk. "I have some packages. Mama wanted to shop for some things for the baby."

Jackson drew his eyebrows together. Had it started already? Had she grown tired of working? Had she begun to long for the days when she'd been able to shop all day?

Had she grown tired of him?

"I was worried," he said tightly.

She searched his expression. "Were you?"

The question, the way she voiced it struck a nerve, and he narrowed his eyes. "You *are* pregnant. With my baby."

"Oh, of course," she snapped. "Silly me, the baby."

"You could have called."

"You're right, I should have. I'm sorry." She ducked past him. "I had things on my mind."

He caught her arm. "What things?"

Bentley looked at him sharply. "I don't think you want to know."

"Try me."

Bentley narrowed her eyes. This wasn't the way she had wanted to broach the subject of his feelings about her and their upcoming marriage. She'd wanted them both to be calm, mellow. Rational. She hadn't wanted to be spoiling for a fight.

And she was, indeed, spoiling for one. And so was he.

Maybe it was better this way, she thought, shaking off his hand and facing him. Maybe if she was angry enough it wouldn't feel as if her heart was being ripped from her body when he forced her to tell him goodbye.

"What do you want, Jackson?" she asked, inching her chin up a fraction more. "Or maybe a better question is, what do you believe?"

"It depends on what the subject is."

"The subject is me. *Us,* our upcoming marriage. Do you think we're going to make it? Or do you think we're going to end up like you and Victoria did?" At his silence, Bentley curled her fingers into fists at her side. "Tell me, Jackson. I need to know."

"I think we're going to end up... apart."

"Divorced."

"Yes," he murmured.

The simply spoken word sliced through her like a dull blade. She caught her breath. "Then why are you marrying me?"

Jackson took a step toward her. "Come on, Bentley. Let's not play games. You know why we're getting married—"

"Say it, Jackson," she said, her voice high and tight. "I want to hear it!"

Jackson tipped his face toward the black sky and swore. "The baby, Bentley. I want the baby to have a father. I want him, or her, to have my name."

"You don't have to marry me for either of those. You are the baby's father. Your name will be on the birth certificate."

"Damn it, Bentley, you know what I mean."

She strode to the edge of his garden, barren now at winter's peak. She stared at the brown leaves and flowerless vines, then swung to face him. "You've never spoken of it, so I have to ask." She inched her chin up, battling tears. "Do you love me?"

"Don't do this, Bentley." He held his hand out to her. "Please—"

"Do you?"

He dropped his hand. "No."

She swallowed past the lump in her throat. "Do you think you will ever love me?" The question ripped at her, but she had to ask. She had to know—and face—the truth.

A muscle worked in his jaw. "Bentley, I don't think this is the time. Why don't we—"

"I have to know now, Jackson."

He swore again. "Why? It didn't matter four weeks ago when we agreed to do this thing. Why now? This moment?"

"Because I've changed. I didn't realize until today how much."

"I see," he said coldly. He pinned her with his angry gaze. "No, I won't ever allow myself to love you."

Bentley brought a hand to her mouth to hold back her cry of pain. She hadn't been wrong about how much hearing those words would hurt. But she hadn't realized just how much she'd been hoping and praying for a different response.

She fought the pain, the denial and tears. "Why, Jackson?" she asked brokenly, wrapping her arms around herself.

"Bentley," he said softly, crossing to her. "Please, try to understand. I've been through this before."

"You're not the only one who's survived a bad marriage. You're not the only one who's been hurt."

"That's not what I mean." He unwrapped her arms and caught her hands, rubbing them between his. "I know you're not like Victoria, but you are from her world. Marriage to me is going to be a big life-style change for you. It's better not to pin hopes on things that will end. And I just know that one day you'll—"

"What?" Stunned, she lifted her eyes to his. "That one day I'll thank you?" His eyes told her everything, and she jerked her hands from his. "I can't believe you would think that. You arrogant, condescending . . . You think I'm going to get bored with you? With my job? With Chloe and the baby?"

Tears filled her eyes, then spilled over despite her vow that they wouldn't. "I love you. And I care deeply for Chloe. Every day she becomes a bigger part of my life." She shook her head. "I've never been happier than in the last couple of months. Yet you think I'm going to get bored." Her voice rose. "How could I get bored with loving you? With loving Chloe? You don't know me at all."

"Bentley..."

He tried to pull her into his arms, but she slapped his hands away. "We have the same exact problem we had the day we met. You don't believe in me. You can't see beyond my family name to see me for who I really am. What if our situations were reversed? What if I couldn't see you as anything but a shrimper's son? I'd be a bigot, wouldn't I?"

She turned to his garden. A tiny purple flower peeked out from underneath fallen leaves and ground cover, and she stooped and moved aside the brush so that in the morning the blossom would have sun.

She lifted her face to Jackson, towering above her, and smiled through her tears. "Something wonderful happened today. I saw David. At first I panicked. I wanted to hide, to run. Then I realized I wasn't frightened any more. It was my own fear, my own doubts, that gave him power over me. I stood up to him. I let him know he couldn't hurt me."

Jackson searched her expression, the panic that he'd been battling on and off all day racing through him once again. "What are you getting at?"

"I'm not going to marry you, Jackson."

He took a step back from her, his world shifting crazily on its axis. "What?"

"I'm not going to marry you. I can't. Even if you didn't love me, if you believed in me, I would try to make it work. But you don't, and I won't settle for less." Her voice cracked and she looked at that tiny, hopeful flower. "I shouldn't have to work for your respect. And without it, our marriage *would* fail."

"This is unbelievable...crazy. It's..." Jackson wheeled away from her, struggling to even his breathing, to slow the frenetic beat of his heart. He crossed to the other side of the drive and for long moments stared blankly at the lighted windows of the house next door.

When he turned to her, he had his emotions and his voice under control. "You convince me to marry you, now you don't want to get married."

"That's the whole point," she whispered, wiping at the moisture stinging her cheeks. "I don't want to have to convince you to marry me. I want you to want me, for me." She pressed a hand to her chest. "And I won't settle for less than everything."

He curled his fingers into fists of frustration. "This is my baby, too. I have rights."

"And I won't deny you them. But I'm not going to marry you only for the baby's sake."

"Damn it, Bentley." His voice thickened. "Don't do this."

"I would have thought you'd be happy, Jackson." Her tears brimmed again. "You're off the hook."

"What if I don't want to be? What if—"

"You don't have a choice. Not unless something pretty drastic changes. Inside you."

Desperation and frustration washed over him, and he strode across the drive. He caught her upper arms. "Do you want me to lie?" he demanded. "I could. I could tell you everything you wanted to hear."

Tears slipped helplessly down her cheeks. "That would be less than I already have now. Is it so wrong to want everything? Don't you?"

Jackson dropped his hands and stepped away from her. That was the damnable thing. He did want everything. But right now that seemed like what they'd had. And lost.

Bentley slid his ring off and held it out to him. "It's a beautiful ring. I loved wearing it."

Jackson gazed at the ring for long moments before lifting his gaze once more to hers. "So, that's your decision?" His chest ached so badly, he had to force the words out.

"Actually, it's yours."

He paused a second more, then took the ring from her fingers, his own closing tightly around it.

Battling sobs, she pushed past him toward her car.

Jackson caught her hand. "Bentley, wait. Please—"

She shook her head and tore her hand from his. "No. Goodbye, Jackson." A moment later she was in the BMW and backing down the drive.

Jackson watched her go, his eyes burning, his chest tight. It was for the best, he told himself, turning to face his dark, empty house. She would be happier; they would both be saved a lot of pain. She'd done the right thing for them both.

Then why did he feel as if nothing would ever be right again?

Chapter Thirteen

The peal of the phone dragged Bentley from sleep. She struggled into a sitting position and, pushing the hair out of her eyes, reached for the phone. "Hello?"

"Bentley. It's Jill."

Disoriented, Bentley looked around her room. Sunlight streamed in from behind the blinds, and she squinted against it, a dull headache beginning to thrum behind her eyes. "What day is this?"

"Sunday. Bentley—" Jill sucked in a sharp breath. "Something terrible's happened."

Bentley sat up straighter, instantly awake, instantly alarmed. "Jackson?" She tightened her grip on the receiver. "Is he—"

"Fine," Jill assured her quickly.

"Chloe?"

"She's fine. It's...there's been an oil spill in the ship channel. Between Texas City and Bluebonnet. A tanker and a barge collided. Late last night."

"Oh, God." Bentley sank back against her pillows. "How bad?"

"I don't know. But it doesn't look good. Not only is the high wind making the containment booms almost ineffectual, it's pushing the oil in toward Bluebonnet."

"Jackson?" Bentley asked. He would be distraught, she knew. Beside himself with frustration and worry. Even as she reminded herself that Jackson's feelings were no longer her concern, she wished she could comfort him.

She couldn't help herself. She still loved him.

"Out there already," Jill answered. "Since about dawn."

"What can I do?"

"Nothing. I just thought you'd want to know."

"Nothing?" Bentley repeated incredulously. "Jill, I know the number of volunteers needed when a spill occurs." She drew her eyebrows together. "What's going on?"

Jill paused. "Jackson didn't want you out there. It's exhausting work, and he's worried—"

Angry heat stung Bentley's cheeks. "He doesn't think I can handle it, does he? I can't believe he—"

"Simmer down," Jill said quickly. "That's not it. He's worried about the baby."

Bentley brought a hand to her throbbing temple. "He has nothing to worry about," she snapped. "I'm taking very good care of myself."

Jill was silent for long moments. "I know now's not the time, but what's going on between you two? One week ago everything was fine. You two left the office on Friday, engaged and walking on air. Monday morning comes and you two aren't even speaking, let alone engaged any more. Talk to me, Bentley. Maybe I can help, maybe there's something I can—"

"There's nothing you can do," Bentley said quickly, her voice thickening with tears. "I don't want to talk about it, Jill. It's not you, and I do appreciate your concern, but—"

"But you're so much in love," Jill murmured. "Don't throw that away."

"That's the problem," Bentley said, hearing bitterness and hating it. "*I'm* so much in love." Her throat closed over the words, and she cleared it. "Please, Jill, just tell me how I can help with the clean-up. I'll go crazy sitting around here all day."

The other woman was silent for a moment, then she sighed. "Okay. The veterinarian in charge of the bird rescue operation needs volunteers desperately. The birds are in real trouble."

"Where do I go?" Bentley asked, climbing out of bed, scrambling around for a pen and paper.

"They're setting up the rescue operation at the Bluebonnet middle school. Dr. Marjorie Friends is in charge. Tell her I sent you."

After Jill had given her the directions, Bentley cleaned up and threw on a pair of jeans and a sweater. Deciding to get breakfast on the way to save time, she raced from the apartment.

The drive to Bluebonnet took nearly forty-five minutes. During that time Bentley tried to focus on the job that was going to have to be done, tried to remember what she'd read about other successful bird rescue operations from other spills.

Instead, she thought of Jackson. And of the words he'd so bluntly handed her. He didn't love her. He never would. An ache speared through her, and she caught her breath. The week before, her path had seemed so clear, her decision either black or white. But a week before she'd been riding high on adrenaline and the feeling of power at having stood up to David.

Today she felt like what she was—a rejected lover, an unwed mother. Today she didn't feel nearly so strong, nowhere near invincible.

Bentley tightened her fingers on the steering wheel. But no matter how she felt, she'd made the right decision. She couldn't marry a man who didn't believe in her.

Tears blurred her vision. Would the pain ever go away? Would the need? She turned into the middle school's parking area, found a space and stopped her car. She rested her head for a moment on the steering wheel. Would a day ever go by when she didn't think of him and ache?

She lifted her head and swiped at the tears that had escaped despite her best efforts at containing them. She doubted it. Because of their child, Jackson would always be a part of her life; she would never be allowed to just forget.

Bentley threw open the car door and stepped out. As she did, the scent of the oil, rich and cloying, hit her. Her stomach lurched, and she put one steadying hand on her stomach and the other on the car.

"You okay?"

Bentley turned and managed a wan smile at the woman who had stopped to help her. "Yes. The smell, it's so potent."

The woman's mouth tightened. "This is a bad one. And a bad time of year, too. Besides all our native species of birds, we've got migrating and wintering waterfowl here right now." The woman held her hand out. "Dr. Marjorie Friends. I hope you're here to volunteer?"

Hours later, exhausted, strung out on coffee and adrenaline, Jackson raced into the gymnasium. He stopped just inside the doors, moving his gaze frantically over the room full of volunteers, searching for Bentley.

When he didn't see her he swore. *Where was she?*

He'd wanted to throttle his office manager when she'd told him what she'd done. Bird rescue was one of the most difficult parts of a spill clean-up. The distraught, oil-soaked birds would fight the volunteers, pecking at them with their razor sharp beaks, screeching their outrage and fear. And the great majority of the birds, despite the volunteers' efforts, would die right before their eyes. It was as emotionally draining as it was physically exhausting.

Jackson dragged his hands through his hair. The last week had been hell. She'd surprised him by showing up Monday morning, ready for work. She hadn't resigned, as he'd expected. So they'd worked alongside one another. Not speaking unless absolutely necessary. Not touching at all.

He'd gotten an idea of what it was going to be like, having Bentley be a part of his life, but not in his life. An agony. And one of his own creation.

He couldn't stop thinking about her. He couldn't stop thinking about what she'd said to him, or about how her words had made him feel. Desperate. Like a fraud and a liar.

And he couldn't stop yearning for her. Her laughter, her companionship. Her love. Jackson brought a hand to the back of his neck and massaged the tight, aching muscles there. He didn't know what the answer was, he only knew that as hour after hour surveying the wreckage outside had passed, he'd been unable to stop thinking of the wreckage inside himself. The wreckage of his life. Of his heart.

He had to see her. He had to assure himself she was all right. After that, he didn't know.

"Jackson!"

He turned. Marjorie Friends had spotted him and was rushing over. She looked as wiped out as he felt.

"What's going on out there?"

He rubbed his hands wearily over his face. "It's looking up some. The wind's died down. The containment booms are doing a pretty good job of keeping the oil off shore. Turns out the barge had a double hull. Most of its oil was caught by that second hull."

"Thank God."

"Don't thank anybody just yet," Jackson said grimly. "The birds are going to keep coming."

"And coming," she added. She narrowed her eyes at him. "What brings you in here?"

"I'm looking for one of your volunteers." Jackson gazed past the woman, searching the room again. "Bentley Cunningham."

Marjorie Friends shook her head. "There are so many—"

"Tall, gorgeous brunette. She's here, I saw her white BMW in the lot."

"Oh, sure." The vet motioned to the corner and a figure huddled under a blanket. "I finally convinced her to get off her feet. She'd been going at it for hours. She refused to rest while there was a bird that needed her."

Jackson stared at Bentley, his heart turning over. *How had he ever thought her shallow and spoiled? How had he ever been so blind?*

"That lady's made of some tough stuff." Marjorie laughed. "Finally, I told her if she didn't eat and rest, I was sending her home. She somebody special?"

Jackson swallowed past the lump in his throat. "Very special. Excuse me."

Jackson crossed the gym, ignoring people who called to him, never taking his eyes from Bentley. Finally, he stopped in front of her and for long moments just gazed at her while she slept. Her eyes were shadowed with exhaustion, her face streaked with oil. One arm had slipped out from under the blanket, and he saw that bright red welts, the result of the terrified birds striking out, dotted the back of her hand and arm.

Dear God, how had he ever believed himself not in love with her? He'd been in love with her almost from the beginning.

His love rushed over him in a crystal-clear, intoxicating wave. And with it came wonder and a kind of freedom, a boyishness he hadn't felt in years. Victoria had stolen the last of his youth from him, he realized. And Bentley had brought it back to him.

Jackson knelt down beside her, tenderness taking his breath. He lifted her hand and brought it gently to his mouth. He kissed one tiny wound after another, aching for the wounds he had caused with his harsh words the week before, praying for the chance to heal them with his love.

He thought of their first meeting and their second, he remembered their first kiss and the afternoon they'd first made love. From the very beginning, she had been everything wonderful and good in life—strong and loving, kind and vulnerable.

What a fool he'd been. What a blind idiot. Because of past unhappiness, he'd almost thrown away his future.

He could have lost her. Maybe he had.

Desperation coursed through him. It couldn't be too late. *It couldn't be.*

Bentley stirred; her eyelids fluttered up. "Jackson," she whispered. "It's you."

"Yeah, it's me." He laced their fingers. "I shouldn't have awakened you. You need to rest."

Bentley blinked and looked around her, realization racing into her eyes, along with the horror. "The birds... Jackson, it's so awful."

"I know." He brought her hand to his mouth once more. "But a lot of them will be saved because of your efforts. You have to focus on that."

Bentley was silent a moment, then she eased her hand from his. The hurt in her eyes tore at him. "What are you doing here?"

"Finding you."

She drew the blanket more tightly around her, sitting up straighter. "I see."

"No, you couldn't possibly." Jackson smiled and caught her hand again, curling his fingers possessively around hers. "Because I've only just seen myself."

She eyed him as warily as one of the wild birds. "Jackson, we've said all there is to—"

"I love you."

"What?"

"I love you," he repeated. "So much I feel like I'm going to burst with it."

For long moments, Bentley gazed at him, her heart a jackhammer in her chest. "And just what caused this epiphany?"

"Fair question, Princess." He laughed and drew her against his chest. "But the answer is so simple. You did."

"Me?"

"Mmm." He drew away from her so he could gaze into her eyes. "My marriage did more damage to me than I'd admitted or even realized. I'd always acknowledged my anger, but never my hurt. I'd admitted to bitterness, but not disillusionment. Not fear. But Victoria *did* hurt me. She stole some of my dreams, a whole bunch of my confidence. I was afraid to love, to trust again.

"When I met you, I stuck you in a box neatly labeled Just Like Victoria. But you wouldn't stay in that box, because you were nothing like her. And even after you'd shown me, time and again, the person you really are, I wouldn't allow myself to see the truth."

He laughed lightly and shook his head. "And God knows, I wasn't about to allow myself to love you. I believed if I didn't allow myself to love you, I couldn't be hurt, couldn't be disillusioned. But I did love you." He laced their fingers. "And being without you hurts like hell."

"I don't want you to feel trapped, Jackson." She looked at him. "I don't want you to mistake wanting the baby for wanting me."

"This isn't about the baby. This is about you and me and the way I feel. And I feel anything but trapped." He brought her hand to his mouth. "Happy, yes. Blessed. Ecstatic. Passionate. Younger than I have in fifteen years."

He laughed again. "The night Chloe ran away I got the first inkling of my real feelings for you. She told me you were in love with me. That terrified me, because on some level I knew I felt the same. So I tried to push you away, tried to distance myself from you."

"So, I was right," Bentley said. "It wasn't just Chloe. You were keeping something from me."

"And from me, too." With his thumb, Jackson brushed at a smudge of oil on her cheek. "You forced me to see the truth, Bentley. You forced me, despite myself, to trust again. You taught me how to give and bend, showed me that everything isn't black and white." His voice deepened. "You showed me how to love again."

He cupped her face in his palms. "I was so afraid of losing you. And I was so sure I would. I told myself, and you, that I only cared about the baby. That was a lie, a way of explaining my feelings without having to face the truth." He ran his fingers over her face. "I love you, Bentley Cunningham. I believe in you. I want to marry you...for you."

Bentley laughed and drew his face to hers. Their lips met in a lingering kiss. When she pulled away, her cheeks were wet with happiness. She smiled through her tears. "I was so afraid I'd lost you," she whispered. "So certain I had no choice but to go on without you."

"But you would have, Bentley. You're strong. Like the flower that blooms despite the cold."

"I love you so much, Jackson."

"And I you."

He kissed her again, this time deeply and with all his heart.

Epilogue

"Are you sure you want to do this?" Jackson asked as they stepped off the elevator and onto the Houston Galleria's second level.

Bentley glanced down at the gift box in her hands. Inside, nestled carefully in layers of tissue paper, rested her music box. She looked at her husband. "Yes. I'm sure."

He shook his head and followed her lead, turning to the right. "Mind telling me why? You love it."

Bentley angled a smile at him. "You're going to think it's silly."

"Try me."

"I have this feeling that somebody else needs a miracle."

"A miracle?" he repeated, lifting his eyebrows in question.

"I told you it sounded silly." She motioned with the box. "You'll understand more when you see the store. It's in the corner, over there."

Moments later they reached Small Miracles, and Bentley caught her breath. A banner announcing a Going Out of Business Sale was draped across the front window. A Closed sign hung in the door.

"Oh, no," Bentley murmured, moving up to the window and peeking inside. The lights were on, and she thought she saw someone moving around in back. She tapped on the glass and a second later Marla appeared at the door.

"Well, hi, sugar. I was wondering when you'd be comin' around." She swung the door wider, smiling broadly at Jackson. "My, you're a big one. You must be the new husband."

"He is," Bentley said. "But how did you...?"

"Know you'd gotten married?" The pixie woman laughed and motioned to the shiny gold band on Bentley's left hand. "You weren't wearing that before. Come on in."

Inside, Bentley moved her gaze around the dismantled shop. "I'm sorry about your business," she murmured sympathetically. "You had some lovely things."

"Heck, don't be sorry. I'm moving because I want to." Marla slipped her hands into the front pockets of her dusty Levi's. "I'm going to New Orleans. There're some folks over there in need of a miracle."

Jackson's mouth dropped, and the pixie woman laughed. "Marla's Small Miracles. Get it?"

Bentley smiled at Jackson's expression. "I said almost that same thing. Which is really the reason I'm here. I want to sell you back my music box."

Marla eyed the gift box, pursing her lips. "It's usually the other way around, sugar. You're supposed to buy things from me."

Bentley's smile faded. "I know. But what you said about miracles... I have the feeling this is the right thing to do."

"Well, since you put it like that—" Marla narrowed her eyes speculatively. "I'll give you seven-fifty for it."

"I paid fifteen hundred."

"I've got overhead." Marla patted her fire-red curls. "Miracles don't come cheap, you know."

That they didn't, Bentley thought, looking at Jackson, happiness washing over her until she was liquid with it.

He was going to think she had lost her mind. And maybe she had. She held out the box and smiled. "It's a deal."

Marla grinned. "I've got cash in my deposit bag. I'll be right back."

After the other woman had disappeared into the store-room, Bentley lifted her face to Jackson's. "Isn't she great?"

Jackson arched his eyebrows in disbelief. "Bentley... darling... she's a little weird. This whole place is a little weird." Cupping her face in his palms, he grinned at her. "Not to mention the fact she took you to the cleaners. You could have held out for more."

"How could I?" she whispered. "I already have everything."

"Ah, Bentley..." He lowered his mouth to hers in a lingering kiss.

"It's nice to see folks so happy," Marla said, coming up behind them. "In fact, it's what I live for. Here you go." She handed Bentley an envelope. "If ya'll are ever in New Orleans, look me up."

"We will," Bentley murmured, tucking the envelope in her handbag as Marla walked them to the door. After another goodbye, she and Jackson stepped out into the mall and started for the elevator.

"By the way," Marla called, poking her head out the shop door. "Congratulations."

Bentley looked at the woman. "What?"

"The baby." The little woman grinned. "And, sugar, don't you worry about a thing, you're going to be a terrific mother."

Startled, Bentley looked at Jackson, then at her still-flat abdomen. When she glanced at the shop, Marla was gone. "But, how did she know?"

"It was a guess," Jackson murmured, slipping his arm around her.

"You think so?"

"What else?"

Bentley shook her head at the wild what elses rampaging through her. "You're right, of course. A guess."

He laid an arm across her shoulders. "Sure."

"Or maybe it was my feet that tipped her off." At Jackson's arch look, she laughed. "Jill told me that as soon as a woman gets pregnant, her feet start to turn out. Like a duck's."

Jackson gave a hoot of laughter. "I presume, to more efficiently waddle in the ninth month of pregnancy." He hugged her tighter. "I like the guess theory better."

"Not looking forward to watching me waddle, huh?"

Stopping, Jackson turned her to face him. He cupped her cheeks in his palms, his expression serious. "Princess, I'm looking forward to watching everything you do, including growing old. I love you."

Bentley lifted her face to his. "Oh, Jackson...I love you, too."

* * * * *

Look for NIGHT JASMINE *by Erica Spindler in September, only from Silhouette Special Edition.*

A Note from the Author

When my editor told me *A Winter's Rose* and my heroine Bentley had been chosen to be part of the That Special Woman! promotion, I was thrilled. A celebration of womanhood—what a wonderful thing to be a part of.

And how appropriate. After all, at the heart of every romance novel is its heroine. A strong, courageous yet vulnerable woman, one who beats the odds, no matter how bad they are, and in the end finds happiness, not only with her man, but with herself.

My Bentley is just such a heroine. She appears to have it all—looks, social status and wealth. But in fact, her appearance is a beautiful facade that hides an insecure and hurting woman, a woman who has faced what many of us face every day in the real world: prejudice, indifference, cruelty. Bentley overcomes. She finds her inner well of strength, she learns to believe in herself. In the end she sees just how special she is.

I believe every one of my heroine's is special. Just as I believe every woman is special. Thank you, dear readers, for celebrating womanhood with me and Silhouette Special Edition this month and every month.

Yours,
Erica Spindler

that Rebecca now swept in a wide arc and let settle behind Samantha as the young woman moved down the three steps and came to a stop beside Seamus.

"Take her hand," Grover whispered from the corner of his mouth.

Then Seamus realized he was standing there with his mouth open, staring at her—finding that she was not only beautiful, as he had remembered her every one of those nights at Adobe Walls and those cold, rainy nights following Mackenzie up and down the Staked Plain, but perhaps the most beautiful woman in the whole world. She held her hand out to him in front of her, a small bouquet of blue bonnets in the other.

"Hold my hand, Seamus," she said to him quietly.

He swallowed and took hers in both of his own. Finding that it was all right. Now they were trembling together.

Then she was pressing her leg against his as the bald-topped minister edged forward from somewhere at the side of the porch and he heard the crowd inch up behind them, the better to hear the vows. Sensing the beads break out on his brow as she pressed her leg to his, Seamus knew no one else would know that she did so beneath the yards of lace and crinoline—that private embrace shared between them at this moment only the merest hint of the fiery passion that he knew would once more be his this night. The first of their new life together.

And for but a moment he remembered that first night he had recited poetry for her. Likely he had smelled of horse sweat and wood smoke and a few more things nigh on to impossible to wash out of a man's body with simply bathing. Despite that, he smiled, Samantha still wanted him.

"Dearly beloved," the booming, stentorian voice of the minister rocked over them all, shade and shadow and sunlight too, "we are gathered here in the sight of God and these witnesses, this community of true believers . . ."

Both Liam and Ian, so richly Irish each in his own way. And his mother. With a sour ball of regret rising to his throat, Seamus wished again she were here to stand with the others at this moment, once more to look upon her face so pale, framed by the auburn hair that curled and fell across her shoulders. How she would look now, so different, older than that day she stood on the dock, waving farewell as she saw her oldest off to Amerikay.

How he owed that strong woman of County Kilkenny who had held their family together the best way she knew after her man was gone. He recalled how he had learned at her knee, listening intently as she read those bible verses, paying heed as she explained the intricate meanings to be sorted out in the proverbs and the tales of those ancient and faraway peoples of so long ago. With warm fondness Seamus remembered how that woman had explained those stories and those people as if they were her neighbors and those truths were her life. Testaments to be lived by when one's own path grew rocky.

Something so strong and abiding, yet something so warm and intimate in those stories of life and living—that perhaps was the woman's greatest gift to her firstborn son.

He was fighting the sting of tears, again wishing she were here to listen to this music, to hear as well the laughter of the children and smell the lilacs on the summer breeze, to enjoy the sunshine she had known so little of in all her life—

—when the crowd gasped, falling into abject silence, all gazing as one at the porch behind the spot where he and Sharp Grover stood.

Slowly, Seamus turned, to look at what had stunned the others into silence, finding Samantha stopped in the doorway behind Rebecca. While he had never seen Rebecca look lovelier, it was nonetheless the sight of her younger sister that had silenced the entire congregation gathered here at the behest of Sharp Grover for this ceremony and celebration.

Samantha slowly moved out of the shadow onto the sunlit porch, radiant in yards and yards of lace Rebecca had ordered in from Dallas to fashion this long, flowing gown